Hat[illegible] for Broken Hearts

BOOKS BY TILLY TENNANT

AN UNFORGETTABLE CHRISTMAS SERIES

A Very Vintage Christmas
A Cosy Candlelit Christmas

FROM ITALY WITH LOVE SERIES

Rome is Where the Heart Is
A Wedding in Italy

HONEYBOURNE SERIES

The Little Village Bakery
Christmas at the Little Village Bakery

MISHAPS IN MILLRISE SERIES

Little Acts of Love
Just Like Rebecca
The Parent Trap
And Baby Makes Four

ONCE UPON A WINTER SERIES

The Accidental Guest
I'm Not in Love
Ways to Say Goodbye
One Starry Night

Hopelessly Devoted to Holden Finn
The Man Who Can't Be Moved
Mishaps and Mistletoe
The Summer of Secrets
The Summer Getaway
The Christmas Wish
The Mill on Magnolia Lane

TILLY TENNANT

Hattie's Home for Broken Hearts

bookouture

Published by Bookouture in 2019

An imprint of StoryFire Ltd.

Carmelite House
50 Victoria Embankment
London EC4Y 0DZ

www.bookouture.com

ISBN: 978-1-83888-002-6
eBook ISBN: 978-1-83888-001-9

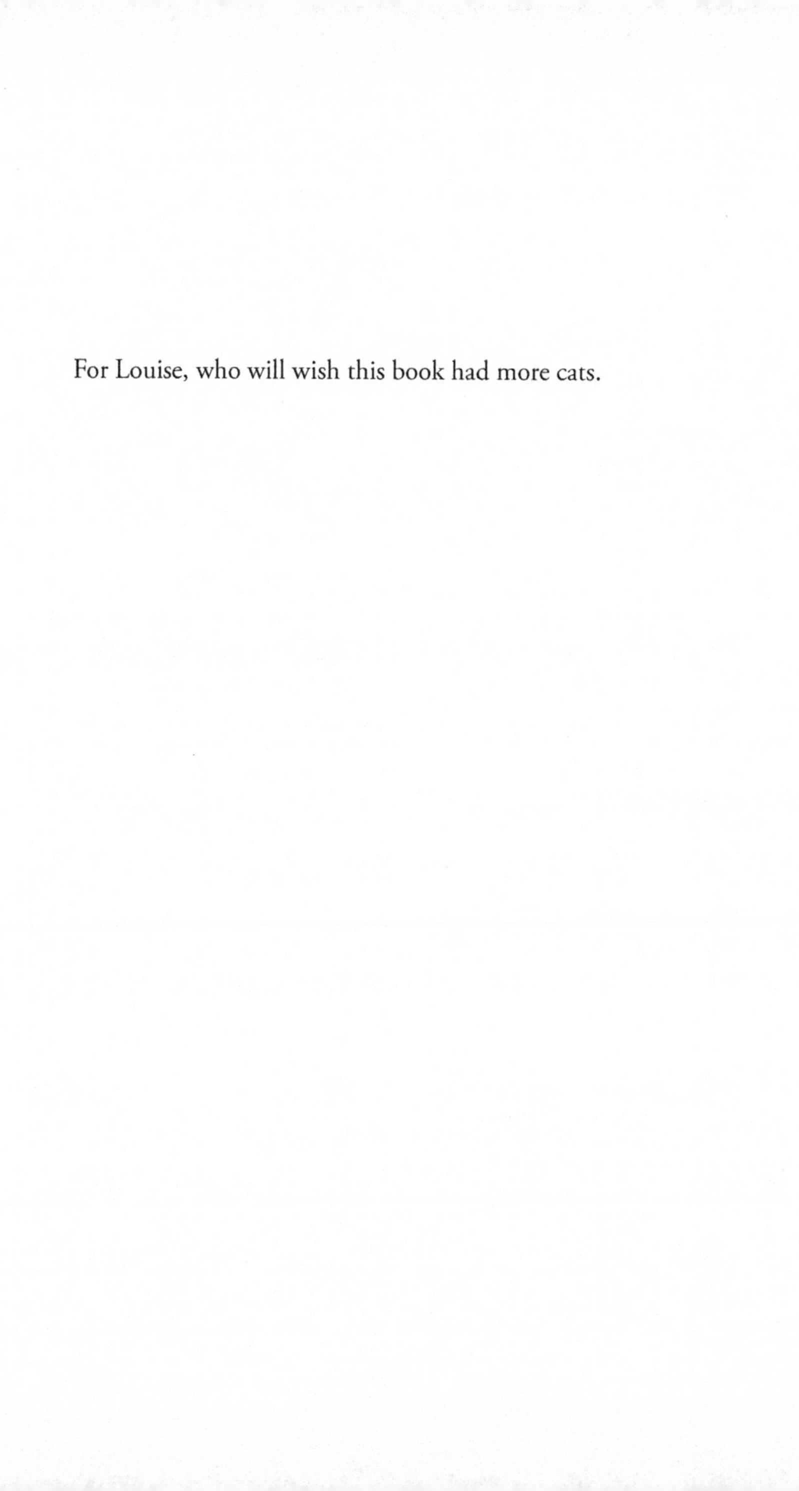

For Louise, who will wish this book had more cats.

Chapter One

Life could be good and sometimes life could be a little less than good, but one constant remained. Paris, no matter what else was happening in Hattie's life, would always be magical. There was something about the place, an indefinable quality. It was in the cobbles, slick in the lamplight, and it was in the welcoming glow of a backstreet bistro. The tourists tramping the Champs-Élysées with weary feet and wondering eyes soaked it up and when they went home their lives were a little richer for it. The French had a phrase for it – *je ne sais quoi*. Trust the French to make *I don't know what* sound romantic.

Hattie sat on the low wall and looked out towards the Seine. A humid dusk embraced the city, indigo skies washed into velvet blackness. Boats cleaved their way through the choppy waters of the river – most of them the low, broad, glass-walled pleasure boats full of tourists that had become such a familiar, unremarkable sight to Hattie over the last two years, dotted with lights that reflected back and scattered into explosions of gold over the dark waters. Along the banks stood rows and rows of pristine and glorious façades, grand and beautiful old buildings brightened by so many lights it was as if they were trying to compete with the stars, and away in the distance the proud Eiffel Tower looked over the city and dared it to argue that it was not the most wondrous sight of all in this most magical of places.

Hattie looked out on the place she had called home for the past two years, and the sights that had become so familiar over that time had never before been such a source of sadness. Her flight back to England was booked. Given time, perhaps Alphonse might have asked her to reconsider, but the damage had already been done. She didn't know if their working relationship could ever get back to the way it had once been and part of her didn't know if she even wanted it to. Perhaps the catastrophe of the opening night of his new collection was a sign. Though she loved Paris, Hattie had been plagued by the vague feeling that something wasn't quite right for a few months now. She'd been employed as his PA, eager to learn about the business, but all she'd done since she began working for him was run around fetching his lunch and dry-cleaning. She'd mentioned it to him more than once, but he'd just tapped his nose and warned her not to run before she could walk and all would be well. That was easy for him to say when the star of his own career as a fashion designer was rising, and soon it would be about as high and bright as it was possible to get. Certainly, it was far above the less impressive orbit of Hattie's own.

Then it had happened: Alphonse had finally trusted her with the task of stage dressing for the opening of his show, and Hattie had been beside herself. But it had all gone horribly wrong and Alphonse's rage had been such that Hattie had feared for his life, if not her own, and he'd sacked her on the spot. He'd repented, of course, once he'd realised that he'd have to run for his own coffee and dry-cleaning if Hattie left, but the incident had made Hattie's mind up for her.

She stood up and drew a lungful of air. *It's been good, Paris,* she thought, *and I'll never forget you… but it's time to go home.*

Chapter Two

No matter how apprehensive the thought of coming home made her, the sight of the foxglove-edged lanes as the taxi drove her towards her parents' house, the meadows of wildflowers and copses of ancient trees that became blurs as the car raced past, the picture-perfect houses of the Dorset village where she'd been born – all thatched roofs, rose bushes and pastel-rendered walls – would always soothe her. Early summer was a remarkable time of year here, when the landscape seemed to burst into life. She'd left many troubles behind when she'd left Gillypuddle, but she'd left good memories and good people too. She couldn't deny that it would be nice to catch up with those people again, relive some of those memories and maybe make some more.

'Nice place,' the taxi driver remarked approvingly as he pulled up outside the sweeping driveway. Hattie never really thought about how posh her parents' home might look to strangers, but every now and again an admiring, covetous glance would remind her that what was unremarkable to her was very remarkable to others. It was just the place she'd grown up in, just home. But as she looked out of the car window now, she really appreciated for the first time just how imposing and grand it was. Unlike a lot of the cottages in the village, the high roof was tiled instead of thatched. It was much larger than the houses surrounding it, the original façade an elegant Georgian design, while sections had been added over the years. It sat in impressive grounds, dressed in an abundance of mature frothing shrubs and leafy trees – a product of her dad's love of gardening. They were a mile or so away from the ocean; while the sea fog sometimes rolled this far inland and smothered the house, they couldn't see the sea from here, though being close enough to walk to the beach had always been one of the best things about growing up here.

'Thanks,' she said, glancing up at the meter and paying him with a note that would cover it. 'Keep the change.'

The driver tipped an imaginary cap and got out to fetch her bags from the boot. Hattie walked round to the back of the car and found he'd already placed them on the ground for her.

'Alright now?' he asked.

'Yes, thanks,' Hattie said. 'I can manage now.'

'Righto.'

With another brief nod, the driver got back into his car and drove away. Hattie looked up at the house and took a deep breath. Her mum and dad would be happy to see her, wouldn't they? Grabbing her bags, she walked up to the house. She'd soon find out one way or the other.

'Helloooo!'

Hattie closed the front door behind her and dropped her bags to the floor. The entrance hall was silent and she called again.

'Hello! Anyone home?'

Nothing. Her parents must have gone out, but she'd half expected that. Perhaps a little part of her had almost hoped for it. One thing was certain, she could hardly complain about it when she'd given no warning of her return.

Her parents had decorated again. The grand entrance – and it was just that, a room that opened out to various doorways and a staircase that curled into the next two floors – had been covered in a heavy paper last time she'd been to visit, but now the paper had been stripped and the walls had been painted in contrasting variations of sage and cream. It looked brighter, cleaner… more optimistic. The usual gallery of photos remained, however, and with them the pervading sense of sadness, reminders of what was lost, the immobility of time that had choked Hattie during the years before she'd left home. She took a slow tour of the walls, stopping to inspect each image as she reached it. There was her older sister, Charlotte, beaming down with her violin award. Charlotte winning the gymkhana. Charlotte in her school uniform proudly displaying her head-girl badge. Charlotte on her sixteenth birthday, Charlotte in her choir robes, Charlotte shaking the hand of the mayor and beaming for the camera…

Then the one at the end of the row, next to the stairs. Hattie and Charlotte together on the beach, squinting into the camera, smiles crinkling their faces as they held hands, the sun somewhere out of shot but bright and fierce. Hattie could still remember the feel of it burning her back. Hattie would have been six or seven here, Charlotte five years older. Hattie had long suspected that the only reason this photo had made it into the gallery was because Charlotte looked so unutterably angelic on it. Hattie herself looked like a smudge on legs and there were far nicer photos upstairs in her mother's album.

Hattie sighed as she gazed at the photo. Her parents would never stop mourning Charlotte and Hattie would never expect them to, but sometimes it felt as if they existed simply to mourn. Since Charlotte's death, keeping her memory alive had overshadowed everything else. It had become such a defining feature of Hattie's own childhood that it had engulfed it quite completely, and she sometimes wondered if they'd forgotten they had another daughter.

And there were the constant comparisons too, the constant disappointment that Hattie was not all that her sister had been. While Charlotte had been alive her parents had been able to celebrate the differences in their two daughters – and there had been many – safe in the knowledge, perhaps, that at least one of them would become all the things they valued and approved of. Once Charlotte was gone, it seemed to Hattie that she herself had suddenly become a living epitaph to their dead daughter, that they now expected Hattie to become all the things that her sister had been, to fill the gap her death had left in their lives. Charlotte, by virtue of never growing up, would never fail. She'd never go off the rails, marry an unsuitable husband, have children too early or too late, never disappoint or make mistakes or lead a messy life. She'd always be there: a perfect daughter in a photo, frozen in moments of achievement and triumph, while Hattie – live and fallible – made all the messes. Like running off to Paris against her parents' wishes and screwing everything up when she got there.

Hattie walked back to her cases and looked down. When it had all gone wrong in Paris, coming home had seemed so appealing, but now Hattie wasn't so sure it had been the best idea after all. The hallway where she now stood represented everything she'd run away from in the first place. She'd been so ready and eager to rush back to it when her life had taken a turn for the worse in Paris, but why? Had she expected her old life to offer some comfort and safety? In financial terms perhaps it would, but emotional comfort might be harder to come by.

She hauled in a breath and pushed her shoulders back. Her parents *would* be happy to see her and it *would* be good to be home again. And, even if they weren't, being back in the village where she'd grown up would offer so much in the way of welcome familiarity that it would be worth spending some time here. It wouldn't be forever anyway – she just needed a breather, time to regroup, decide what to do next with her life...

Dragging her cases into a corner of the hall, she went through to the kitchen. Sunlight was pouring in through the glass roof, bouncing from gleaming marble worktops. To judge from the smell of disinfectant, Carmen, their cleaner, had recently been in. Hattie went to the fridge and opened it to find the shelves groaning with food. Her flight had been delayed and she hadn't eaten since her early-morning check-in; she didn't think her parents would mind if she opened a pack of ham and made herself a sandwich. It was good ham too, Hattie remarked silently as she eyed the packaging – better than the stuff she'd been forced to eat living away from home. Her parents had always liked the best of everything and Hattie had grown up with no idea of what value brands looked like – until she'd gone to Paris, of course. There, with her extortionate rent and low wage, she'd soon found out the meaning of value. At first, she'd sort of enjoyed having to economise – it had almost been a kind of rebellion against her upbringing – but she soon realised just how privileged her home life had been and been filled with a sense of guilt for all she'd had before. She'd wanted to distance herself from that life and she would never tell new friends about it. Right now, a slice of luxury ham was very welcome – maybe she could forgive her parents' high standards just this once.

She'd just settled on a seat at the kitchen island with a ham and pickle sandwich and a large glass of cold, fresh orange juice when a voice floated into the kitchen. It was quiet and distant but unmistakable. With a faint look of regret at her lunch, she got up and went to the entrance hall to investigate. The letterbox of the front door was open and a mouth filled the slot.

'Dr Rose…? Mrs Rose…?'

Hattie smiled as she recognised the voice. Rushing to the door, she yanked it open and a tiny old man almost fell into the house. He looked up, his expression of shock and bewilderment giving way to a beaming smile.

'Hattie!' he cried, and she threw her arms around him.

'Rupert!'

'Nobody told me you were coming home!' Rupert said, holding her at arm's length now to look at her, smiling all over his face.

'I didn't know I was coming myself until yesterday,' she said, trying not to think about the events that had led to that decision. It was far too lovely seeing her old neighbour to let that sort of melancholy ruin the moment. 'How are you? It's so good to see you!'

'All the better for seeing you, my dear,' he replied cheerily. 'I expect your parents are thrilled to have you home.'

'They don't know I'm here yet – I've just arrived and nobody's home.'

'Ah,' Rupert said. 'That answers my question. I wanted to have a word with your father about my gammy knee.'

Hattie raised her eyebrows. 'Still not a fan of the new village GP?'

Rupert looked faintly guilty. He was of the generation that held anyone of any qualification in the utmost esteem and reverence, and he must have been half afraid that being less than complimentary about the village's new doctor would cause a bolt from heaven to strike him down.

'I'm sure she's very good but Gillypuddle is not the place for someone like her. She'd be better suited to a big city where she doesn't have to care about being part of the community.'

'Dad says she's very professional; that's why she doesn't get involved personally with her patients.'

Rupert gave a dramatic sigh. 'I suppose it's a modern thing. It's a sad sign of the times, though, when your family doctor can't stay for a pot of tea and a slice of cake.'

'I expect she's got a lot of work to get through,' Hattie said carefully. She was used to hearing all about Rupert's disgruntlement from phone calls to her mum and dad. 'I'm sure it's nothing personal.'

'It isn't and that's precisely the problem,' Rupert continued, determined that Hattie's assessment wouldn't sway him to have even the tiniest bit of sympathy with the new doctor's probably massive workload. Her dad had started his career back in the days when the village GP was everyone's friend, when people who worked in the health service had time to spare, but for many years now he'd been saying that it wasn't like it was in the old days and that the job got tougher every year. It had been one of the deciding factors in his recent decision to take retirement.

'So Dad's still seeing patients?' Hattie asked.

Rupert tapped the side of his nose. 'Not officially. He'll only give informal advice if his friends ask, and we mustn't say anything in case it gets back to the new woman – could cause all sorts of trouble.'

'I understand. I'm not really surprised either – I suspected Dad wasn't enjoying retirement much, even though he'd said for years he was going to take it as soon as he could.'

'Sixty's no age to retire these days, is it? You're still in the prime of your life at sixty. He's getting plenty of golf in though, so he's keeping busy.'

'Yes, so Mum tells me.' Hattie smiled. 'Why don't you come through to the kitchen and have a cup of tea? I'm sure Mum and Dad won't mind if you wait for them.'

'Where have they gone?'

Hattie paused. 'That's a very good question; I don't actually know!' It seemed ridiculous now that she wouldn't have warned her parents that she was coming home, but it had been such an impulsive, sudden decision that she'd barely thought about it. Now, it seemed rather arrogant to have assumed that her return would just be OK with them, that they'd accommodate her regardless. But all she'd thought about when she'd booked her flight back to the UK was how much she wanted to be home. And perhaps a small part of her had been desperate to delay for as long as possible the conversation about why she was giving up a life in Paris, when it had been the subject of such a fierce fight before she'd gone to chase it.

For the moment, she tried to push all this to the back of her mind and gave Rupert her brightest smile.

'In that case, perhaps I'd better not,' he said. 'It's not that I'm not enjoying your company, but there's no telling how long they'll be and Armstrong will want feeding.'

Hattie blinked. 'Armstrong?'

'Oh, I've still got him.' Rupert laughed. 'He's toothless and half deaf but I think he might be immortal.'

'I don't know about that, but I'm sure I've never heard of a cat as old as he must be now.'

'Twenty-three,' Rupert said proudly. 'Give or take a few months because we were never quite sure how old he was when he came to us.'

'Well, it must be a good life living with you. I ought to try it.'

'Ho ho, you practically did live at our house when you were little – you and your sister. Kitty loved having you both over – God rest her soul.'

'It's nice of you to say so but I'm sure we must have made absolute nuisances of ourselves, turning up at all hours and expecting you to drop everything to entertain us.'

'Never! We loved it. Kitty always said it was better than having our own children because we could send you back when we'd had enough.' He chuckled. 'Not that she'd ever have had enough. I think she would have adopted you both if Dr Rose had allowed it!'

Hattie's smile grew, but a small part of her thought that it was a good job she'd never known this fact when she was younger, because she might have campaigned quite vocally to put this arrangement into place. Not because she didn't love her parents or appreciate the home they'd given her, but because at least then the years after Charlotte's death wouldn't have been characterised by the overwhelming sadness that had eclipsed all else. Perhaps, in Rupert and Kitty's care, Hattie might have blossomed into the vibrant, individual flower she'd always felt she was meant to be instead of trying to grow into a shape that fitted the hole Charlotte had left behind. Perhaps she wouldn't have been gripped by the compulsion to rebel in quite the same way, and perhaps she wouldn't have dropped out of education or run off on a whim to Paris with a man twice her age. Perhaps she would have understood with more certainty where she fitted in the world and what she was capable of achieving. She'd had a lovely time in Paris, of course (until the last bit anyway), but she'd realised very soon after her arrival that the relationship that had taken her there had been a huge mistake and nobody – least of all Hattie – could argue with that.

'I'll pop back later,' Rupert said, speaking into her thoughts, 'when your parents are home. You'll be staying for a few days more?'

Hattie gave an uncertain nod. If her mum and dad would have her, she'd be staying for a lot longer than a few days, but she wasn't sure how welcome she'd be to move back in when she thought about how hard she'd tried to persuade them that Paris was the right place for her. The phrase *I told you so* was bound to feature in conversation when they returned and found her there, and she'd have to bite her tongue when it did.

'I expect so,' she said.

'Wonderful! I'll look forward to hearing all about your adventures in Paris then! I can't promise any fancy French wine if you pop round but I do have some bottles of bramble wine that I made last autumn.'

'That sounds lovely.' Hattie gave him a brief hug and a peck on a whiskery cheek. 'I'll look forward to that.'

Rupert smiled affectionately. 'You both were such sweet, polite little girls,' he said, 'you and your poor sister. Not many would spare time for an old man like me.'

'I've always got time for you, Rupert,' Hattie said.

She saw him to the door and, with a final farewell, she watched him go and shut it again. Her sandwich was waiting in the kitchen, but somehow she wasn't quite as hungry as she'd been when she'd made it. She walked back anyway, Charlotte smiling down at her from another row of photos on the wall. Hattie had returned to Gillypuddle to fix something, though she didn't even really know what it was that needed fixing. She'd thought coming home would make everything better, but now she wasn't quite so sure.

Chapter Three

Hattie was asleep on the conservatory sofa when the sound of a key turning in the lock of the front door woke her. She hadn't meant to fall asleep, but the sun pouring in had been so warm and the cushions so plump and soft, and she'd been up so early that morning, and in the end, it had been so easy to drift off. She leapt up now, groggy and disorientated, and rushed to the entrance hall, where she found her parents inspecting her suitcases with a puzzled look. At the sound of footsteps, her mother looked around and broke into a broad smile.

'Oh, how wonderful!' she cried. 'Why didn't you warn us you were coming?'

'I'd only just made up my mind for certain last night,' Hattie said, rushing into her mother's open arms. 'I'm sorry I didn't call ahead but…'

'But what?' Hattie's father asked, offering a slightly stiffer, more formal hug.

Hattie gave a vague shrug. 'It was all a bit sudden really and I didn't know how you'd react.'

'You're always welcome to visit us, any time,' her mother said. 'You know that. We hardly see you enough so we're not going to complain about a lovely surprise like this. How long are you staying? More than a day or two, I hope?'

'Maybe,' Hattie began slowly. 'How would you feel about me staying for good?'

'Coming home?' Hattie's mum looked to her husband. Hattie caught the uncertainty and her dad's answering frown.

'So what's happened?' he asked, turning to Hattie now.

'Nothing.'

He raised his eyebrows and Hattie felt fourteen again, making excuses for the cigarette butt he'd found at the end of the garden.

'I just decided that Paris is not for me after all. Not somewhere I want to live forever anyway.'

'What about that job you were so determined was going to change your fortunes? You didn't need a degree to be a success – that's what you told us. All those years of school fees down the drain so you could run away from home and play at fashion designer and now you don't even want to persevere doing that?'

'I know I said that but…' Hattie fell silent.

'And what about this man you were supposed to have been madly in love with? That ended well too, didn't it?'

'Dad…' Hattie's jaw clamped so tightly it almost felt like it would never open again. Didn't her dad know how much it hurt when he brought Bertrand into the conversation? It made her feel silly and ashamed for the way things ended there, and surely her dad could see that? 'I wasn't madly in love with him,' she said in a sulky tone that hid her real feelings. 'And I'd rather not talk about it if you don't mind.'

'So now you're home, what are your plans?'

'Nigel…' Hattie's mum cut in, 'perhaps we should have this conversation later?'

'Why?'

'Because Hattie's only just got here and I'm sure she's tired after her journey.'

'It's OK, Mum. Dad's right – I should have plans – but I'm afraid I don't have a clue. There. I messed up in Paris – is that what you wanted to hear?'

'Nobody's accusing you of that,' Hattie's mum said, but Hattie shook her head.

'It's what you're thinking.'

'It's what you think we ought to be thinking,' her dad said, 'but it wouldn't make any difference if we were or not. Nobody's ever been able to offer advice or the benefit of their wisdom to you without a fight and I'm not about to start trying again now. I expect you'll do what you always do – exactly what you want. And when you're bored you'll fly off on the next breeze. Is that about right?'

'I don't fly off on the next breeze,' Hattie returned sourly. 'I went to Paris to chase a career.'

'You went to chase a fantasy.'

'It was a job.'

'You'd have been better finishing your education.'

'I have an education – a very good one, as you keep reminding me.'

'An unfinished education. It's a competitive world out there and the best jobs go to those with the best qualifications.'

'Academia never suited me – I thought we'd established that.'

'You couldn't possibly have known that after only four months.'

'It was enough. If I'd studied for four centuries I wouldn't have liked it any better.'

'It's not about what you like and don't like. Charlotte understood how important it was and she worked hard even when she didn't want to. If she'd made it to her graduation…'

His sentence tailed off and Hattie saw her mother's gaze float to the row of photos on the wall. Everything always came back to Charlotte. If Charlotte had lived she would have become a consultant surgeon or a GP like her dad or something worthwhile. Charlotte would have been a success, not like her hopeless little sister who couldn't even stay away from home and rebel with any degree of efficiency.

'I'm sorry,' Hattie said quietly. 'It was a mistake.'

'I always said running off to France was a mistake.'

'Not that,' Hattie said. 'I shouldn't have come home.'

'Of course you should!' Hattie's mother cut in.

'But I've made Dad angry.'

'I'm not angry,' he said, and Hattie waited for him to add the usual: *I'm just disappointed.* Disappointed was what he'd always been in Hattie and why would that change now?

'Please stay,' her mother said.

'Rhonda…' Hattie's father began, but she fired a warning look and this time he backed down.

'I'll get a job, I promise,' Hattie said. 'I wouldn't be scrounging.'

'Nobody said you would,' Rhonda replied. 'We can talk about your options over dinner. How does that sound?'

Hattie hesitated. Exactly what options would these be? She wasn't sure she had all that many left. Twenty-six and no real education to speak of apart from some very expensive school certificates, and a CV that was frankly embarrassing. And it wasn't as if she was going to get a glowing reference from Alphonse in Paris any time soon, even if she dared to ask for one. But she looked into her mum's dazzling green eyes, the ones Charlotte had inherited, while Hattie's own were dull and brown like her dad's, and she could see that her mother was desperate to help.

'I'd like that,' Hattie replied finally. 'I'd appreciate any advice you could give me.'

'But would you be willing to take it?' Nigel asked.

'I'd be willing to think about it,' Hattie said. 'Would that be enough?'

He only frowned at her through his wire-framed glasses and offered no reply.

'I'll go and make up your old room,' Rhonda said into the silence.

'I'll help.' Hattie grabbed for the nearest suitcase and followed her mum up the stairs. She heard footsteps behind her and turned to see her dad bringing the other one.

'Is this all you have?' he asked.

'Yes.'

'It's not much to show for two years in Paris.'

'Well, the flat was furnished by the landlord and I didn't see the point in bringing back anything that I didn't really need.'

'So what did you do with the things you didn't need?'

'I gave them to a homeless charity,' Hattie huffed as she hauled her suitcase onto the landing at the top of the stairs and paused for breath. Her dad gave a nod of approval. At least she'd got that right if nothing else.

'I'll let you and your mother sort out the bedroom while I start dinner. We're having salmon if you're interested.'

'Sounds lovely,' Hattie replied absently, her gaze falling on a fresh row of childhood photos at the top of the stairs, the lion's share once again of Charlotte. She couldn't understand how, but she'd quite forgotten about this collection, though she'd seen them often enough over the years. The sight of them threw her. Her dad was right – if Charlotte had lived to be a hundred years old, she'd have never cocked up as often or as impressively as Hattie did.

Chapter Four

Hattie pushed her empty plate away. 'That was *so* good! The best chefs in Paris can't cook like you, Dad. Not that I got much of a chance to try out the best chefs on my wages…'

Nigel nodded his thanks with a wry smile. 'Do the best chefs in Paris have someone to clean up for them?'

Hattie grinned. 'I see what you did there… I'll clear the table.'

'I'll help you,' Rhonda said, finishing her wine.

'Thanks, Mum.'

Hattie began to collect up the dirty dishes with her mum. In the kitchen they stacked the dishwasher together.

'It's so lovely to have you home,' Rhonda said.

'Do you think Dad feels the same way? It didn't seem like it at dinner. I know he wants to talk seriously about what I'm going to do now I'm back in England, but honestly, Mum, I just don't think I'm ready yet.'

'I know, darling. It doesn't matter – when you're ready.'

'I don't think Dad would agree with you there.'

'He does. Oh, don't listen to him… you know what he's like. He's spent too many years calling the shots in his career – it's hard for him when something is out of his control.'

'Something like me?'

'He really does only want what's best for you. That's all he's ever wanted for his children.'

'I know. And Charlotte would have listened to him too.'

'You're not incapable of listening.'

'The trouble is, I can listen but I can't always agree. I can't help that I'm not the same as you and Dad.'

'That's not what we're asking of you; we don't want a carbon copy. We realise that you might have different hopes and aspirations to those we might have for you. We realised that a long time ago, but it doesn't stop us from sometimes thinking you're making a mistake and wanting to do something about it.'

'Even if they're mistakes, they're my mistakes and I want to be able to make them. I'm twenty-six, Mum. I'm not your little girl anymore.'

'You'll always be our little girl, no matter how old you are.' Rhonda's smile was melancholy and Hattie guessed that she might be thinking about her other little girl, the one who would never grow up and never be able to make mistakes now.

'Thanks, Mum,' Hattie said. 'I appreciate that.'

'So…' Rhonda said in an obvious attempt to banish the gloom that had settled over the kitchen. 'What are you planning to do now you're home? Don't worry, I'm talking in the short term here, nothing more.'

'Apart from sleep for a week?' Hattie smiled. 'I suppose I'll need a job.'

'In Gillypuddle? I think you'll find your options rather limited. I imagine you'll have to look further afield if you want something above minimum wage.'

'For now, I'll take minimum wage if I have to. As long as it allows me to give you and Dad a little.'

'We don't need money and we don't care if you contribute to the house or not.'

'It's the principle, Mum.'

'But we wouldn't have you slogging your guts out in some horrible job just to give us money.'

'I think Dad might see it as a matter of principle too. Or at least pride. I don't think he would be able to hold his head high at the golf club if his loser daughter was scrounging from him.'

'You wouldn't be scrounging,' Rhonda said, though Hattie thought that, privately, her mum probably agreed with her. Hattie's dad had always been big on image and social standing.

'Well, regardless, it might have to be a minimum-wage job considering my qualifications and recent work record.'

'You had a perfectly good job.'

'Maybe, but I don't suppose a casual working arrangement with a temperamental Frenchman is going to count for much back here in England and I don't think Alphonse will be too forward with the references either.'

'So…' Rhonda wiped her hands on a dishcloth and reached for the washing tablets from the cupboard. 'Are you going to tell me what really happened in Paris?'

Hattie held up a serving dish. 'Do you maybe want to rinse this before I put it in the dishwasher?'

'Hattie…' Rhonda said sternly.

Hattie put the dish in the sink with a heavy sigh.

'Honestly, I don't really know. I mean, I messed up but it wasn't really anything I wouldn't have been able to put right with an apology and a bit of grovelling.'

'So why didn't you do that?'

Hattie shrugged. 'I suppose the bright shiny career working in fashion that I thought I was going to have one day wasn't looking quite so bright and shiny anymore. I had friends and, even though Bertrand had left me high and dry, I was having a good time. Living in Paris was like a dream, of course, but… something was just missing. I can't explain it, but I think now that maybe I was using the thing that went wrong as an excuse to give it up and come home.'

'What do you think was missing?'

'All that stuff didn't mean anything. You know – like Dad's job made a real difference and so did your law career. You did important things – Dad saved lives and you saved innocent people from prison. They meant something and my job with Alphonse just didn't. It was like an empty sweet wrapper – all tempting and pretty on the outside, but when you got into it, there was just nothing there.'

'So…' Rhonda smiled. 'While others leave home to find themselves, you've had to come back to do that?'

Hattie gave a small laugh. 'I suppose you could look at it that way. I just need time to figure out what I want.'

'It's not too late to go back into education.' Rhonda closed the door of the dishwasher and switched it on.

'I know that's what you and Dad would like, but it's just not for me.'

'How do you know if you don't give it a chance?'

'I just do.'

'Well, if you say you want to do a job that matters like your father and I had, that's all very noble, but careers like that don't come with half an hour's on-the-job training before your first shift starts.'

'I said I wanted to make a difference, but I'm sure there are other ways of doing that without having to take exactly the same career path as you or Dad did. There has to be something out there for me, something that I'm meant for, and I just need to find out what it is.'

'But opening yourself up to educational possibilities might help.'

Hattie frowned. 'You're starting to sound like Dad.'

'Because I actually think your father might have a point. What if we made some enquiries, found out what it would take to get you on a course somewhere? We could go and look at some nearby universities, talk to some people…'

'That's not what I want, Mum.'

Rhonda pursed her lips. 'Sometimes what you don't want is exactly what you need.'

'Yes, but if I don't want it then I don't really care if I do need it or not because I don't want it. And that sentence *does* make more sense in my head.'

'At the very least, don't dismiss the idea out of hand. Please say you'll give it some consideration. You did say you'd listen to our advice.'

'I suppose I did.'

'So you'll think about it?'

'I'm not making any promises.'

'Good,' Rhonda said, apparently choosing not to acknowledge Hattie's negative response. 'Your dad will be pleased to hear that the idea is not completely dead in the water.'

'But I am going to look for a job in the meantime.'

'Of course. You know, now that I think about it, I'm almost certain that Lance and Mark were looking for someone to help out at the Willow Tree.'

'They're still running that place? I thought they'd sell up after Mark's heart attack.'

'It was touch and go for poor Mark and we all thought that, but I suppose the Willow Tree is their lifeline. Lance told me they'd thought long and hard about keeping it on but decided that they'd be so bored if they sold up they'd probably eat themselves to death anyway.'

Hattie was thoughtful for a moment. Lance and Mark were fun, and it couldn't be that hard working in a sweet little café like the Willow Tree where the lunchtime rush mainly consisted of the ladies of the village choir or the odd passing tourist on their way to the coast. It might just be the breather she needed while she worked out a bigger life plan.

'I'll call in tomorrow and see if the job is still going,' she announced.

'Right.' Rhonda peered into an open cupboard. 'Now that's settled would you ask your father if he wants mint or chamomile tea?'

As Hattie made her way back to the dining room, her mum called after her. 'In fact, when you've taken his order you can make it – it'd be good practise for your new career in catering.'

Hattie turned to her with a grin. It was a shame more conversations with her parents didn't go this way, but when they did, she loved being at home with them again.

'Oh!' she said, suddenly recalling something she'd needed to tell them. 'I don't know why I just thought about it but I forgot to tell you that Rupert came looking for Dad earlier. He wants him to look at his knee.'

'In that case we'll skip the tea for now and pop next door. I'm sure Rupert will have one of his fruit wines open. Want to come?'

'That sounds nice, and I did say I'd try to see him anyway now that I'm home.'

'Perfect! I'll go and fetch my jacket; I could do with giving old Armstrong a cuddle…'

Despite her long day of travelling, the three glasses of warming bramble wine shared with her parents and Rupert, the easy conversation with her affable neighbour and more than her fair share of fussing an old cat with a purr that could still shake tiles from the roof, regardless of his advanced age, Hattie still struggled to sleep that night. She woke early the next morning with the future on her mind. She'd told her mum that she didn't want to go back into education and it was true, but she did have to concede that they had a point about where her life was going without it. She could train for something – but what? The fact was, it bothered her more than she'd let on. And she couldn't shake the feeling of failure that had clung to her, even though she'd left Paris. Everything had gone wrong there in the end, no matter how hard she'd worked to make it go right. First Bertrand had abandoned her, and then she'd messed up with Alphonse.

As quietly as she could, she went downstairs as the sun was rising to make herself a chamomile tea.

As she pulled up the blinds in the kitchen to let the sunlight in, she was forced to smile at the sight of Rupert's old cat, Armstrong, sitting on the windowsill, staring impassively at her. She opened the window and he stepped in, rubbing his face against her outstretched hand and purring so loudly that Hattie half wondered if it would wake her parents. Half an hour with Armstrong gave her more peace than any amount of sleep could have, and half an hour was all she got. Armstrong, as was his fickle way, decided he'd had enough mid-stroke, turned tail and stalked off. Hattie watched him leap down from the windowsill and pad across the garden, keeping a keen eye on a family of sparrows that were flitting noisily around the bird table.

She closed the window and filled the kettle. She'd been so engrossed with Rupert's cat that she'd totally forgotten her tea. But then her gaze went to the bright meadows beyond her dad's beloved garden. A walk. Maybe a good long walk would tire her out and she could head back to bed for an extra few hours.

Putting the kettle to one side, she headed upstairs to pull some clothes on over her pyjamas.

Hattie had only intended to do a circuit of the nearest field and then go back, but her thoughts had been so absorbing that before she knew it, she was treading the old path that led to the beach and the cliffs that overlooked it. She didn't know what had taken her there, but now that she was on her way she longed to see the sea. So she quickened her step. She knew exactly where she wanted to go – to the secret spot where she'd always gone with Charlotte. They'd play, and later, when Charlotte got too old to play with Hattie, she'd take Hattie anyway. Then she'd show her patterns in the rocks or they'd hunt for shells. Sometimes they'd look for creatures in the pools and sometimes they'd see how many different types of birds they could spot. Hattie thought with a melancholy fondness on those times now and though she knew it was pointless to wish them back, it didn't stop her from doing it. Perhaps Charlotte wasn't a perfect teenager, but she was always perfect in Hattie's memory.

As Hattie approached the path that would lead to the beach, she heard a noise, carried on the breeze. It seemed to be coming from the cliff top. It sounded like… Hattie frowned. It sounded like braying.

Nobody, as far as she knew, kept donkeys around here. There was old man Ferguson's farm up there, but he'd never kept donkeys and, besides, he'd been dead for years. Her mum and dad hadn't mentioned anyone buying the place. Then again, she supposed it probably wouldn't be a priority in their minds to tell her if someone had.

It came again and Hattie was intrigued enough now that she just had to go and look. So she changed direction and headed up to the cliff path.

At the top, sure enough, there was an enclosure and in it perhaps half a dozen or more donkeys. She was sure it had never been there before. So did that mean someone had bought the farm? If someone had, she wondered what else they were keeping.

She walked up to the wire fencing. Watching her idly was a smoky brown donkey. Hattie smiled. Within the enclosure, further away in a cluster as if they might be gossiping about the first one, stood the others. Hattie went up to the one on its own and approached it cautiously.

'Hey, fella...'

The donkey shuffled forward and nuzzled into Hattie's outstretched hand. She giggled and rubbed its velvet nose.

'What's wrong with that lot?' she asked, nodding at the others. 'Gossiping about you? I'd take no notice – gossips only gossip because they've got nothing useful to do.'

The donkey snorted down its nose at her and she leapt back with a giggle. But then it stretched forward and started to nose into her coat pocket.

'There's nothing in there, I'm afraid.' She yanked a handful of wild grass from around the fencing and offered it, but the donkey didn't seem interested. Instead, it went for her pocket again and she had to push him off.

'So who owns you?' she asked thoughtfully. Maybe she could take a walk to the old Ferguson place and see if anyone was living there now. But then, perhaps if someone saw her it might look like she was trespassing. At the very least it would seem incredibly nosey and she had the feeling that she shouldn't even be here now with the donkey, let alone visiting the farm. But the donkey was so adorable that she decided it was worth taking the risk and she fussed him for another ten minutes before finally deciding that she ought to go back to her original plan and head to the beach.

Before she went, she walked the length of the fencing to see if she could get a closer look at the other donkeys. They were only vaguely interested in her, though she did notice that a grey one had now wandered over to the brown donkey Hattie had been fussing and was now standing silently alongside, both of them looking out to sea together like two old men sharing views on the weather. Hattie smiled. They were so cute. She'd always loved animals and she couldn't bear to think of one suffering. In Paris, she'd fed any cat that came near the balcony of her flat, much to the annoyance of her landlord and flatmates. When she'd said that they looked like they were starving, her flatmates had only laughed and told her that if they were hungry they'd be keener to keep the rat population at bay.

With a last fuss of her new friend, Hattie turned back to the path that led to her secret cove. Not secret, of course, because everyone in Gillypuddle knew about it, but it was always the way she'd thought of it – hers and Charlotte's secret. It was the place where they'd shared childish confidences, the place where she'd always felt she could have her sister's undivided attention.

Once she got to the grassy steps, cut into the cliffs, memories overwhelmed her. When it was wet the steps were dangerous, but Charlotte would always cling to Hattie's hand until they were down safely. When the weather was dry they'd flatten grass that had grown along the steps as they walked, disturbing bees and dandelion seeds and sending them into the air. The air now was salty, as it was back then, and the sea dashed itself against the rocks in a steady rhythm as it had always done and as it would continue to do. This coast, this landscape, this sea… they were forever – it was only the people who lived here who weren't.

Hattie sat on the sand. It was damp. She poked her finger into it and wrote her name. Then she wrote Charlotte's, and she tried to pretend that Charlotte herself had just written it. Even after all these years, just like her parents did, Hattie still missed her terribly. But unlike them, she just didn't think that Charlotte would want to see her sad forever.

Chapter Five

Hattie had returned home from her hour on the sand feeling peaceful but still not tired. Her parents had gone out and left her a note to get her own breakfast, so she hadn't been able to catch up with them or ask whether Sweet Briar Farm had a new owner. It meant the mystery would have to wait for now. So she'd got showered and dressed and had headed into the village on her quest to find work. The first port of call was to check out her mum's recommendation.

The Willow Tree café was a little old-fashioned by most standards, but what it lacked in modernity it more than made up for in atmosphere. It was spotless, cosy and welcoming, due in part to the continued efforts of the owners, Lance and Mark. Wooden tables were dressed in clean red gingham cloths with fresh flowers in slender white vases and watercolours of the local scenery painted by Mark's mother on the walls. Lance and Mark ran it with pride, and they loved it almost as much as they loved each other. Lance was ten years younger than Mark, dark-haired, trim and neat, while Mark carried a little weight (which actually rather suited him) and more grey in his perfectly groomed hair. Mark had met Lance in a bar in Amsterdam, where he'd been living and working after leaving his home in rural Wales for a spot of adventure, and by the time the night had been over Lance had already promised to move to

England to be with him – or so the legend went. Hattie had never actually asked them how they'd met, but she didn't think the story sounded all that unlikely.

They were both standing behind the counter of the Willow Tree now, side by side in matching deckchair-striped aprons, Mark looking suitably apologetic as he spoke.

'I'm so sorry, my love,' he said. 'If only we'd known you were back we'd have snapped you up.'

'You'd have certainly added a bit of glamour to the place,' Lance agreed with an equally apologetic expression.

'But Phyllis Roundtree came about it yesterday,' Mark continued. 'And we gave the job to her.'

Lance shot Mark a look that could have meant anything, but knowing the two of them of old, Hattie guessed it was a look that said they'd had some disagreement about Phyllis's employment. She'd lived in the village for all of her... well, Hattie didn't know exactly how old Phyllis was, but she knew she was old, and she kept herself busy and active. Hattie had no doubt that she'd keep up the pace in the café, and she was very popular on account of her sunny disposition, but she was known to be a little accident-prone. Quite a lot accident-prone, as it happened; her exploits including falling into a pub cellar because she'd failed to notice the trapdoor was open, getting caught in the closing doors of a bus as it started to drive away and knocking down the maypole in her out-of-control Mini Metro. And that was just the stuff that was big enough to become village news.

'I don't know that it would have been enough hours for you anyway,' Lance added. 'It's only a little job and we can't afford to pay a lot – it's just to take the strain off Mark occasionally.' He threw an affectionate glance at Mark. 'Don't want any more silly heart attacks, do we?'

'So I have to take it easy,' Mark said. 'Even though it's driving me mad. Doctor's orders.'

'My dad's by any chance?' Hattie asked.

Mark looked sheepish.

'It's OK.' Hattie laughed. 'I saw Rupert yesterday and he's still asking Dad for medical advice too.'

'I am very sorry about the job, though,' Mark said.

Hattie shrugged. 'It's not your fault. I was just hoping to get a little something in Gillypuddle for now that would save me having to commute.'

'If it doesn't work out with Phyllis we'll be sure to come to you next,' Lance said.

'I'd appreciate it,' Hattie said.

'Stay for a latte,' Lance said. 'On the house. You can tell us all about the glamour of *gay Paris...*'

'Oh... I suppose it wouldn't hurt to stay for one,' Hattie said. 'And I don't suppose you have a copy of the *Gillypuddle Newsletter* lying around?'

'What on earth do you want to read that drivel for?' Lance asked with a laugh as he poured milk into a steel jug. 'Unless you're desperate for an update on that family of ducks after their highly traumatic attempts to cross the A road last winter.'

'No.' Hattie giggled. 'Nothing like that. I just wondered if there might be any other jobs in there.'

'I doubt it,' Lance replied and Mark nodded agreement. 'We'd usually be first to hear any news around here and we haven't heard anyone saying they need staff.'

'Apart from Medusa on the hill,' Mark added in a meaningful tone and Lance laughed.

'Nobody in their right minds would work for her,' he said. 'Besides, didn't she say it was a bed-and-board arrangement only?'

'No pay?' Hattie asked. Surely she had heard it wrong.

Lance nodded.

'Really?' Hattie frowned. 'Are you sure?'

'Well, perhaps she's paying some kind of wage, but whatever it is, it won't be enough. I'd want a gold pig to work for her.'

Hattie was thoughtful for a moment. 'Should I know who this person is?'

'Jo Flint,' Lance said. Hattie shook her head. 'She's been here for a good couple of years now,' he continued. 'She bought old man Ferguson's place on Sweet Briar Cliffs.'

'I don't know her,' Hattie replied. But that did confirm Hattie's suspicions that someone had bought the farm. So did this woman own the donkeys Hattie had seen too? 'Maybe she moved in as I was moving away…'

'Perhaps so,' Mark said, the sound of frothing milk drowning out the rest of his reply.

'Mum and Dad have never mentioned her to me,' Hattie said to Lance.

'They've probably never had cause to run into her. Keeps herself to herself.'

'And she's got a job opening?'

Mark placed the latte on the counter in front of her. 'She might have but you wouldn't want to take it.'

'Why not?'

'For a start, she's hell on toast. Horrible woman – so rude and obnoxious. Doesn't care a fig for Gillypuddle or anyone in it. She didn't even come down from the cliffs for the Round Table Christmas charity do last year!'

'Maybe she's just very private. What does she do then if she wants help?'

'She's got some sort of donkey prison,' Lance said.

Hattie had to laugh at his expression of mischief. 'Donkey prison? I did see some donkeys up there this morning when I went for a walk but they didn't look too distressed to me.'

'It's supposed to be a donkey sanctuary,' Mark cut in. He offered Hattie a biscotti.

'But imagine being a poor defenceless donkey and being forced to go and live with that miserable old trout,' Lance continued. 'You'd have to phone Donkey Line to be rescued or something, wouldn't you?'

'So she looks after donkeys? What does she need help with? Cleaning them or something?'

'Haven't a clue,' Lance said airily. 'Perhaps she needs someone to polish her horns of an evening.'

'You're terrible.' Hattie laughed. 'Both of you!'

Mark looked at Lance with an affectionate grin. 'Aren't we just? It must be why we're so well suited.'

'So this Jo Flint may have a job?' she asked thoughtfully.

'If you can call it that. The pay is terrible and I'm almost certain she said she wanted whoever she employs to live there. That's probably why nobody's been stupid enough to apply for it.'

'Nobody's applied for it?'

'Not that I'm aware of.'

'I think I might like to have a go at that. I like animals, and the donkeys were very cute.'

Lance and Mark exchanged a look and Hattie laughed again. 'She can't be *that* bad.'

'Oh, you poor misguided child,' Mark said, shaking his head as he eyed Hattie with mock solemnity. 'I think you'll find she can.'

*

'Dad… can I use the laptop?'

Hattie peered around the door of her father's study. The walls were lined with bookcases – most of the books housed there guides to various medical issues, volumes containing anatomical diagrams and lists of encyclopaedias of exotic-sounding diseases that most people had never heard of. His desk faced out towards the window and looked onto a picture-perfect view of gently rolling hills and distant trees. Her father was sitting at his desk poring over a copy of *The Lancet*. So much for retirement, Hattie thought wryly.

'What do you need it for?' he asked as he picked it up from his desk and handed it to her.

'Really, Dad?' Hattie frowned.

'I'm not prying – I simply wondered if you'd decided to act on the discussions we had last night.'

Hattie had. She recalled now very vocal and detailed debates about her options for the future. Most of them had involved going back into education in some form or another. Hattie had decided to act on their discussions in a very general way, and perhaps not quite in the way her dad had hoped. The fact was, she couldn't stop thinking about this mysterious Jo Flint and her donkey sanctuary on Sweet Briar Cliffs. Mark and Lance had told her more about Jo – about how very private she was, how miserable she seemed, how she went out of her way to avoid any kind of community involvement, how she spent all her time up on the cliffs with her donkeys. Hattie was intrigued. She wanted to know why Jo was all these contradictory things. Contradictory, because if she was so miserable and selfish, why did she care so much for the donkeys? If she hated everyone in the village so much, why was she asking for help? If she hated company, why was she willing to have someone live with her? To Hattie, it could only mean that she cared so much about her donkeys that she was willing to make these concessions and, in Hattie's eyes, that made her far less scary than she might have everyone believe. It made her like Hattie – an animal lover – and how could anyone who loved animals be all that bad?

Hattie had decided to see if there was a visitor website or such for the sanctuary – perhaps even a number so she could phone for more information about what sort of help Jo was looking for. She had some experience of horses – she and Charlotte had shared a pony called Peanut for many years – and how different could a donkey be?

'I'm doing some research,' she said evasively as her dad waited for a reply. 'I wouldn't have it for long.'

He was clearly pleased by the incorrect assumption that she'd be looking up mature student entry routes into university and not looking for photos of an elusive and unpopular local. 'Take as long as you like.'

'Thanks, Dad.'

'Oh, and your mother wanted you earlier. I think you were in the shower or something – goodness knows… She's popped out again now but she wanted me to tell you she ran into Melinda this morning and told her you were back. Melinda's going to call later to see if you'd like to meet up.'

Hattie smiled broadly. 'How many of her kids will she be bringing? How many does she even have now?'

'Oh, I should say a least half a dozen,' Nigel said with a wry smile as he dropped his reading glasses back onto his nose.

Hattie laughed lightly as she closed the door to his study and took the laptop to the kitchen. Melinda had been Hattie's best friend all through primary school. And even when Hattie had gone to a different, fee-paying secondary school outside the village, they'd stayed good friends. Partly because the teenage population of Gillypuddle was so small it was hard to do much else. In their final year of high school, Melinda had started dating Stu. They'd been inseparable ever since and by the age of eighteen were married, with Melinda expecting her first baby.

Melinda and Stu were thrilled and everyone could see how devoted they were to one another and what fantastic parents they'd be. Melinda and Stu's own parents clubbed together to give them a deposit on a little cottage and their first child, Sunshine, was born a few months later. Ocean followed after a year, Melinda getting caught almost immediately after Sunshine's birth, then Rain another year after that, and finally Daffodil after a more respectable two-year gap, until even Melinda had declared that four children by the age of twenty-four was quite enough for anyone. It wasn't viable for Melinda to work because the childcare bill would be so enormous, but Stu worked long hours in the local garage to support them. His dad had built an extension onto their tiny cottage to house their own little population explosion, and Hattie suspected that both sets of parents sent regular rescue packages to Melinda and Stu's home.

Daffodil had been tiny when Hattie was last over, but she'd been a delightful baby even then. All of Melinda and Stu's children were perfectly adorable and angelic and an absolute pleasure to be around. Hattie couldn't imagine how Melinda and Stu had managed to bring them up so well when their lives must have been far from easy. It would be good to see Melinda and her brood again and catch up on the latest instalment of the Melinda and Stu love story. There'd been plenty of messaging while Hattie had been away in Paris, but it just wasn't the same as a natter in person. Hattie decided she'd give her friend a call as soon as she was done with her dad's laptop.

After pouring herself a juice, Hattie fired up the laptop. She didn't have a name for Jo's sanctuary – mostly because Lance and Mark didn't think Jo had ever chosen an official one – but she knew it was based at Sweet Briar Farm, so she keyed that into the search box, alongside Dorset and donkey sanctuary, and a second later a lot of random results came up. There were pages for tourism, pages about the area in general, a website dedicated to the flora and fauna of the cliffs, something about the geology, another listing nearby holiday accommodation and an amateur photography account, but there was no website for Jo's sanctuary.

Strange, Hattie thought, and clicked through to the second page of results. Nothing there either, and only at the bottom of the third page came a clue – a link to a now defunct page of an estate-agent listing of Sweet Briar Farm from two years before. This must have been how Jo had come across the property to buy. The photo showed a tumbledown place with higgledy roof slates, rotten windows and frames and crumbling render surrounded by overgrown gardens. Despite the disrepair – or perhaps because of it – the place had a sort of wild beauty about it. The listing said that the house came with a large amount of land, including its own orchards and paddocks, but acknowledged that extensive repairs and modernisation were necessary to restore the house and outbuildings. The price was still eye-watering, though. Jo must have either had a tidy sum put to one side or taken on a crippling mortgage. Hattie didn't know much about saving donkeys but she guessed it wasn't cheap, and if there was no website inviting paying visitors, then she couldn't imagine Jo was making much money for the upkeep of the place either. All this information only served to intrigue Hattie further.

Closing the page down, she went onto a telephone directory site to see if she could find a number listed but – as she'd half expected – there was none. It looked as if she was just going to have to go and visit in person to see if she could catch Jo. The problem with that was she couldn't ask her mum or dad to drive her up there without telling them why and, as she didn't have a car of her own and the local taxi service was so unreliable it was practically non-existent, it would mean borrowing a car or begging a lift from someone else and she couldn't think who because it seemed like a big ask. Failing that, it meant another hike up to Sweet Briar Cliffs – it usually took a good hour at least there and back. She looked out of the window. At least it looked likely to stay fine for the next few hours.

Having finally made up her mind, Hattie hopped off the kitchen stool and went to find her shoes.

Chapter Six

Up on the winding path that climbed the cliffs there was a brisk salted breeze. The sun was warm when it dropped, foam-topped waves dancing in the bay, twisting and rolling and breaking in tiny explosions onto the rocks below. The grass was strewn with daisies and buttercups, and pockmarked with rabbit burrows. Paris was beautiful and magical, but Hattie had forgotten how beautiful and magical her home could be. Her dad had always said that this was what heaven would look like for him, and for the first time Hattie understood what he meant.

Once again, as she emerged from the path onto the cliff top, she saw the new wire fencing circling the field. The donkeys were milling about looking perfectly content. Hattie went up to the fence and clicked her tongue onto the roof of her mouth to call them over.

'Here donkeys!' she called. 'Come and say hello!'

One or two simply looked at her and then turned back to whatever pressing thoughts of life, the universe and everything had been occupying them. But the brown one who'd come for a fuss earlier came over again.

'Hey!' Hattie smiled as she rubbed a hand down his nose. He nuzzled at her. She wished she'd brought a treat to give him now, but she hadn't thought about it when she'd left the house.

'I wonder if you're a Victor or Victoria,' she said. 'You're a friendly little soul anyway,' she continued. 'I reckon I could look after you.

What do you know about the job? Come on, you can tell me and I won't squeal that you gave me inside information—'

'Hey!'

Hattie whirled around to see a woman striding towards her. She was well-built, hair scraped back into a severe ponytail, dressed in grubby jeans and a wax jacket, and carrying a bucket. And she didn't look happy.

'This is private property,' she bellowed.

'I'm sorry,' Hattie began, but she quickly realised that the wind was taking her words in the opposite direction. Instead, she walked to meet her. This had to be Jo. The woman was breathing heavily as she ran a critical eye over Hattie, who squinted as the sun moved from behind a cloud. 'I didn't know I wasn't supposed to be up here – I thought the cliff path was a public thoroughfare. Are you Jo?'

'Depends who's asking,' the woman said, giving Hattie another obvious once-over. Hattie was suddenly very aware of how un-workmanlike her flippy skirt and denim jacket must look. Perhaps she should have worn something that made her look more practical and capable.

'I heard you needed some help,' Hattie replied, deciding that the woman probably was Jo.

'Maybe.'

Hattie tried not to frown. Either she did or she didn't.

'Well, I was looking for work,' Hattie replied uncertainly.

'Know anything about donkeys?'

'I know about horses,' Hattie said brightly. 'A little, anyway. I used to ride a pony.'

Jo – Hattie was fairly confident now that this was Jo – sniffed. 'Horses are not donkeys.'

'I know that – I only meant that I'm good to muck out and do a bit of manual work because I used to muck Peanut out. If that's the sort of help you need, of course… I love animals if that helps…' she added, immediately feeling a bit silly. It was like going for a job as a teacher with no qualifications and saying that you liked kids.

'I can't pay more than minimum wage. Did you hear that from your source?'

'Minimum wage?' Hattie repeated, quickly running the figures through in her head.

'I can offer bed and board too – makes it better than a minimum wage in the end.'

Hattie shoved her hands in her jacket pockets. 'Bed and board where?' she asked, casting her mind back to the photos of Sweet Briar Farm she'd seen on the estate-agent listing. She knew the farmhouse lay beyond the rise of the paddock they were now standing next to so she couldn't see from here what changes – if any – Jo had made. Surely she would have made some improvements if she was expecting someone else to be happy living there?

'My house,' Jo said.

'Sweet Briar Farm?'

Jo put the bucket down and folded her broad arms across her chest. 'Been doing your homework, have you?'

'I was just trying to find out a bit more about what you might need.'

'Help with the donkeys,' Jo replied, as if this was the most obvious thing in the world. She wasn't exactly making herself personality of the year but still, if she was trying to put Hattie off for some reason, it wasn't working. The idea of living at the Sweet Briar farmhouse – or wreck, depending on how much had been done to it – wasn't exactly appealing, and neither was Jo if Hattie was honest. But she did need something to fill her time, and she had promised herself it would be something worthwhile, something that mattered. Jo and her donkeys mattered, didn't they?

'Right,' Hattie said.

'And you reckon you could do that?'

'I'm sure if you showed me the ropes I could.'

Jo nodded shortly, silent again as she sized Hattie up.

'And I wouldn't actually want any bed or board because I'm good for that, so I'd just take the wage; I wouldn't mind that at all.'

'I'd need you to be on site,' Jo said. 'If you can't move in then I can't give you the job. Donkeys need looking after night and day.'

'Oh. Well, when do you take time out? Surely you're not working twenty-four-seven?'

'I don't take time off.'

'You'd have to give an employee time off.'

'Anyone who works for me works the same as me.'

'But the law—'

'Doesn't concern me. What concerns me is that these donkeys have all they need.'

Hattie stared at her. Maybe this wasn't such a good idea after all.

'Look,' she began. 'I'm sorry I wasted your time—'

Hattie stopped mid-sentence as something nudged into her shoulder and almost knocked her off balance. She turned to see her new donkey friend, pestering for another fuss.

'Norbert's oldest one here,' Jo said, nodding at him. 'Friendliest donkey you'll ever meet. Good judge of character too. If Norbert likes you then that's usually alright with me.'

Norbert pushed his nose into Hattie's neck and she giggled.

'He does seem very affectionate,' she said, pushing him off with a smile. 'I bet your visitors love him.'

'Don't get visitors.' Jo picked up the bucket. 'Just me and the lads up here.'

'You don't have visitors? Don't people want to come? I mean, I did notice you had no website but...'

'Don't need people coming round and upsetting the donkeys,' Jo said briskly. 'Peace and quiet is what they need. Most of them have come from bad places – treated cruelly, abused or neglected. Some of them have lost good owners and that's almost as bad. I'm here to give them a safe home, not turn them into something to be gawped at by misbehaving school trips.'

That all sounded very noble, Hattie thought, but where was the money coming from to look after these lucky donkeys? She thought better of saying so, but she couldn't deny it was just another thing about Jo that intrigued her.

'Do you want the job or not?' Jo said into the gap.

'I'd have to live here?'

Jo nodded.

'And you wouldn't be able to pay more than minimum wage?'

'No, afraid not.'

'And I wouldn't be able to have time off?'

'Maybe I could see my way to the odd day. Depends what the donkeys want.'

Nobody in their right mind would see this as an attractive employment package. Jo would wait for a hundred years to get help on those terms. Hattie glanced back at Norbert and reached to rub his neck as he gazed at her through melancholy, pleading old eyes. Maybe it would be fun to take care of him for a while. She looked at Jo, who wore the slightly worrying expression of someone who might just punch her in the face if Hattie dared refuse the offer now that she'd made it. OK, maybe not fun, but maybe it would be interesting, and she hadn't got anything better to do.

'Is there a trial period?' she asked.

Jo sniffed, wiping a hand on the back of her jeans. 'Stay if you want, go if you've had enough. I don't need to trial you – Norbert looks happy enough.'

If Hattie took this job, it would possibly be a more stupid and impulsive decision than the one she'd made to leave for Paris. Her dad would say so, but something about the idea was pulling her in and wouldn't let go.

'Alright,' she said finally. 'When would you need me to start?'

'Sooner the better,' Jo said, starting to walk to the gates to the field.

'Next week?' Hattie asked, needing to put some sort of date on it.

'If you like.'

Jo continued to walk away.

'Don't you want details from me?' Hattie called after her. 'Name, address, previous employment…?'

Jo waved a dismissive hand as she shut the gates to the field behind her and started to march up the gentle slope to the main group of donkeys.

'My name's Hattie!'

'Great!'

'Hattie Rose!'

At this, Jo stopped and turned around. 'Dr Rose anything to do with you?'

'My dad.'

Jo nodded, seemingly satisfied, and turned back to the donkeys.

Hattie watched for a moment, uncertain whether she ought to stay or go. But then she left Norbert with a last neck rub and began to walk back down the cliff path. She wasn't altogether sure how it had happened, and she had no idea what to expect, but it looked as if she was moving into Sweet Briar Farm with the strangest woman she'd ever met.

Chapter Seven

'Well,' Lance said as he placed a pot of tea on the table in front of Hattie, 'I can't say I'm surprised at any of it. I told you she was a one.'

Hattie had arranged to meet Melinda at the Willow Tree on the day after her encounter with Jo. Lance and Mark were used to dealing with Melinda's brood and even had a corner of the café set up with toys to keep them occupied, along with any other little ones who might visit. So far, Melinda had failed to materialise, but Hattie noted from the Disneyland clock on the wall that it was only twenty minutes or so past their agreed meeting time and she wasn't worried. With four young children in tow, Hattie would be surprised if Melinda ever got anywhere on time.

'After what you've told us,' Lance continued, hands in the pocket of his apron as he stood back, 'I'm more surprised you didn't turn tail and run.'

'I'm not really sure why I didn't,' Hattie agreed. 'I might have to get Dad to look at my head in case I've bumped it without realising.'

'And all your common sense fell out?' Mark laughed as he came over to join them. 'Perhaps you should.'

'When does Phyllis start working for you?' Hattie asked.

'Why? Are you going to sabotage her shift so you can have the job rather than having to go off to the scary house on the hill?' Lance asked.

Hattie giggled. 'I'm just curious.'

'Next week,' Lance said. 'She's a little sweetie, of course, but I do wish we'd known you were on the market. You'd be faster than her for a start.'

'She's not *that* slow,' Mark said.

'Coastal erosion is faster than Phyllis,' Lance shot back.

'They do say slow and steady wins the race,' Hattie said, pouring her tea.

'Slow and steady might win the race but it also gets you cold bacon sandwiches,' Lance said pointedly as he looked at Mark, and Hattie guessed immediately which of them might have pushed harder for Phyllis's appointment and who might not have been so keen.

'It's probably for the best that I didn't get a job here,' Hattie said. 'I'm not sure my dad would have been any happier about me taking a job with you than he will about me taking the one with Jo when I tell him. No offence,' she added quickly.

'None taken,' Mark said cheerily. 'I realise working shifts at the Willow Tree is not everyone's greatest ambition.'

'But we do have fun,' Lance added.

'I'm sure you do,' Hattie said. 'I can't pretend I'm not a bit sorry that Phyllis beat me to it but I've taken the post with Jo now so I've got to give it a go.'

Lance looked at Mark and twirled his finger at his temple to indicate a less than stable mental state. Hattie laughed.

'Oi!'

'All I can say,' Mark replied, 'is that if she's mean to you, come and tell us and we'll sort her out.'

'I hope it won't come to that,' Hattie said. 'She's a bit gruff but she didn't seem all that bad to me. I actually think underneath it all she might even be a big softy.'

'Wow, now I know you definitely did get that bump on the head,' Lance said. He looked up as the bell above the door tinkled. 'Here comes your date, by the way.'

Hattie followed his gaze and leapt to her feet as Melinda came in, the two older children walking at her side, the third on safety reins and Daffodil in a pushchair. She wore jeans and a simple cream ribbed top, and she looked as trim and perfect as ever – incredibly so for a woman who'd had so many children in such quick succession. Her peachy complexion was glowing and she wore her tawny hair gathered up in a loose bun.

'Hattie!' she cried, throwing her arms around her. 'How are you?' she asked, stepping back with a broad grin.

'I'm good!' Hattie said. 'You look great!'

'I can assure you it's good make-up,' Melinda said with a musical laugh. 'Most of the time I look like an extra from *The Walking Dead*. I've only made an effort today because I'm out in public and I don't want to frighten anyone. You're looking pretty good too – I love the dress!'

'Well, you know, if you can't look good after living in Paris for two years then there's really no hope for you. French clothes even make me look good!'

Melinda took hold of Hattie's hands in hers and squeezed them as Rain – the child on the reins – took advantage of her sudden freedom to toddle off at top speed. Mark was one step ahead and grabbed hold of the trailing handles. Melinda glanced across but didn't seem too concerned – her second-youngest child was never really going to come to serious harm with the two best babysitters in Gillypuddle on duty.

'It's so exciting that you're home!' Melinda squeaked, turning back to Hattie. 'And you're really staying this time?'

'That's the plan. At least for now.'

Hattie looked down and smiled at Sunshine and Ocean, while Mark brought Rain back.

'You've grown,' she said. 'You're completely enormous!'

Sunshine smiled shyly while Ocean giggled and puffed out his chest. Hattie peered into the pushchair.

'Hello, Daffy the Daffodil,' she said. 'You've grown a bit too.'

Mark pulled lollipops from the pocket of his apron and handed one each to the older three.

'For my favourite kids in the world,' he said. Then he tickled Daffodil under the chin to make her laugh. 'Sorry kiddo, no lollies for you just yet.' He straightened up and turned to the other three. 'The toy corner awaits your patronage, my young prince and princesses.'

Sunshine, the oldest girl, looked up at her mum uncertainly. 'I want to talk to Hattie.'

'Maybe in a little while,' Melinda said. 'For now, could you play with your brother and sister for me so I can catch up with Hattie first? She is my very best friend, after all, and I'm sure if you hadn't seen Suri for a long time you'd want to catch up with her too?'

Sunshine nodded, though she looked disappointed.

'It's just the same for me and Hattie,' Melinda said patiently.

'Come on…' Mark offered his hand. 'Give the ladies half an hour to gossip and then we'll all have ice-cream sundaes – how does that sound?'

While Sunshine, Ocean and Rain followed him to play in the corner, Melinda parked the pushchair containing Daffodil at Hattie's table and took a seat herself. She handed her youngest child a juice cup and a jumble of bright plastic keys and stuffed animals attached to a teething ring.

'So, come on.' Once satisfied that Daffodil was suitably occupied, Melinda turned to Hattie. 'Fill me in. What's happening? How come you're home? Why didn't you want to tell me about it on the phone?'

'It wasn't that I didn't want to tell you, it was just that it's a bit complicated to do on the phone – I'd rather have seen you.'

'So, now you can see me. Tell me everything.'

'Don't you want to order something to drink first?'

Melinda waved an airy hand. 'Lance knows what I like – he'll bring something over. Right now, I'm more interested in what's been happening in the world beyond Gillypuddle. Sometimes I forget there even is a world beyond Gillypuddle.'

Hattie smiled and gave a vague shrug. 'It's not as exciting as you might think. In fact, I'm looking forward to forgetting about the world beyond Gillypuddle for a while.'

'Oh dear – things have been that bad?'

'No – it's just that life is calmer here and I need a little calm right now.'

'You mean dull.'

'I don't think it's dull. It's certainly less competitive. You're not constantly comparing yourself to everyone else, worrying that you're falling behind, that you're not popular or clever or funny enough, and you don't wake at night worrying that you've forgotten to do some really important thing that you need to do.'

'I wouldn't say that's entirely true,' Melinda said mildly. 'People have different worries here. Try having four kids for a start – that'll keep you awake at night worrying about important things you might have forgotten to do.'

'I know,' Hattie said. 'I sound a bit whiny, don't I? I can't really explain what I mean, only that I think it will be nice to just be myself for a while – just plain old Hattie Rose – rather than spending all my time pretending to be someone far more exciting.'

Melinda looked blank. Clearly she still didn't see what Hattie was trying to say. Perhaps Hattie didn't really see it either. She'd simply had a vague notion of something missing from her life, of something not quite in its right and proper place, and that was the thing that had brought her home. The incident at Alphonse's show had been only the catalyst that brought the change – Hattie could see that now. She couldn't give the exact feeling shape or form, but it was there just the same. Nor could she say what she wanted from her life now; she only hoped that it would become clear as the weeks and months went by.

'You said something had happened at a show,' Melinda pressed. She wanted gossip and Hattie supposed the least she could do was oblige. She couldn't help a sheepish smile, though.

'I sort of burnt a building down.'

Melinda's mouth fell open. 'Talk about not doing things by halves! How the heck did you manage to do that?'

'Alphonse had designed this real gothic-inspired, vampy collection and finally, after months of me begging, he agreed to let me dress the set for the showing. I went all out with candelabras all over the place and the most gorgeous red drapes. Turns out his collection might have been manufactured from flame-retardant material, but the cheap drapes I bought to go along with all the candles weren't. All it took was a nudge from a wobbly model, the candles fell onto the curtains and everything went up like dry grass.'

Melinda let out a gasp.

'Nobody got hurt,' Hattie added quickly. 'Thank goodness everyone evacuated *tout de suite*. Alphonse wasn't best pleased though.'

'I can imagine.'

'I thought I'd been so clever saving all that money by going to the flea markets for the set dressings. I was trying to make him so pleased he'd let me do the job again instead of Colette, who always got all the best jobs. Goes to show, he should have asked Colette after all. I suppose he always asked her because he suspected I'd be crap – that's why he'd never given me anything important before.'

'Rubbish!' Melinda huffed. 'He gave you a job in the first place and you had no fashion experience back then. He must have seen something in you or he wouldn't have taken you on.'

'Cheap labour?'

Hattie raised her eyes to Lance, who was approaching with a tall mug topped with a peak of swirled cream.

'Madam…' He grinned, handing it to Melinda. 'Just as you like it.'

'Cream as well?' Melinda scooped some onto her finger and licked it off.

'Mummy's got to keep her strength up.' He turned to Hattie. 'Anything else for you, my love?'

'A slice of that Victoria sponge would be good. I've got to have *something* for lunch.'

'An excellent choice,' Lance said. 'Nutritious and delicious.'

'I'll get one of those too,' Melinda said. 'To hell with the housekeeping budget.'

'I'll get it—' Hattie began, but Melinda held up a hand.

'No – it's fine. You need your money right now.'

Hattie didn't push it, because Melinda had her pride like everyone else. It didn't mean that Hattie wasn't aware that sometimes things were a bit tight for Melinda and Stu. A young couple trying to raise four kids were bound to have money worries, but Melinda would never say so to Hattie, and she would never ask for pity. It had been their decision to have every single one of their children and they were happy with the life they'd chosen, even when the bills waited to get paid just a little longer than they'd like.

Melinda's grey eyes crinkled into a smile as Lance left them to get their order. Hattie often thought that the old saying about the eyes being a window to the soul had probably been invented for Melinda, whose inner joy and peace with her life shone out.

'I haven't had a Victoria sponge for ages,' Hattie said.

Melinda wrinkled her nose and grinned as she licked another blob of cream from her mocha. 'God, I'm going to be a whale eating that along with this. But it's soooo good! Lance just knows how to make a mocha like nobody else.'

Hattie looked across at Melinda's three oldest children, chatting happily amongst themselves as they worked their way through Mark's treasure trove of toys. Sunshine had taken charge and was playing a more supervisory role as she instructed the other two how to organise their game; already it was easy to see Melinda's more maternal, caring traits in her. Mark glanced across every now and again as he wiped the counter down, surreptitiously keeping an eye on things – though he needn't have. Melinda might have looked relaxed and unconcerned as she chatted at their table, but Hattie knew she was keeping a close eye on things too.

'Well,' Melinda continued, 'I know I shouldn't say this but I'm glad you set fire to Alphonse's show and had to come home.'

'Maybe it will turn out to be a good thing…'

'Of course it will. And even though it's totally selfish on my part, I get my best friend back.'

'Isn't Stu your best friend?'

'Sort of. He's my best friend with benefits.' She laughed lightly. 'But I can hardly complain about Stu to Stu, can I? That's what you're for.'

Hattie laughed now. 'I'm glad to hear I'm useful for something.'

Melinda scooped another fingerful of cream from her mocha and stuck it into her mouth. 'So, have you found a job yet?'

Hattie's reply was cut short by Lance coming back to their table with two generous slices of Victoria sponge.

'So when do you start your job with Medusa on the hill?' he asked, winking at Hattie as he set their cake down on the table.

Melinda's eyes widened. 'What do you mean – *start your job with Medusa on the hill*? You mean Jo Flint?'

'You know Jo?' Hattie asked.

'Everyone in Gillypuddle knows Jo,' Melinda said with another light laugh, but it wasn't the laughter that suddenly unnerved Hattie, or that everyone in Gillypuddle knew Jo, it was how easily Melinda had recognised who Lance was talking about from the nickname he and Mark had given her.

'So,' Hattie began carefully, not certain she wanted to hear the answer to her next question, 'what do you think of her?'

'Soooo friendly,' Melinda said.

'Life and soul,' Lance added.

'Always the first to get stuck into community projects,' Melinda continued.

'Always down for coffee mornings… such a gossip…' Lance grinned, and Melinda returned it.

'Alright, alright – very funny,' Hattie said. 'I did manage to speak to her and she didn't seem all that bad. I mean, she's a bit gruff but she seems OK.'

'A bit gruff?' Melinda pulled her plate towards her and dug the delicate silver fork into her sponge. 'Well, I suppose you have been surrounded by Parisians for two years so you'd know what gruff looks like. Anyone else would call her downright misanthropic.'

'What's that mean?' Hattie asked.

'She hates people,' Lance replied as Melinda chewed on a mouthful of sponge with a look of zen-like contentment on her face.

'Maybe she's just socially awkward,' Hattie said. 'A bit shy. That can come across as stand-offish, can't it?'

'Or she could just be rude,' Lance said.

'Or she could be harbouring some secret heartache that makes it hard to interact with people,' Hattie continued.

'Or she could just be rude,' Melinda said, exchanging another grin with Lance.

'So, do you know how she managed to pay for that farm?' Hattie asked, curiosity getting the better of her even though she ought to have been telling Lance and Melinda off for their comments about Jo.

'No idea,' Melinda said absently. 'She doesn't tell anyone anything.'

'I'll bet it was an inheritance,' Lance said sagely. 'It's how most of us get money, isn't it?'

Hattie blinked. 'Is it?'

'I suppose she could have borrowed it,' Melinda said.

'Yes,' Hattie replied, 'but who would lend money to someone to start a donkey farm?'

Melinda shrugged. 'I didn't say that was the answer; I was just saying it's a possibility.'

'She could have stolen it. A huge big heist,' Lance said with a wicked grin at Melinda. 'Perhaps she's a fugitive and that's why she doesn't let anyone go up there.'

'Yes! Or maybe she did some elderly relative in to get their money.'

Hattie sighed, though she couldn't bring herself to feel annoyed. 'You two are impossible.'

'I just hope you don't set fire to her gothic drapes – she'd skin you and feed you to her donkeys,' Melinda said.

'She can't be that bad,' Hattie insisted.

'Daffodil bursts into tears every time she sees her.'

Hattie frowned. 'I'm sure it will be fine.'

'I'm sure it will,' Melinda said serenely as she went back to her cake. Lance left them to serve a customer at the counter because Mark was now talking to Melinda's children in the toy corner. But then Melinda spoke again. 'Have you told your parents yet?' she asked, her tone still casual but loaded with meaning nonetheless.

'I haven't had the opportunity yet.'

'But you think they'll be OK with it?'

'I'm sure they will. And even if they're not, I'm an adult now so they can hardly stop me taking a job if I want to.'

'Oh, but they know how to complain, though, don't they?'

Hattie dug into her own cake and shoved a wedge into her mouth. 'They know how to do that alright,' she said as she chewed. 'World champion complainers.'

'I suppose you'll just have to be world champion at not listening then,' Melinda said innocently. They both knew the not-listening thing was harder than it seemed. Melinda had been friends with Hattie for years and even she'd been on the receiving end of Nigel or Rhonda's – or even both their – displeasure on occasion during that time. It had usually happened when Hattie had got into trouble and her parents had decided it had been Melinda's fault.

Melinda pushed her plate away with a contented sigh. 'So good!'

'I don't know how you stay so slim,' Hattie said. 'You inhaled that cake.'

'I run around after four kids all day, that's how.' Melinda reached into the pushchair and unfastened a now restless Daffodil to sit on her lap.

'She's so cute,' Hattie said. 'The absolute image of you.'

'Everyone says that.' Melinda smoothed Daffodil's curls from her forehead. 'Stu hates that none of them look like him.' She turned to Daffodil again, kissing her lightly on the head. 'But we all know that's a blessing, don't we?' she cooed.

'I think Stu would probably agree if it came to it,' Hattie said with a smile. 'How is he anyway?'

'Good,' Melinda said. 'Working too hard but there's no change there.'

'And you've finished now?' Hattie asked with a meaningful nod at Melinda's children playing over in the corner.

'Finished?'

'Having kids. Surely you've got that covered now?'

Melinda grinned. 'I do say that after every one. But then they start to grow up and I think, maybe just one more. I don't think you can ever have enough really, but there's a limit to your time and money that even I have to acknowledge. So, I think enough for now but I never say never, and I've got plenty of years left to change my mind.'

'I think you might have earned a break.'

'When the big ones are older it'd be easier to have another baby because they'd be able to help a little.'

Hattie shook her head with a wry smile. By the look on Melinda's face, she wondered whether she and Stu weren't already hard at work on baby number five, despite what she'd just said. She supposed she'd find out soon enough – Melinda and Stu were about the most fertile couple in Britain and if they were trying for another baby it probably wouldn't take them long to conceive.

'You still don't fancy motherhood?' Melinda asked serenely. 'I can recommend it.'

'That's because you're good at it. Besides, I'd need a man first.'

'You haven't left anyone behind in Paris then? No hot-to-trot Frenchman whispering "*Je t'aime*" in your ear? Nobody after the dreaded Bertrand?'

'The men I met mostly shouted rather than whispered. And it was usually "Out of my way" when they were trying to push in front of me on the Metro. And they weren't even hot. So there was nobody waiting to mend my broken heart after Bertrand, but really, I wasn't all that bothered anyway. You get burnt by one dodgy Frenchman and they all look a bit dodgy after that.'

'Well, that's disappointing. I don't think I'll bother visiting Paris then.'

'I don't think you need to visit Paris if you're only going to look for a man to father children,' Hattie laughed. 'I think you've got that well and truly covered. Leave poor Paris alone – what's it ever done to you?'

Melinda giggled. 'How rude! As you're free, I can give you the inside info on the very yummy new vet at Castle House practice. Although, after that last insult I'm not sure you deserve my inside information.'

'Come on – spill!'

'Well, he's a new vet…'

'Yes.'

'And he's very yummy.'

'That's it?' Hattie crossed her arms in mock annoyance. 'That's your insider information? How old is he? What does he look like? Is he single?'

'I don't know how old he is and I think he might be single. He looks like that man who does the history programmes.'

Hattie looked at her blankly.

'You know,' Melinda said, 'the Scottish one.'

'I haven't been watching a lot of British television in Paris and what I have seen certainly hasn't been about history. I have no idea who this man is.'

Melinda pulled out her phone and typed something into a search page. She turned the screen to Hattie to show a selection of images of the man she was talking about. In most of them he was wearing a forest-green corduroy jacket with brown elbow patches teamed with a pair of jeans and heavy walking boots, dark silky hair resting on his shoulders and pushed back from his face, or sometimes tied in a ponytail at his neck.

Hattie burst out laughing. 'Are you serious?'

'I think he's good-looking,' Melinda said defensively.

'Have you seen his hair?'

'I think long hair looks good on some men.' Melinda snatched away the phone and locked the screen. 'I wish I hadn't shown you now.'

'You think he's attractive?' Hattie asked. 'But he looks nothing like Stu…'

'That doesn't mean anything. I'm not saying I'd marry him or anything. I'm just saying that if I was single I wouldn't kick him out of bed for eating crackers – that's all.'

Hattie grinned. 'I'm sorry. It's not that I don't appreciate the heads-up but I really don't think your vet sounds like my type.'

'Well, that's all I've got, I'm afraid. If you're going to be that fussy then you're going to have to look a lot further afield than Gillypuddle. Apart from the new vet there's only one other eligible bachelor and he's got BO that could cut cheese.'

'Bobby Wye?'

'See – some smells just haunt you forever.'

'I'll bear it in mind if I ever get my sense of smell removed. I appreciate your concern, but I don't see me meeting my very own Stu any time soon.'

'You're not going to find him when you're being so fussy.'

'I don't think turning down a walking cesspit and Mr Corduroy Jacket is being fussy. Besides, I'm not going to worry about it – I've got bigger fish to fry. Like what I'm going to do with the rest of my life now that I'm home from Paris.'

'I suppose I can see why that might be a little concerning,' Melinda said with a solemn nod. Daffodil was trying to prise the phone out of her hand so she lifted it out of reach, prompting a petulant squeal from the toddler that momentarily had the entire café – including Daffodil's siblings – turning to look. But everyone soon decided that their own affairs were more important – including Daffodil's siblings, who were very probably used to her tantrums – and went back to their own business while Melinda dug into the changing bag for a doll for Daffodil to play with.

To Hattie, watching Melinda care for her children was like watching a swan glide across a lake. Her friend made motherhood look so effortless, and yet every minute of every day she had to be frantically paddling beneath the surface just to keep the barest order. Life was no easier or better for her than anyone else, but she seemed to make it look so. Hattie had never been very good at hiding the frantic activity beneath the surface where her own life was concerned – when things were going awry everyone could see the desperate paddling to stay afloat.

'So, what is it you'll be doing for Jo Flint?' Melinda asked.

'I don't know exactly – something to do with her donkeys.'

'That's one thing I do have to give her. People around here find her difficult but they would help if she asked because it's for a very good cause. She just doesn't give anyone a reason to offer.'

'But they'd want to help if they were allowed?'

Melinda shrugged. 'It's hard to say. People have busy lives and, even though they love the idea of what she's doing, nobody wants to give their precious time to someone who's so ungrateful.'

'Maybe she'll turn out to be different than everyone thinks. I suppose I'll find out when I get to know her.'

'Well, good luck with that because we've been trying to get to know her for two years and we're still no further on than when she arrived.'

'But she took me on so she's not completely averse to company.'

'All I can say is that she must really be desperate for help around the place.'

Hattie raised her eyebrows. 'Thanks.'

'You know what I mean.' Melinda laughed. 'You're a better woman than most round here for trying to make friends with her.'

'I've got to do more than make friends with her – I've got to live with her.'

Melinda's eyes widened. 'What?'

'She said she needed someone twenty-four-seven. She says donkeys need someone there all the time so she'd only give me the job if I agreed to live on site.'

'*She's* there all the time! Why do you have to be?'

'Maybe she's sick of being there *alone* all the time. Maybe it's a cry for help. Maybe it's her way of telling the world she needs company.'

'It's a funny way to go about it,' Melinda said doubtfully. 'If she wanted company she could just come down to the village every now and again and she'd have all the company she needed.'

Hattie nodded. She was forced to agree with Melinda on that point, but there had to be more to it. Maybe there was something else going on, some deep trauma, something that made Jo nervous of human company. Yes, Hattie decided, that had to be it.

Chapter Eight

Nigel didn't need to rant – the disappointment was plain enough on his face. Even Rhonda looked bitterly let down and she often tended towards the more tolerant position where Hattie was concerned.

'What on earth would you want to do that for?' she asked now, shaking her head in disbelief.

'I know you think it's a terrible job, but sometimes jobs are about more than money. Like nurses and carers. This is a caring role, isn't it? I just think it will be good for my spiritual fulfilment...'

Spiritual fulfilment. Even Hattie thought that sounded ridiculous but it had come out anyway. Clearly her mother and father agreed, and Rhonda repeated the phrase, looking blank.

'You know,' Hattie struggled on valiantly though she knew her argument was going nowhere, 'working to care for animals without any of the trappings of luxury I have here...'

'It's hardly *Médecins Sans Frontières,'* Nigel said haughtily. 'And this excuse for your current madness is only marginally better than the excuse you gave us last time you suffered a bout of temporary insanity.'

'I've never suffered temporary insanity,' Hattie replied, her own patience fraying a little at the edges now. She was trying to ignore the quiet voice in her head that was telling her that, even though she disagreed outwardly, her dad might have a bit of a point. Sometimes, it was possible she gave way to spontaneity just a little too easily.

'What do you call running away to Paris?' he asked. 'And that time you were learning to stand on your own feet or some such nonsense. You could have done that by finishing your education and embarking on a worthwhile career.'

'I told you I didn't want to do any of that.'

'Your father and I have done a lot of things over the years we haven't wanted to do,' Rhonda put in. 'It's called being an adult.'

'I *am* an adult,' Hattie replied testily. Why did everything have to be their way? Why couldn't they accept that not everyone embraced their vision of what a successful and happy life looked like? 'At least, I could be an adult if you treated me like one.'

'We just feel that your choices are sometimes…'

'You deliberately set out to rebel like some silly teenager,' Nigel finished for his wife. 'If you insist on acting that way then how else are we supposed to treat you?'

'I've never set out to rebel,' Hattie said. 'I mean, I suppose sometimes it just happened that it might look that way, but I've never done any of it to hurt you. I just need—'

'We only want you to make the right decisions,' Rhonda said gently.

'I am making the right decisions! I'm making the right decisions regardless of whether they seem bad or good because they're *my* decisions – that's what makes them right. They're my choices, made for me by me, and they feel right to me.'

Nigel fired a look of exasperation at Rhonda, but she simply gave a heavy sigh.

'I suppose we can hardly stop you from going.'

Hattie relaxed. She was sure they'd come around eventually, even though it didn't look that way now. She hated to be at loggerheads with her parents, who only wanted what they thought was best, but they had to start accepting that what they thought was best for her wasn't always what she felt was best for her, and it was her life, after all. She knew they wanted another Charlotte, but she'd never pretended she could be that for them and she wasn't about to start now. She just wished they'd stop trying to interfere all the time and accept her choices more readily. Melinda's parents had never made any secret of the fact that they'd considered her and Stu too young to marry and that they thought the couple were taking on too many children at once. But they'd never tried to interfere so forcefully and, once the choices had been made by Melinda and Stu, they'd supported them fully, no matter what they might have said on the matter. That was all Hattie was asking for from her own parents. She didn't want to seem ungrateful, of course. Materially, she'd had everything she could ever want from them, but money and comfort weren't everything.

'Thanks,' she said. 'I need to get my stuff packed then.'

'How are you going to get it all up to Sweet Briar without transport?' Rhonda asked.

Hattie looked sheepish because she knew her reply was going to be a cheeky one, especially given the conversation they'd just had.

'I was hoping you might be able to drive me up in the Range Rover?'

At this, Nigel stalked off, making his feelings on the request very clear.

'I suppose I could take you,' Rhonda said wearily. Hattie had often felt sorry for her mother over the years. She was caught between wanting to make her only surviving daughter happy and her agreement – at least in part – with her husband's stance on the matter of Hattie's life choices. It must have been hard when she was forced to take sides in an argument she wasn't entirely certain of herself.

'I could pop next door and ask Rupert if it's a problem…' Hattie began. 'Or Stu might be able—'

Rhonda shook her head. 'Of course not. I'll take you. When do you want to go?'

'Give me an hour or so to get some things together?'

Rhonda nodded. Without another word, she went through to the conservatory – presumably to find her husband and smooth some ruffled feathers – which left Hattie, feeling partly guilty but also relieved that the conversation was out of the way, to go and finish packing.

Hattie sat in the passenger seat of the Range Rover, arms wrapped around the overnight bag on her lap.

'Thanks, Mum – I really do appreciate this.'

'There's no need to thank me again,' Rhonda said briskly. 'It's no bother – it's not all that far to Sweet Briar Farm.'

'I don't mean the distance or the inconvenience,' Hattie said. 'I mean for not siding with Dad on this.'

'What makes you think I haven't sided with him? Frankly, I think he makes a very good point even if I might not agree entirely with the way he makes it. I just don't see how we're supposed to stop you from doing what you want to do and I don't think being deliberately obstructive is helpful.'

'I don't mean to make things difficult.'

Rhonda gave a tight smile. 'I know.'

'I just can't be something I'm not – even for you or Dad.'

'You've never been good at taking advice, even as a little girl – we should have realised by now that you're never going to be good at it; it's been going on for long enough.'

'Charlotte always had the good-girl thing covered. I suppose I thought I didn't have to worry about it. And I guess it was easier to let me get on with things when she was around because at least one of us would turn out right.'

'You were a good girl too and we've always been very proud of you – even if you might not think so.'

'Just more proud of her.'

'That's nonsense and you know it. Honestly, we don't compare you, and if you feel we do then I'm sorry – it's not intentional.'

'Because you understand that I can't ever be like Charlotte was.'

'Of course I do.'

Rhonda's tone was emphatic, but Hattie recognised the emotion in her mother's voice just the same. She looked across. Rhonda stared straight ahead, eyes on the road, but they were glazed with unshed tears. It still hurt, after all these years. Hattie knew that because she felt it too. With Charlotte gone there would always be a corner missing of their solid square, a weak point that could collapse them at the slightest pressure. Her mum and dad must have woken every morning marking another day of loss, and they would continue to do so no matter how many years passed. Charlotte would have been thirty-one now. Hattie often wondered what sort of woman she would have been. She'd just turned eighteen when she died and they'd seen glimpses of it then, before the meningitis that took her so swiftly even her father wouldn't have had time to diagnose it.

But her father hadn't been given the chance to save Charlotte because she'd been away on a sixth-form residential trip to celebrate the end of exams. She'd been in a remote part of rural Croatia in a hostel when she'd refused to get up for breakfast with the others because she felt so ill. Nobody could have foreseen how it would unfold and the Roses didn't hold anyone responsible, but it must have been a constant source of torment that perhaps, if Charlotte had been at home, Nigel would have recognised the signs quickly enough to save her. As it was, the teachers had sent her back to bed and taken the rest of the class out white-water rafting. By the time they'd returned that evening, Charlotte was dead. She'd died completely alone in a strange bed in a foreign land, and that was the thing that had broken her parents for a very long time. They felt somehow that they'd failed in their duty as parents, that they'd failed to protect her, that they'd failed to keep her safe.

Perhaps that was why, since then, they'd craved such control over Hattie's life choices, because they wanted to be able to protect her too. But Hattie could see what their grief had blinded them to – that they would never be able to protect her from everything, no matter what they did, and their urge to keep her safe only created other problems. She'd felt controlled, hemmed in, desperate to break free from the confines of her home and parental influence since her teenage years. At first she hadn't dared to go too far – she'd gone to Torquay, only around eighty miles away, to work in a bar at eighteen – though it was perhaps the job guaranteed to disappoint her dad more than any other, so what she'd lacked in geographical daring she'd more than made up for in occupational bravado.

There had been other jobs in Torquay after that one – children's party assistant, fast-food cook, deckchair attendant – and then she'd met a French artist called Bertrand who'd crossed the Channel on a whim to travel the West Country – the ultimate bohemian ideal. He'd taken a deckchair on the beach and refused to pay for it when Hattie had gone to get the fee, offering philosophical arguments against payment that tied her brain up in knots, but his overwhelming charm and wit had been such that she'd ended up putting the money in herself and agreeing to model for him that evening. She ought to have known then that he was going to be trouble and that she ought to have left well alone. It was funny what clarity hindsight gave to a situation.

He was almost twice her age and her parents hated the idea of him (though Hattie had been careful never to let their paths cross) and so, naturally, young and rebellious Hattie thought he was the most fascinating man she'd ever met. He was wild, impulsive and unpredictable with no regard for rules or norms, and he showed Hattie a life that was a world away from the rigid order and respectability of her parents' home. It was no great love affair, and Hattie had never pretended to believe that it was, but she'd been fond of him and perhaps fancied she loved him a little. His charisma was such that when he suggested she return to his home in Paris with him and move into his flat, she readily agreed. It was fun for a month or so, but then, inevitably, the ex-wife – Catherine – crawled out of the woodwork. It was obvious to her now that a little thing like a marriage wouldn't have got in Bertrand's way if he fancied someone else. Catherine was almost as crazy as he was, and she made life nigh impossible for Hattie.

It was also shortly after Hattie's arrival in Paris that Bertrand introduced her to Alphonse and that had turned out to be a more fortuitous meeting in the end. Bertrand announced one summer's evening that he was going back to Catherine and they were moving to Corsica to paint landscapes, and he'd left the next day with barely a nod to the English girl he'd abandoned. The flat had been repossessed and Hattie had been forced to think on her feet to find a new home that she could afford. Strangely, she hadn't been scared because it had felt like the greatest adventure of her life.

Alphonse had helped her. He was temperamental but kind, and he needed a cheap assistant for his fashion house. Hattie was eager to learn all he had to teach about a world that seemed glamorous and mysterious. She soon found that it wasn't as glamorous as it might seem from the outside and that Alphonse was hardly a celebrated name in the Paris fashion circles, but it was fun. At least at first.

When Alphonse's partner, Raul, left him broken-hearted after their acrimonious break-up, he became more morose, more demanding and temperamental. He relied more upon Hattie to take care of the minutiae of his everyday tasks but also more impatient too. Until the final event that had brought her back to Gillypuddle and led her to where she was now. Which was where, exactly? Even Hattie couldn't answer that right now.

'I haven't heard many favourable reports of this woman, Jo,' Rhonda said.

Hattie turned to her with a small smile. 'Neither have I, to be honest.'

'Are you sure this is wise then?'

'Maybe not. Since when did I ever do wise?'

'That's true.'

'But the one thing that's good about it is, even if things don't work out, I'm not so far away from home this time… if you'd have me back, of course…'

'You know we would. You have a home with us for as long as you need it and for as long as we're able to provide one.'

'Thanks, Mum – I can't tell you how good that is to hear. It makes me feel safe that I can try things. I know you don't really approve of this, but I really want to try it. I don't know why, but I just have such a good feeling about Sweet Briar Donkey Sanctuary.'

'And why would that be? From what I've heard, Jo Flint really is the most misanthropic woman in England and you're… well, you're more or less the exact opposite of that.'

'Exactly. Maybe she's just crying out for someone to take the time to try and understand her. Maybe she's the way she is because she's reacting to the instant opinions people form of her. Like a self-fulfilling prophecy – you know? Maybe she just needs someone to see a bit deeper, someone who doesn't care about all those opinions, someone who might see the real her.'

Rhonda raised her eyebrows as she navigated a sharp bend in the road. 'And you think that person is you?'

'I know what you're thinking and maybe you're right. But why not? If I could put up with Alphonse's tantrums, then I can probably handle flak from anyone.'

'I hate to throw cold water on this but you didn't exactly part from Alphonse on the best of terms.'

'Oh, that's all water under the bridge now. I expect if I met him today we'd be just fine again.'

'If you thought that were true, why didn't you go back to Paris? I thought you loved living there.'

'I did, but something changed. Paris isn't what I want anymore.'

'And living at Sweet Briar is?'

'Mum – you said—'

'I know, I'd support you and I wouldn't interfere. I'm just saying.'

'I think this could be really good, Mum, a win-win. I get to do something worthwhile and interesting, Jo gets the chance to open up to someone and the donkeys get a new person to care about them. How can there be anything wrong with any of that?'

'Hmmm,' was all that Rhonda said. Hattie chose to ignore the warning, because she was going to make a real go of this, no matter what anybody else might think.

Chapter Nine

Jo hadn't come out to greet Hattie on her arrival, though she must have been able to hear the car arrive and she had been expecting her. Instead, after waiting in the courtyard for a few minutes, Rhonda had reluctantly left Hattie, at her insistence, standing on the old cobbles of the house's yard with her belongings and a reminder to call right away if things went wrong – and by *if*, Hattie knew Rhonda meant *when*. Hattie had watched the car leave and then gone to search for Jo.

As she searched, she was given the opportunity to look more closely at her new home – from the outside at least. She could see that there had been some improvements made from the photos she'd seen on the estate-agent listing, though she wasn't filled with hope that she was in for a five-star stay. She was optimistic, however. Just because the rendering still needed a lick of paint and the old wooden window frames were a bit gappy, that didn't mean the inside would be as run-down. Perhaps Jo had concentrated on making the inside of her home comfortable before she tackled the arguably more cosmetic aspects of the house's repairs. And it didn't need to be trendy or even modern to be homely and snug.

Hattie eventually found her new boss in one of the outbuildings, soldering an electrical circuit board for some appliance or other. The draughty old building looked as if it had once been a barn, but was now filled with tools and bits of old vehicles and the workbench that Jo was leaning over.

'Oh.' Jo looked up from her soldering on hearing Hattie clear her throat. 'You're here then.'

'Yes.' Hattie stood and waited for something else, but Jo put her head down again and continued to work. 'Um… where shall I put my stuff?'

'Your room's at the front,' Jo said without looking up. 'I need the bigger one at the back.'

'That's OK – I don't need much room.'

Jo simply grunted.

'So… can I go in and unpack?' Hattie asked.

'Nobody's stopping you.'

'Are you going to let me in?'

'Door's never locked – no point up here.'

Though she disagreed in principle, Hattie could at least see Jo's point on that much. Sweet Briar Farm was well off the beaten track and, unless someone was expressly coming to visit the house, it was very unlikely that they'd have any other reason to come here. Maybe there'd be the odd intrepid climber who'd make the effort to the top for the spectacular views, but most people headed to the beaches and rock pools at the foot of the cliffs. And as Jo hadn't opened her sanctuary to visitors, Hattie didn't imagine she had anything to worry about as far as locking her house was concerned. If the outside of the house was anything to go by, there probably wasn't much worth stealing even if someone did come all the way up the cliffs to break in. It felt safe nonetheless. Perhaps that was why Jo had decided it was the perfect place for her sanctuary – nice and peaceful for her more skittish residents. It was beautiful too – the air was brisk and clean and the ocean was like a wave-powered metronome, beating out the rhythm of a briny lullaby.

If you'd endured a life of neglect, abuse or overwork, this was the sort of place that might just heal your soul – although on first impression it didn't seem to have done much for Jo Flint's.

Hattie took herself to the front of the house. Opening the door, she dragged her suitcases inside and took a moment to get the measure of her new home. There was no grand entrance hall here like the one at her parents' house. The front door opened onto grey flagstones, warped and worn with age, with panelled doors in need of a paint opening onto various rooms and dusty stairs straight ahead, muffled by a worn patterned carpet. There were no prints or photos, no wallpaper panels or soft muted shades of elegant sage or peach. It felt as if Hattie had stepped into a sepia print taken a hundred years before. The ceilings were low and beamed, and the small windows meant there wasn't much natural light in the entrance space once the heavy front door was closed.

The stairs creaked and protested as Hattie climbed them with her things. It took three trips to get everything up there by herself. She'd opened and closed doors along the upstairs landing to find one room after another filled with clutter. One of them had a made-up bed which looked as if it had recently been slept in. Hattie assumed this was Jo's as it was at the back of the house overlooking the courtyard. The bathroom had no shower, a cracked porcelain bath and a toilet that still flushed with a chain. Then Hattie came to the bedroom at the front of the house, the one she assumed Jo had meant was for her. There was a single bed in here but it wasn't made up, though there was a pile of clean sheets and blankets sitting on the bare mattress. It also housed a teak wardrobe, a wooden chest and a faded armchair sitting in the corner, and that was it. Thin curtains dressed the window, the pattern almost faded away by decades of sunlight. It smelt of damp and general lack of use. Hattie crossed to the window to open it and let some air in, and that was when she saw properly the view that had been gifted to her.

Jo had said she needed the bigger room but Hattie would have gladly swapped space for this any day. Beyond the rolling fields that stretched away to the cliff's edge lay a shimmering ribbon of blue, embraced by the walls of the cove on either side where briars and shocks of yellow broom grew. Gulls circled overhead, their cries echoing across the bay, darts of black against a patchwork sky. Hattie stared, mesmerised by the sight. Her parents' house had lovely views of the fields and meadows around Gillypuddle, but they couldn't compare to the drama of this. For however long she chose to stay at Sweet Briar Farm, this was hers, and suddenly, it didn't seem to matter how damp and run-down the house was or how taciturn Jo might be, or how hard the work was.

Besides, she thought as she tore herself reluctantly from the window and set about making up the bed, if this was her room then surely Jo wouldn't mind her making it a little more comfortable and personal – perhaps a lick of paint and some new furniture. When she could catch Jo in the right mood (and she might need time to learn what that looked like) she'd ask.

Before she knew it, an hour had passed. Hattie had spent it staring thoughtfully at her new living quarters, wondering what she could scavenge from her parents' house to make it more homely and what colour paint might best liven up the dull walls. She hardly noticed the passing of time until a commotion downstairs snapped her out of her reverie. She went down to find Jo in the kitchen running her hand under the tap and muttering curses under her breath.

'You're there,' she said, looking up as Hattie came in. 'I thought you'd decided to go home.'

'What do you mean? Why would I do that?'

'How should I know? You were quiet, though. Pass me that towel, would you? Bloody blowtorch.'

Hattie rushed to retrieve a towel slung over the back of a chair. It hardly looked sanitary enough to be allowed anywhere near a wound, but she had the feeling that Jo wasn't the sort of woman who would let that worry her.

'What happened?' she asked as she handed it over.

'Grabbed the wrong end. Could have been worse – at least it had been lying idle for a couple of minutes so it hasn't seared my skin off. I'll live.'

'What were you doing with a blowtorch?'

'Bodywork on the tractor's had it.' Jo dabbed the towel gingerly over her wet hand. 'I've done my best, but I doubt it's ready for anything but the scrapyard.'

'Do you use it a lot?'

'I can probably do without if push comes to shove but it helps make life easier.'

Hattie nodded at Jo's hand. 'Do you need to go to hospital with that?'

'Hospital? No point for this – they wouldn't do much with it anyway.'

'My dad could take a look at it for you.'

Jo was examining her hand but she looked up at the offer. Hattie was sure she'd almost smiled, but she'd never swear it in a court of law.

'I'll do for now,' Jo said.

'He wouldn't mind just giving you something for the pain,' Hattie said. 'He'd clean it properly too.'

'It's clean just as it is.'

'Oh, I didn't mean it wasn't *clean* clean. I mean, like, doctor clean… you know?'

Jo just stared at her and Hattie couldn't really say whether the offence she'd inadvertently caused had dissipated or not. She gave an uncertain smile in reply. She didn't want to get off on the wrong foot with Jo before they'd even begun to work together. It seemed that Hattie was going to have to tread carefully for a while.

'You eat stew?' Jo asked, tossing the towel onto the kitchen table and going to the fridge. She pulled out an enamel plate. Sitting on it was a hunk of what Hattie assumed was beef, richly red and marbled with creamy veins. 'Not one of those vegans, are you?'

'No – I like stew,' Hattie said cautiously. At least she thought she liked stew. Her parents weren't stew sort of people so they rarely ate such farmhouse fare. Hattie couldn't actually remember the last time she'd eaten stew, though she'd had beef bourguignon and stroganoff plenty of times in her favourite Parisian bistro. It was still beef and vegetables just the same.

Jo slammed the meat down onto the chopping board and set about hacking it to pieces with a large cleaver. Clearly her love of animals didn't stretch to ones she wanted to eat. Hattie made a brief but very important mental note to make sure she didn't annoy Jo because she looked pretty handy with a blade.

'Is there anything I can do to help?' she asked.

'You can peel some carrots if you like. In the larder. Fetch the potatoes and onions while you're at it. We'll get this on the stove and then I'll walk you across to meet the donkeys properly.'

'I'd like that.' Hattie followed the direction of Jo's outstretched finger to a door set in the kitchen wall. Inside, rows of sturdy shelves lined a whitewashed wall stacked with all kinds of produce, from jars of pickles to teabags. On the bottom shelf she found crates filled with fresh vegetables. They weren't washed and neatly shrink-wrapped like the ones her dad bought in from the supermarket, but dusted with earth. Carrots topped with sprays of green lay side by side with parsnips, broad beans, cabbages, potatoes and onions, and things that Hattie couldn't quite recognise without washing them.

'Do you grow these?' Hattie asked.

'Might as well if I've got the land.'

Hattie was glad she'd put on some old jeans and a sweatshirt as she grabbed an armful of dirty carrots and took them to the sink, because already they were grubby, and a coating of soil wouldn't do her more expensive items a lot of good. Though she had a feeling she wouldn't have much use for designer clothing for a while.

'I bet they taste amazing,' Hattie said.

'Taste like carrots.'

Hattie couldn't help a smile. 'I bet they taste like amazing carrots,' she said, running the tap into Jo's cracked old Belfast sink. 'My dad pays a fortune for organic ones and I bet these still taste better.'

Jo only grunted. Hattie was learning fast that Jo wasn't exactly the most talkative woman on the planet. If she did feel the need to speak she used as few words as she could get away with, but Hattie had sort of expected this and she didn't mind, perhaps because she'd been prepared for it by just about everyone she knew in Gillypuddle. So she hummed quietly to herself as she helped to prepare the vegetables and, when everything was diced and cubed, Jo threw it into a large steel pot with the meat and stock and set it on the stove. Then she went to change into heavy boots and a coarse sweater; when she returned, she gave a brisk nod towards the back door.

'Ready?' she asked.

Hattie nodded and followed her out into the courtyard, shutting the door behind her and noting that Jo didn't go to lock it, nor did she ask Hattie to lock it. She really did trust in providence that nobody was going to disturb her house while she was gone. Hattie didn't know whether it was stupidly naive or endearingly trusting. She had a good idea what most people in Gillypuddle would say about it, although there was nobody she could think of in the village who would disturb Jo's house, unlocked or not. She resolved not to mention it to anyone anyway, just in case – you never knew who might be listening.

The afternoon was on its last legs as they walked up to the high field where the donkeys spent most of their days. Come dusk, Jo explained in her own succinct way, they'd have to walk them down to the stables and tuck them in for the night. Then – weather permitting – she'd walk each one back up to the field again the next morning. If the weather was especially unkind then she would either leave them in the stables until it cleared or she had a more sheltered paddock close to the house where she could let them wander under the protection of a variety of broad, spreading trees. According to the individual personality of each donkey (and they did have individual personalities, Jo assured Hattie), they'd either be happy braving the elements or want to stay close to their warm stables.

To Jo, these animals were like family. She obviously wasn't one for warm words or overstatement, but you could hear the love and pride in her voice whenever she talked about her donkeys. She went over the schedule of their daily care in meticulous detail with Hattie as they walked – what time they had to go to the field in the mornings, what time they came down again (depending on the season and hour of sunset), what day she did their regular health checks, how often she exercised them, and so on. Then Hattie got more specific information – which donkeys were friends and which ones had to be kept away from the others from time to time, which ones liked to make the odd bid for freedom and which ones would probably live in the house if she'd let them. She went over all this twice just to make sure Hattie understood. Hattie almost expected to be told that there'd be an exam on it when they got back to the house and that if she failed it, she'd have to go to bed with no stew.

As soon as they arrived at the gates to the field, the head of every donkey swivelled in their direction. As one, they all began to trot over, making an obvious beeline for Jo. Hattie watched as the lines on Jo's face seemed to melt away and she transformed, her expression brightening and softening. It was amazing to see, and it only confirmed Hattie's belief that she really couldn't be as awful as everyone in Gillypuddle seemed to think. Each donkey shuffled forwards, jostling for prime position and maximum access to Jo, but Jo made sure each one got a fuss and a tasty treat no matter how the more dominant ones tried to muscle in. With obvious pride, she introduced them all to Hattie.

'Norbert you've already met,' she began. 'Oldest fella here. Loves his food – should have been a goat. Lola and Loki are brother and sister. Lola wears the trousers, though. Pedro came all the way from Spain. That's why he's called Pedro. Such a state when he came to me I could have committed murder for him. Blue… Norbert's best mate, a beach donkey – did years up and down on Blackpool front; as gentle as anything you've ever met. So's Minty – worked on Yarmouth beach. Speedy's one you've got to watch. A bit bossy and still gets a bit frisky with the girls so you have to keep an eye on him when he's in the mood. Daphne's the youngest, though still an old girl. Worked at an industrial museum – they were kind enough to her, but then it closed down and there was nowhere for her to go, so she came here.'

Hattie approached each one with trepidation but she needn't have. As a girl going to Peanut's stables she'd learnt that not all horses were as friendly as hers, but every one of Jo's donkeys were gentle and affectionate and happy to be fussed over.

'What do you think?' Jo asked. 'Think you could get on with them?'

Hattie turned her back to the fencing and opened her mouth to reply. But then she felt hot breath on her neck. She spun around to find Daphne trying to get a good sniff down the collar of her coat.

'Oh…' Hattie giggled. 'Get off, you daft thing.'

It didn't take long for the others to think that Daphne might just be onto something and soon there was more than one donkey trying to get into Hattie's coat. Perhaps they thought Daphne had found food there, but whatever it was, it made Hattie laugh uncontrollably.

'Which one's this again?' she asked, pushing away a smoky grey donkey with a white spot on its nose.

'That's Blue,' Jo reminded her. 'You can tell it's him on account of his colour.'

'And I think this is Lola… or Loki?' Hattie asked as one started to nose in her coat pocket.

'Loki. Probably thinks you've got treats in there…' Jo's hand went to her own pocket and she pulled out a handful of brownish pellets. She offered them to the donkeys and all Hattie's fans suddenly switched allegiance and crowded around Jo.

'Fickle!' Hattie laughed.

'So,' Jo said, turning to her, 'you've seen enough to decide you?'

'Absolutely!' Hattie said, her grin full of childish glee. 'I can't wait to get stuck in! What will I be doing?'

'A bit of everything. Don't see the point in your duties and mine; as long as it all gets done it's all the same to me. If you see something needs doing in the house and you have time, do it. Same goes for everything else. I don't expect to have silliness about it.'

'There wouldn't be.'

'Good.'

'So… just to be clear, I'd cook and clean and look after the house?'

Jo nodded. 'When it was needed.'

'And help look after the donkeys?'

Jo nodded again. 'Sometimes gardening. If you want to eat, at any rate. I do my own tree surgery in the orchard too, so I'd expect you to pitch in.'

'Would I have to do mechanics? Like with the tractor?'

'If I do it I don't see why you can't.'

'It's just that… I know someone who could do that for us. My friend's husband is a mechanic—'

'Don't need him. No point in getting someone else to do what I can do myself.'

'Oh. But you said—'

'You'll soon pick it up.'

'Right…'

Norbert nuzzled Hattie and she turned to fuss him. Jo watched and Hattie could sense her approval. The situation seemed relaxed, and Hattie felt they were getting on well – perhaps well enough to ask the thing she'd thought about earlier that day.

'Jo… can I do stuff to my room?'

'Something wrong with your room?' Jo asked sharply.

'No… of course not. I just wanted to make it feel a bit more like mine… you know what I mean?'

'It's yours – I don't know how much more like yours you want it to feel.'

'Well, yes, I know, but I wanted to put my mark on it.'

'You're not painting it.'

'OK. So nothing permanent. Maybe I could just grab some stuff from home. Creature comforts?'

'You're not here to be comfortable.'

'When I'm not working I'd like to be.'

Jo was silent and for a moment Hattie wondered if she was going to tell her to get lost and that their arrangement wasn't going to work after all. But then she nodded. 'Nothing permanent but you can put some of your own things in.'

'Like furniture?'

'Yes.'

'What about pictures? Photos?'

'I don't want holes in the walls.'

Hattie resisted the urge to raise an incredulous eyebrow. She really didn't see how a couple of extra holes in the wall could make the farmhouse look any less run-down and dated than it already did, but she supposed it was Jo's home and she got to call the shots.

'No holes. Got it. Thanks.'

Jo looked at her watch. 'Time we started getting them to bed.'

'Right.' Hattie waited expectantly for Jo to tell her what she wanted doing first. But Jo simply frowned.

'Who shall I take?'

'They all need to go – doesn't matter.'

As Norbert was badgering Hattie anyway and seemed to have decided she was his new best friend, it looked like he was going to be the very first donkey she tucked into bed on her very first day at Sweet Briar Sanctuary.

Chapter Ten

Over the next week Hattie got stuck in, just as she'd promised. Whenever Jo showed her how to do something she itched to try it by herself and, although her attempts weren't always successful, often she was pleasantly surprised that she could do things she'd never imagined she was capable of. She learned how to keep the donkeys' hooves trimmed and disease-free (they were animals born for dry climates, so Jo told her, and the damp grass of Sweet Briar didn't really suit their feet at all, which meant they had to take extra care). She also learned how to check their teeth – though none of them ever made it easy for her – and she learned how much feed was too much, and that they had to move the fencing around the paddock from time to time to stop the donkeys overdoing it on the lusher grass. Hattie imagined them like a load of old drunks who couldn't stop eating their juicy grass once they'd started, and even Jo had to be impressed with the analogy when she told her. Jo showed her how to take the engine of the tractor apart and – perhaps more importantly – how to reassemble it, though Hattie was certain she'd never remember a single step and would always ask Stu if any kind of mechanical job was given to her in the future.

Hattie and Jo shared most tasks equally apart from cooking which, for some reason, Jo seemed to covet. Whenever Hattie offered to take a turn Jo would direct her to do something else and, when Hattie finished it and came back, supper would either be well underway or ready. She'd allow Hattie to offer limited assistance but that was about it, and she always decided what they were going to eat. It was mostly simple, wholesome food – stew, sausages and mash, chicken casserole – but it was always good and Hattie didn't mind that it was just plonked in front of her without having been consulted on the menu. And after a day spent working outside she was always so hungry that she wolfed it down and looked longingly at the pot for seconds.

Midway through the week Hattie's mum came to see how she was getting along. She seemed a little taken aback to see Hattie looking so happy and well. Even though Jo was taciturn and almost monosyllabic in her communications and they rarely sat and chatted in the evenings once the donkeys had been put to bed, she was content to let Hattie head out for a walk along the cliffs or down on the beach or watch TV in her own room on the laptop borrowed from her dad. And when Melinda phoned for a chat, she sounded as surprised as Rhonda that Hattie was getting on so well.

It was a quiet life after the bustle and stress of Paris, but Hattie quickly settled into it. Better still, she was quickly growing to love Jo's little band of misfits who lived on the high field. The more time she spent with the donkeys, the more she got to know each one's little quirks. Just like people, they had distinct personalities and habits, and just like people they had best friends and also frenemies. Lola and Loki were practically inseparable; Norbert and Blue bickered like an old couple but got skittish when they couldn't see each other; Minty always got under the feet of all the other donkeys, as if she was determined to remind them that she was there, just in case they'd forgotten; and Daphne seemed to get excited at the sound of a car engine for some reason.

Hattie loved spending time with them so much that she didn't even mind the muckiest of jobs – like cleaning sick from Norbert's fur because he'd vomited some mystery item he'd eaten and then decided to roll in it. Jo had been worried, and if she was honest, Hattie had been too, but try as they might, they couldn't figure out what he'd eaten or where he'd got it from. They just hoped it was a one-off and that he wouldn't find any more of whatever it was. He seemed fine after he'd got it out of his system, and so perhaps they needn't have been so concerned. Hattie was very fond of the old boy already, though, and she hated the thought of him coming to harm.

It was Sunday of her first week and Hattie was getting changed into some cleaner clothes after a day spent weeding the vegetable patch and debugging (by hand because Jo wouldn't permit pesticides) the plum trees in the orchard. Her phone sat on the windowsill, and when it rang she went to answer, expecting it to be her mother or Melinda checking on her, as they had done periodically during the week. But her brow knit into tight folds as she saw the number on the display, a number she'd never expected to see flashing up on her phone again after the way they'd parted.

'Alphonse! *Salut! Ça va*?'

'Hattie! Is that you?'

'Why are you calling me, Alphonse? Is something wrong? What's happened?'

'I went to your apartment but they told me you'd left Paris!'

'Well, yes… I came home.'

'England?'

'Yes.'

'*Pourquoi?*'

'You know why. I didn't have a job so I had to come home.'

Hattie's frown deepened. She'd been gone from Paris for three weeks now and she'd thought she'd made it clear before she'd left why she was going. What did he think had happened? Where did he think she'd gone? He can't have been expecting her to come back, surely? He'd told her in no uncertain terms what he'd thought of her and, although he'd expressed remorse shortly after the event, it was difficult for Hattie to forget the unkind words. She had decided that their working relationship would never recover after a bust-up like that and she thought the same now.

'I have no help,' he said.

'You wanted me to help?' Hattie said, unable to keep the note of incredulity from her voice. 'To work for you again?'

'I have Colette but…'

At this, Hattie had to smile. Colette had worked alongside Hattie and they'd socialised a fair bit too. She was around Hattie's age, another wild Gallic spirit like Bertrand, and although Hattie enjoyed spending time with her, she could be tiring in too large doses. If she was doing Hattie's old job now she probably wanted more money than Hattie had ever earned. Colette wouldn't take Alphonse's shit and she could give as good as she got. Colette probably didn't care if Alphonse's morning coffee was just the way he liked it, she probably didn't call into Pâtisserie Margot for his almond pastry before she came to work, and she probably didn't open his post and divide it into bills that needed paying before the bailiffs called and those that could wait.

And Colette slept with almost all of his new models, broke their hearts and made it so they'd never work for him again. Colette was a liability, but it sounded as if she was all he had. Hattie might have felt guilty for leaving him and a little bit sorry for his predicament, but a tiny part of her was still hurt by his unreasonable behaviour after the accident. After all, she hadn't *meant* to set fire to his show and accidents happened to the best of people. Before that, she'd been loyal and she'd worked bloody hard for him.

'Surely you can find someone else?' Hattie asked.

'You will not come back?'

'I don't think that's really a good idea. Besides, I'm settled here now.'

'You have more work?'

'Yes, I have work and I like it.'

There was a pause. And then he asked: 'Another designer…?'

'No, Alphonse, not another designer. I've done with fashion, so you don't need to worry that I'm taking your secrets anywhere else.'

'That is not what I meant.'

It was and Hattie knew it. He might be a little put out at losing her services, but he'd have been seriously livid if he'd thought she might be telling a rival all about his operation.

'I don't think fashion is where my heart lies. I don't think it ever really was, though I had fun working with you.'

'You are happy to be at home?'

'I am.'

'And your parents…?'

Hattie had told Alphonse all about the disagreements she'd had over the years with her mum and dad, and she'd told him many times how much better the relationship was when there was some distance between them. Absence made the heart grow fonder but, in this case, it made the mouth behave too. But Hattie truly believed now that once she got onto the right path as far as her life was concerned, the relationship with her parents would get on the right path too. Once she was settled and happy, they'd have to be pleased for her and see that being happy was more important than any high-flying career they might want for her.

'I'm not living with them.'

'So… you will not return to Paris?'

'I don't think so. Not to live anyway. But if I visit I'll be sure to look you up.'

'I would like that. I miss your funny smile – it would light up my mornings, and when Raul left me…'

'I know; I miss you too, Alphonse, but that life is behind me. I have a new one now, one I want to make good.'

'You are working in the bar again?'

'No, actually…' Hattie braced herself for Alphonse's likely reaction. But what did it matter? It would be good for the entertainment value if nothing else. 'I'm working at a donkey sanctuary.'

'A… what is that?'

'We care for abandoned donkeys.'

There was a delay – a moment's silence. And then Alphonse said: 'Donkeys?'

'You know: *hee haw*. Like horses but not as glamorous. They carry things.'

'*Les ânes?*'

'Yes – that's it.'

'*Mon dieu*! You clean them?'

'When they need it.'

'You walk in the mud?'

'When it rains.'

'They smell terrible!'

'Occasionally they're a bit ripe.' Hattie laughed. She could imagine Alphonse at the other end of the line sitting in his chic apartment, the windows dressed in silk drapes and the walls covered in opulent paper, wearing his smoking jacket and leather slippers, the ever-present cigarette held in a hand that wafted it around as he spoke, shaking his head in disbelief. He'd die if he so much as looked at a hay bale, let alone picked one up.

'This is what you want?' he asked after another pause. Hattie had expected perhaps some ridicule, but it didn't come.

'It is,' she said.

'Then there is nothing to say. *Bonne chance*, Hattie. I will miss you.'

'Come and visit any time – I'll introduce you to the donkeys.'

'Perhaps,' he said, but Hattie knew he'd have to get surgery to remove his sense of smell if he were to ever set foot on the fields of Sweet Briar Sanctuary, and possibly surgery to remove his sense of *haute couture* if he were ever to set foot in Gillypuddle. Hattie's home was about as far from the café society of Paris as it was possible to get.

'Is there anything else?' Hattie asked. 'Only…'

'You are busy. I understand.'

'It's not that, it's just…'

'That is all I have to say, Hattie. Goodbye.'

'Bye, Alphonse. Take care of yourself.'

'I no longer have you, so I will have to,' he said, and Hattie could hear the sad smile in his voice.

The line went dead. Hattie watched as the screen of her phone went black. She'd often imagined that Alphonse might call like this, and that she'd feel some regret over her decision to leave Paris if he did. But now, though she regretted losing his presence in her life – for better or worse he had been a huge part of it and she cared deeply for him – she was unexpectedly content with her decision to come home. Even more than that, she was content with life at Sweet Briar Farm – at least this far, although she realised it was early days.

'Dinner's getting cold!' Jo yelled up the stairs. Hattie smiled. It was cottage pie with a distinct lack of sentimentality. She'd watched Jo grind the beef herself that afternoon. If nothing else, Hattie had never eaten so well. Pulling an old cardigan around her and poking her feet into a pair of soft plimsolls, she raced downstairs.

Jo had almost cleared her plate by the time Hattie joined her at the kitchen table.

'Sorry,' Hattie said. 'I didn't realise you'd already served up.'

Jo sniffed. 'Thought you weren't hungry.'

'I'm always hungry when you cook.'

Jo offered no response to the compliment but Hattie was getting used to that now; she didn't mind and she gave them anyway, in the hope that even if Jo didn't acknowledge praise, it might still please her to get it.

'I thought I'd go down to the village later,' Hattie said as she dug into her meal.

'Will you be back late? It's worming tomorrow and I need to get an early start. Vet's coming and I don't want him waiting around – just another excuse to charge more.'

'The vet's coming? Can't we just give them tablets?'

'I'd rather have him here.'

'Oh.'

'He's checking Speedy over too – back leg looks a bit off to me.'

'I didn't notice that.'

Jo grunted, as if to say that Hattie wouldn't because she herself was the only person who saw everything that the donkeys needed.

'I don't think I'll be too late,' Hattie continued. 'I'm going to my friend Melinda's house, and as she has young children she gets tired early anyway. Which reminds me – do you think they could come up and see the donkeys?'

'Who?' Jo asked, wiping a crust of bread around her plate to mop up some leftover gravy.

'Melinda's kids? They're good kids – they'd be no trouble at all and they'd love to come up here. I thought it might be nice.'

'I'd rather not.'

'No?'

Jo shoved the last morsel of bread into her mouth and chewed slowly.

'Only…' Hattie continued, 'I sort of told them it would probably be OK. They wouldn't get in the way at all and they wouldn't stay for long. I'd literally just nip them up to the top field with a pocket full of apple and then send them on their way.'

Jo took her plate to the sink and dumped it into the bowl.

'It would really mean a lot to me,' Hattie said. 'I'm so proud of this place and the donkeys and I just want my friend and her kids to meet them – I know they'd love them like we do.'

Jo turned to Hattie and leaned back against the sink. She was silent for a moment and Hattie steeled herself for another flat refusal.

'They can come for an hour,' she said finally. 'But I don't want them hanging around the place all day – too much to do.'

'Thank you!' Hattie beamed.

Jo tugged the liner from the bin and took the rubbish to the dustbin outside while Hattie fell upon her meal. Jo had said yes. It felt like progress.

Chapter Eleven

Hattie was staring at the vet. She was trying very hard not to but she couldn't help it. He was striding towards them, hand extended in greeting, having just parked his four-by-four on the courtyard of Sweet Briar farmhouse.

'Jo,' he said, giving her hand an enthusiastic shake. And then he turned to Hattie. 'And you must be the new assistant I've been hearing about.'

Hattie glanced at Jo, whose expression was unchanged from its usual inscrutable state. When the vet said he'd heard about Hattie, it was likely to be from gossip in the village rather than from Jo who, apart from sharing chores and making extra food, hardly seemed to register that Hattie was there at all.

'Hattie…' she said, taking his hand. His grip was firm and confident. Strong. He had dark hair and blue eyes – movie-star eyes, her mum would have said. Movie-star bone structure too. Alphonse would have been swooning and dying to dress him in one of his creations. Hattie's thoughts veered more on the side of *undressing* him.

Blushing, she shook off the thought. Perhaps Melinda was right – perhaps Hattie really did need a boyfriend after all. She'd been wrong about this guy, though – he didn't look anything like the nerdy TV presenter Melinda had shown Hattie photos of. This guy was far, far better looking.

'You're American?' Hattie asked.

'Right.' He laughed. God his laugh was sexy too – all wicked and smouldering. 'The accent confuses you Brits every time. I'm Canadian. I guess we all must sound the same to you.'

'Oh, I'm sorry.'

'Don't be. You all sound the same to me too…' He grinned. 'I'm Seth, by the way. Pleased to meet you, Hattie.'

Jo cleared her throat loudly, as if to remind them that fun and banter were not things she tolerated. Seth now turned his good-natured smile to her. On any lesser mortal, the effect would have been stunning, but Jo hardly flinched.

'So which fella are you having trouble with?' Seth asked.

'Speedy.'

'Only he's not so speedy right now,' Hattie put in. Jo glared at her and she blushed again. 'I only meant because of his leg,' she mumbled.

'OK, cool.' Seth clapped his hands together. 'Want to tell me about it while we walk up to the field?'

Jo began to fill him in on her concerns, her tone brisk and business-like, while Hattie followed, feeling more than a little like a chastised child. She could put up with Jo's stony silences and monosyllabic instructions forever and a day, but somehow this had offended her, because of the way it had happened – in front of Seth. It mattered because Seth had seen it, and in some way it had diminished her in his eyes. She was also beginning to wish she'd made a bit more effort with her appearance that morning. However, a later than planned finish with Melinda the evening before, as well as her flawed assumption that the new vet wouldn't be worth getting up half an hour earlier to comb her hair, meant that she'd got up in a hurry, thrown on some old jeans and scraped her hair back into a ponytail that felt almost as limp and lifeless as the one Jo usually sported. At least Hattie's mum had treated her to a top-up of her auburn hair colour on arrival back in Gillypuddle, because the only thing that would have made her hair look worse than it did right now would have been the very visible roots she'd had when she'd come back from Paris.

As Jo talked, Seth glanced behind and threw Hattie a warm smile. Hattie's misbehaving heart began to gallop and she suspected it was a lot faster than Speedy could move right now.

Stop it, she warned herself, *this is absolutely ridiculous.*

But then Seth dropped back, slowing his pace so that he was level with Hattie. Jo hardly noticed and continued to walk with purpose, face forward, and soon she was way ahead of them.

'So,' he asked Hattie, 'how are you settling in here?'

'It's great! I love it here already. I love the donkeys. In fact, I just love animals.'

Ugh. Stop it, Hattie!

'You do?' Seth asked. 'A girl after my own heart then. So Jo's not working you too hard?'

'Well, of course she is – it wouldn't be Jo if she wasn't. But I don't mind that.'

'Word on the street is you just got back from a couple of years in Paris.'

'What street's that then?'

'It's…' Seth looked confused and Hattie wanted to slap herself for such a stupid comment.

'Sorry, I'm being silly. It's a bit early for my brain to be working,' she excused. 'Yeah, I got back a few weeks ago.'

'I guess it's quite a culture shock then? Swapping Paris for Gillypuddle.'

'Not really. I mean, obviously they're very different places but I grew up in Gillypuddle so I'm used to it.'

'Ah, that's right. Now that you say it, I had heard that.'

Hattie wondered who'd been volunteering so much information about her. She'd bet it was Lance at the Willow Tree – he was the biggest gossip in Gillypuddle and there was some serious competition for that accolade.

'So you speak French?' he asked.

'A little. Probably not as well as I should considering I lived there for so long. I think my boss partly employed me because of my English really.'

'I had to learn both at school – French and English. You know, on account of the French-speaking regions.'

'Oh, right. Do you use it much?'

'Not so much these days – there's not much call for it in these parts. Unless you ever fancy a conversation in French for old times' sake?'

Hattie blushed deeply again. Was this flirting? Surely not considering the state she looked this morning. Now more than ever she wished she'd got up a little earlier to do something with her hair. Next time Melinda told her someone was hot, maybe she'd take a bit more notice.

'Why did you come to Gillypuddle? Where were you before?'

'Oxford for a while with my… well, I lived in Oxford when I first came to the UK.'

'What made you come to the UK?'

'A friend,' he said with a smile that looked sad and far away. Hattie wondered who this friend was, but it didn't seem like a question she could ask.

'And you swapped Oxford for Gillypuddle?' she asked instead.

'There was a job here with good prospects and the village looked OK.'

'Now that you're here… it can be a culture shock if you're not used to village life.'

'I like it. The community's good and the work is interesting.' He shrugged. 'I can see myself staying here.' He turned to look directly at Hattie. 'You liked Paris?'

'It was wonderful.'

'What made you leave?'

'Oh, I lost my job. Nothing serious – the work just wasn't there anymore.' Hattie didn't think now was the time to bring up her accidental arson. 'I just thought maybe it was a sign to come home.'

'I guess life is quiet here after somewhere like that.'

'It is but I don't really miss it. I think being there for so long got all that out of my system. Although I do miss some things about it.'

'Like what?'

'Like the air of excitement. Everywhere is buzzing, something is always happening. And I miss the culture – the galleries and interesting people doing interesting jobs. Sometimes I miss the food too, although I have to say that Jo's cooking is so amazing that she's definitely helped me get over that.'

Seth raised his eyebrows. 'Jo's a good cook?'

'Amazing. I mean, it's basic stuff but she does it so well.'

'Wow, I never had her down as the cooking sort.'

'Well, she has to cook if she's going to eat.' Hattie laughed lightly. 'That alone makes her the cooking sort.'

'I guess that makes us all the cooking sort then.'

'Do you cook?'

'When I have time, which is not nearly as often as I'd like. How about you?'

'To be honest I probably could if I tried but I'm a bit lazy. I help Jo out but she likes to do it, so I don't really need to. I didn't cook a lot in Paris either. I either ate out with friends or ate sandwiches and crisps at home.'

'Too busy to cook?'

'I worked pretty unsociable hours.'

'What did you do?'

'I was sort of… well, sort of a dogsbody really.'

'Now I'm intrigued.'

'It's not nearly as interesting as it sounds.'

'What line of business was it?'

'Fashion.'

'Wow…' At this, Seth looked genuinely impressed. 'Working in Paris in fashion? And you swapped that for *this*?'

'Like I said, it's not nearly as glamorous as it sounds. I mostly ran about fetching coffees and pastries for my boss.'

'It's still running about for coffee in Paris – makes it glamorous in my book.'

Jo cleared her throat loudly again. Hattie had almost forgotten she was there and she wondered if Seth had too because his line of questioning had been about pretty much anything except what he was there for. She wondered if Jo disapproved of it, but, as always, it was hard to tell from the inscrutable look on her face. But they'd arrived at the field anyway. As always, the little band of donkeys turned as one as they walked to the gate and Jo clicked to call them over. It seemed that some of them were familiar with Seth and had perhaps had less than pleasant dealings with him because, for once, not all of them trotted over in the hope that Jo's pockets would be filled with treats.

'It looks like Muhammad will have to go to the mountain,' Seth said with a grin. He didn't wait for Jo to open the gate, but vaulted over the fence and strode off across the field towards a donkey whose coat was a sort of malted chocolate colour. Hattie gazed after him and even Jo looked a little bit impressed. She let herself and Hattie into the field and then closed the gate. They followed Seth.

'He knows which is Speedy?' Hattie asked.

'He knows them all.'

'Does he come up here a lot then? It took me ages to get used to who's who and I've been living here.'

'It's what he does.'

'I suppose so. I suppose he notices features the rest of us don't on account of being a vet and really into animals.'

Jo grunted. Hattie looked back across the field to see Seth trying to steady Speedy as he ran a hand down his leg.

'There's a bit of swelling,' he said, straightening up as they approached. Hattie couldn't help but be impressed again – they hadn't even had the chance to tell him which leg it was; he'd just spotted it straight away.

'Will it need an X-ray?' Jo asked.

'I'll be able to tell you better when I've had a good look – might not be a bad idea to rule things out, though I doubt it's a break of any sort. But of course, there's extra cost involved…'

He looked at Jo, his expression somewhere between expectation and sympathy. For the first time, Hattie thought she saw worry in Jo's own. And then it came to her – Jo couldn't afford expensive treatment for Speedy. But she nodded anyway.

'Do what you need to. If Speedy needs treatment then he'll have to have it. I'll work something out.'

'I'm sure I could work something out too,' Seth said in a tone full of meaning. Hattie was lost as to what that meaning was but Jo seemed to understand.

'Thank you,' she said, and her tone was about as humble as Hattie had ever heard it. It wasn't that Jo was arrogant; she just didn't do please and thank you in the same way most people did. She seemed to view them as if they were a precious commodity not to be wasted on frivolous platitudes. When Jo said thank you, she really meant it.

Seth smiled and turned his attention back to the patient. Hattie watched as he began a gentle but more thorough examination. She wondered if love at first sight was a thing after all, because if it wasn't, she didn't know what was making her feel so giddy.

Speedy behaved himself, though it was obvious now that Hattie looked that when Seth handled a particular spot on his leg it caused some discomfort, which Speedy would show by trying to get out of his reach. When he did this, Jo settled him and held him steady. Seth was so gentle, his voice as he talked to the donkey so soft and full of concern, that Hattie thought his bedside manner was better than that of many doctors she'd seen treating humans.

After a few minutes, he stood back and scratched his head.

'What do you think?' Jo asked.

'I don't think it's anything serious,' he said, looking at Speedy. 'I can't feel anything too worrying anyway, though he's clearly bothered by something.' He turned to face Jo. 'What do you want me to do? We can watch and wait – see how he gets on.'

'It might get worse.'

Seth nodded slowly. 'It might. But I'd bet against that.'

Jo looked at Speedy, and then back at Seth. 'Check him thoroughly,' she said. 'Whatever you need to do I'll pay for it.'

Seth looked as though there was something he wanted to say and Hattie waited for a moment, sure that it was going to be something significant. But then he simply nodded. 'If that's what you want.'

'It is,' Jo said firmly. 'Donkeys have to come first.'

Chapter Twelve

Melinda had left her youngest in the care of Stu's mum. Getting a buggy up to the top field at Sweet Briar would be a nightmare and carrying Daffodil – small as she was – would be just as awkward and exhausting. Sunshine and Ocean were excited, chatting non-stop on the way up, running ahead, skulking back when Melinda shouted a warning, only to forget and run ahead again a few minutes later. Rain, who was a little more apprehensive, kept hold of Melinda's hand.

'Where's Medusa now?' Melinda asked. 'I thought she might be coming up with us to keep an eye on things.'

'So did I,' Hattie said. 'I think she must have bigger fish to fry, though.'

'Like what?'

'Like money.'

'Like not enough money?'

'I don't know. I left her going through a ledger or something. At least, I think it was a ledger; it was basically an old exercise book with numbers written in.'

'Is that why she pays you peanuts?'

'Well, it's not all that bad. When you factor in all the food and a roof over my head, it's as good as I'd get anywhere else. Maybe better.'

'Better than Alphonse?'

'Well, no. But living in Paris was expensive. I think it's a decent deal.'

'I don't call having to live in that scruffy house with Misery herself a decent deal.'

'It's really not that bad when you get used to it. I've got a few bits and pieces in my room from my mum and dad's house. There's running water, heating and electricity. That's all anyone needs, isn't it? And I'm not in the house much anyway.'

Melinda threw her a sideways look. 'You really do like it up here, don't you?'

'Are you shocked?'

'I wouldn't be the only one.'

'Shocked because it's me? I'm not that high maintenance.'

'Shocked that anyone would be happy living in that place with her.'

'She's really not as bad as everyone thinks. She doesn't like to talk much but I suppose some people are just like that, aren't they? Doesn't make them bad. She was weirdly more chatty when Seth was here, but I suppose that's because she had to tell him about any concerns she had with the donkeys.'

'You mean she spoke more than single-word sentences?'

'Yes,' Hattie laughed. 'In some of them I counted three.'

'Wow, he must bring out the chatterbox in people.'

'He brought it out in me,' Hattie said with a smile.

'Ah…' Melinda's smile was rather more sheepish. 'I'm afraid I owe you an apology.'

'Why?'

'Because I was trying to persuade you to flirt with him, but it's recently come to my attention that he's not available after all.'

'He's not?' Hattie couldn't deny the sudden swooping disappointment. She had been very obviously flirting with him – what must he have thought of her?

'Well, in my defence, I hadn't heard anything about this Eugenie woman.'

'He's married?'

'Long-term girlfriend, I think. Living in Oxford, though, apparently, where she's completing some postgraduate studies. She's supposed to be coming to join him when she's done.'

'So she's ridiculously clever and accomplished?'

'Sounds like it. Posh too with a name like Eugenie.'

'I bet my dad would love her,' Hattie muttered.

'Oh, Hattie…' Melinda laid a gentle hand on her arm. 'I'm sorry.'

'It's OK. So, who told you this?'

'Lance – who else?'

'Figures. He ought to be recruited by MI5 – he'd be brilliant at getting information on people.'

'Who says he hasn't been already?' Melinda laughed. 'The Willow Tree could be one hell of a cover – nobody would suspect a microscopic place like Gillypuddle of harbouring an international man of mystery.'

'Nobody would expect Gillypuddle to harbour any sort of mystery,' Hattie said. 'Lance sees to that. Even our deepest, darkest thoughts are no secret when he's around.'

'You can say that again. Somehow he knew I was pregnant with Daffy before I did!' Melinda laughed.

'I can't deny it's a shame, though.'

'What is?'

'Seth. You were right – he's yummy. Very yummy.'

'Oh dear. I should have kept my big mouth shut.'

'It's OK. I suppose it will have to be a case of look and don't touch.'

'At least the looking is enjoyable. I've been making the most of that particular pastime since he arrived in the village.'

'You're terrible! Does Stu know about this dark side you have?'

'Of course he does! I've got to keep him on his toes, haven't I? I can't have him getting complacent.'

'I should imagine, living with you, that complacent is one thing he's not. Here we are…'

Hattie had no need to announce that they'd arrived at the field because the squeals of delight from Sunshine and Ocean did that for her.

'They're so cute!' Sunshine squeaked.

'They're lovely!' Ocean agreed.

'Come on…' Hattie opened the gate to let everyone in. 'Don't run,' she warned. 'Approach them slowly and let them get used to you – they've never met you before and if you go tearing up you're going to make them nervous. We don't want nervous donkeys…'

Melinda gave her a sideways look. 'Careful – you're starting to sound like you know what you're doing.'

Hattie laughed. 'God, I wouldn't want that.'

Sunshine and Ocean gave solemn nods, but their eyes were desperate with excitement. Only Rain, still clinging to Melinda's hand, looked apprehensive.

'I don't want to go,' she said, shaking her little head.

'They're not going to hurt you.' Hattie held out her own hand for Rain to take. 'Come with me – I'll introduce you. You'll be quite safe.'

Rain backed away, holding Melinda tighter and looking more uncertain than ever.

'OK,' Hattie said. 'Why don't you just stay with your mummy and watch for a while. If you feel like coming to say hello later then I'll come to get you.'

Rain gave a small nod and Hattie took Sunshine and Ocean to meet Jo's gang. For the next half hour childish hands reached tentatively to pat docile noses. Each time the children would get a little braver, stroking a neck or flank, but this would be quickly followed by giggling and nervous pulling away. Hattie couldn't have asked for better, more patient behaviour from the donkeys. Norbert was her main man, of course, and Minty was brilliant too because she'd been used to working with children on the beaches of Yarmouth. Pedro kept getting bored and wandering off while Loki and Lola were only interested if they noticed sugar-beet lumps – their favourite treats – coming out of Hattie's pockets.

After a while, Rain decided that there was too much fun to be had to be left out and then all three children were happy to rub each donkey's coat. Hattie produced a brush she'd brought up and showed them how to groom Norbert, who stood patiently, ears flicking from time to time as he gazed out at the ribbon of sea that lay beyond the cliff tops. Each child had a go but they were so gentle that he probably barely noticed it, and, certainly, he didn't complain.

'Is he your favourite?' Sunshine asked as she stroked the brush down Norbert's flank.

'I don't have favourites,' Hattie said loudly. But then she leaned in and whispered: 'Yes he is – just don't tell the others.'

Sunshine giggled and Hattie straightened up to see Melinda smiling with evident pride.

'These donkeys are like your kids.'

Hattie laughed. 'Yeah, I don't need any actual kids now. I'll leave it to you and Stu to top up the human population.'

Melinda grinned but then Hattie saw her attention wander to a spot beyond her. She turned to see Jo striding up towards the field. Hattie was about to call to her to ask if anything was wrong when she stopped. Jo was wearing a peculiar look and, if Hattie hadn't known her better, she could have sworn it was almost a smile. Jo halted at the gate to undo it, but then paused and watched as Melinda's kids fussed over her donkeys. She'd been reluctant to let this happen and Hattie had been forced to give every reassurance she could think of, but now she looked… well, she looked happy. But then her eye caught Hattie's and immediately she closed down again, her expression returning to the stone of its usual state.

'Delivery!' she shouted. 'Could do with a hand when you've finished playing around. This lot will have to come back when it's more convenient.'

'Delivery?' Hattie repeated, ignoring the dig. 'I didn't know we were expecting a delivery. Of what?'

'Chickens,' Jo said before turning on her heel and walking back the way she'd come.

'Chickens!' Ocean gasped, apparently having been distracted enough by Jo's arrival to abandon his rapturous donkey fussing for long enough to hear the conversation. 'Can we see them?'

'You've seen plenty of chickens,' Melinda said. 'The school has some.'

'But I like chickens,' Ocean replied.

Melinda looked uncertainly at Hattie. It hadn't sounded as if they'd be very welcome judging by Jo's tone. Then again, Jo hadn't explicitly said that they couldn't at least see the chickens. Maybe she wouldn't mind them staying for five minutes longer so they could have a look. Hattie had to admit she was curious too. Jo hadn't mentioned getting chickens to her. How many were they expecting? Where had they come from? What was Jo planning to do with them? She really hoped the last question wasn't anything to do with her organic dinners, because it was one thing watching Jo grind her own beef mince but quite another to watch her pluck a chicken they'd seen scratching around the courtyard the day before.

'I'll take you down to the yard,' she said. 'There's a tap to wash your hands – you must always wash your hands after you've handled the animals, you know. I expect you'll get to see the chickens then.'

Then Hattie showed them how to make sure the gate to the field was properly shut and she explained how important it was to check that it was always secure, and then they all trooped back down the path to the farmhouse. The kids were bubbling with excitement, swapping stories amongst themselves about what they'd seen each donkey do, which was their favourite, which ones made them laugh, which ones went off to lick at a salt block in the corner of the field, which ones pulled at the grass and which ones came back from the feeder with hay sticking out of their mouths. Hattie couldn't stop thinking about Jo's face as she'd watched them. On reflection, she ought to have been more surprised that Jo had let them on the field at all, but now that she thought about it, maybe Jo wasn't as distrustful of little people as she was the bigger ones they'd grow to be.

Spots of rain were darkening the stones of the courtyard as they arrived back.

'It's probably a good thing we came back down when we did,' Hattie said. 'Looks like the heavens might open at any time.'

'Will the donkeys get wet?' Sunshine asked, looking worried.

'They've got a shelter up there for the odd shower,' Hattie told her. 'They'll be fine.'

'I don't think a bit of rain would have bothered my lot,' Melinda said. 'They'd have been happy to huddle in the shelter with the donkeys.'

A van was parked up and a man Hattie had never seen before was talking to Jo. The back doors were open to reveal crates of hens – perhaps a dozen of them – all clucking and scratching and looking very annoyed at the humiliation of having to sit in cages. Jo glanced across and waved an impatient hand at Hattie.

'Come and help.' She didn't comment on the fact that Melinda was still there with her kids.

'What needs doing?' Hattie asked.

'They can't sit on the van all day.'

'Where are we taking them?' Hattie asked, making her way over.

'I've set up a coop in the orchard.'

'When did you do that?' Hattie asked incredulously.

'Before you got up.'

'Where are they from?' Hattie went to pull a crate from the van.

'We'll have to take them one by one,' Jo said. 'The crates are too heavy. Like this…' She reached for a bird and ignored its indignant flapping as she tucked it firmly under an arm.

'So they're ours?' Hattie asked, eyeing them with a little apprehension. Jo made taking one out of the crate look easy, but she suspected it wouldn't be when she herself tried.

'Yes.'

'Where did they come from? Did you buy them?'

'Rescued,' Jo said shortly and that was all the information she volunteered before striding off with her hen.

Rescued. Of course they were. This was Jo Flint they were talking about, and Jo wouldn't have stood idly by if she'd heard that a bunch of chickens needed rescuing. She probably hadn't even stopped to think about the practicalities of keeping them.

Hattie looked at the van driver, expecting him to come and grab a bird too, but he simply got back into the front seat of his van and opened out a newspaper. Apparently, his obligations had ended with their delivery. Hattie wondered if he was the previous owner of the chickens or had just been hired to bring them. Either way, she thought he was ignorant, but there was too much to do to worry about it now.

'Can we help?' Sunshine asked.

'Maybe it's best if Hattie and Jo handle it,' Melinda said. 'We should probably go and leave them to it.'

There was a chorus of dissent, but Melinda shushed them.

'I expect you'll be able to come again another day,' Hattie said, not entirely sure if that was a promise she'd be able to keep.

'You can feed them once they're in.' Jo was standing at the van again. She must have run with the first hen and now she was back for another one while Hattie hadn't even got to grips with her first yet. But Jo couldn't have been too annoyed by this if she was still being civil to Melinda and her children. She grabbed another chicken and continued on her way back to the orchard.

Hattie stared after her for a second, and then looked at Melinda, who seemed as surprised as she was. Could it be that Melinda's kids were the key to cracking open the stone heart of Jo Flint? And if so, what might they find inside?

Chapter Thirteen

'It's lucky that Speedy's leg isn't anything serious after all, isn't it?' Hattie said. They were eating steak and kidney pie. Jo had made it using frozen pastry but it was still amazing. Seth had decided to X-ray Speedy's leg and had then been happy to give him a clean bill of health – he'd perhaps caught his leg, turned it awkwardly and made it tender for a couple of days. Whatever the problem, it seemed to be resolving itself now. As for the rescued chickens, Hattie discovered that they'd come from the farm of an old man who'd recently died, leaving the property to his children. They were currently busy dismantling it and systematically selling each bit off, including all the animals. Many had either already gone or were promised to buyers, and some weren't as lucky as the hens that had come to Jo, going to market for slaughter.

The newest residents of Sweet Briar Farm were settling in well. Jo had warned that she and Hattie shouldn't expect too much in the way of eggs from them as some of them were past their prime but, so far, the brood had pleasantly surprised them and provided eggs for breakfast for the last three days. Hattie wondered whether Jo had been asked to pay for the hens and how much – it seemed likely. She also wondered whether Jo had wanted to take any of the other still homeless animals, but she hadn't liked to ask for fear of touching on a sore point. Jo was never what you'd call open, but Hattie suspected, from what she could gather, that there were things beyond her control and they probably involved money – something that Hattie suspected there was a serious lack of.

'Was Seth's bill big?' Hattie asked. 'Vets are expensive, aren't they?'

'Haven't had it yet.' Jo shoved a forkful of steak into her mouth.

'But it might be?'

Jo reached for the salt and didn't say anything.

'Can we afford it?' Hattie asked.

Jo took another mouthful and chewed for a moment. 'Not your problem,' she said finally.

'It sort of feels like it is. I mean, we're a team now, right?'

Jo looked at her. 'You want to pay the bill or something?' Hattie noted the barest trace of amusement. Was this more progress? If she kept tap-tapping away at this armour, could she break through?

'Well, no… I don't think I could afford it. But we could borrow the money,' she added brightly, the idea suddenly occurring to her. 'My dad would help if—'

'No,' Jo interrupted, her expression stone again. 'I don't need charity.'

'You *are* charity!' Hattie exclaimed. 'You're saving animals! Every other animal-rescue organisation or shelter I know of raises the money they need through donations. What's the difference between what they do and what you do? Why can't you take charity? It's not like the money's for you.'

'They're proper registered places.'

'So? Can't you be registered?'

'Too much paperwork.'

Hattie was silent for a moment. Sometimes Jo could be so exasperating. As far as Hattie could see, the solutions to all her problems were staring her in the face and she wouldn't even entertain them. Why did she have to be so stubborn?

'Do you mind if Melinda and the kids visit again?' she asked, deciding to let the argument drop for now. She sensed an atmosphere building and it didn't seem wise to push it.

'As long as they don't get in the way. And I won't be responsible for accidents. We're a working farm, not an adventure playground.'

'Melinda keeps a close eye on them and they're sensible kids.'

Jo gave a brisk nod. That she'd agreed – however reticently – felt like another point scored in the battle to save her soul. If Melinda and Hattie could get Jo to love Melinda's kids then maybe the question of getting paid visitors up to Sweet Briar would be one she'd be more open to consider.

The more Hattie had thought about it, the more she was convinced that, along with fundraising like she'd just mentioned, paying customers would be the answer to all Jo's money worries. It might even enable her to save many more animals. The only thing standing in the way was Jo's refusal to engage with almost everyone, but Hattie thought she might have a solution to that too. She could be the public face of Sweet Briar Sanctuary, the person who welcomed visitors, who gave press interviews and who fronted appeals. Jo could quietly continue her work in the background and she'd never have to deal with any of that while she had Hattie. Hattie had been cooking these plans up for a while now, and she was slowly but surely trying to work Jo, to get her to a place where she might agree. She didn't think they were there yet but she hoped they might be soon. In the meantime, she wondered whether she ought to put the feelers out, gauge interest in visiting the farm, and she'd asked Lance and Mark to put the question to people who came into their café – particularly if they were tourists. So far, the response had been favourable, but Hattie would have to make more concrete plans soon because hypothetical visitors only brought in hypothetical money.

Jo scraped up the last of her pie and chewed slowly, her gaze on the window.

'You get the hens cooped up,' she said, eyeing the darkening sky. 'Make sure they're safe – I've seen a fox. I'll get the donkeys down for the night.'

Before Hattie could reply, Jo pushed her chair away from the table and got up to dump her plate in the sink before heading out, still chewing on the last of her dinner.

One of these days, Hattie would get to have a full, meaningful conversation with her boss that didn't end prematurely with her marching wordlessly out of the room.

Three days had passed since the steak and kidney pie. Since then, Hattie had been treated to cod mornay (the first time Jo had ever cooked fish but still excellent), chicken and leek bake (chicken from the farm shop and not from the new hens, and Jo showed no guilt at all that she was likely eating one of their distant cousins), and another rich beef stew. They tended to grab sandwiches or other quick snacks on the run during the day, a hearty breakfast being enough to see them through till dinner without the need for much else. It was all excellent but, although Hattie was a huge fan of Jo's cooking, she had been thinking that as she hadn't seen much of her parents that week, and her dad had called tempting her with offers of Moroccan-style jewelled couscous with slow-cooked lamb (which did sound very good), she might skip her evening meal with Jo that night and take him up on the offer.

It had rained heavily that day and Jo had decided to get all the animals tucked up in their shelters early that evening anyway, so she and Hattie were free for more of the night than they'd usually be. She asked Jo, and all she got in reply was a warning that Hattie would be forced to eat her portion of hotpot the following day as Jo was not about to throw good food in the bin. Hattie had absolutely no opposition to that plan – she was sure Jo's hotpot would be just as good a day older as it was fresh. So she pulled on her wellies and raincoat and took a slow walk down the winding path that would take her away from the isolation of Sweet Briar and into the relative metropolis of Gillypuddle.

An hour later she was in the warm and dry of her parents' house, rain drumming on the conservatory roof as her mother handed her a milky coffee, chastising her for getting soaked through and trying to persuade her husband that he ought to be checking Hattie out for early signs of pneumonia.

'I'm absolutely fine, Mum,' she said. 'In fact, just lately I feel really healthy.'

'She does look well enough,' Nigel agreed, casting a critical eye in her direction as he laid the table. 'The air up at Sweet Briar must agree with her if nothing else.'

'She looks flushed,' Rhonda insisted, placing the back of her hand against Hattie's cheek.

'I think it's called a healthy glow, Mum,' Hattie said, pushing it away. 'Jo really looks after me – I've never eaten so well and she makes sure the house is warm when we're in; you don't need to worry.'

'I expect you're developing a healthy immunity to lots of farmyard diseases too,' Nigel said dryly.

'I try not to think about those, Dad,' Hattie said. 'Sometimes having a doctor in the family is no fun – you're not allowed to cheerfully ignore any medical risk.'

'There has to be some perks,' Nigel said, rubbing a streaked knife on a napkin.

Hattie grinned. It felt nice that they could share banter about this, even though she knew all the same that it was hard for her parents to accept a situation that put her at any sort of risk at all – especially given what had happened to Charlotte – and how much it pained them to let her do what she was doing up at Sweet Briar.

'I met Seth Bryson the other day,' she said, trying to steer the subject towards something that might feel more neutral for them all. 'He seems nice.'

'Is that the new vet at Castle House?' Rhonda asked.

Hattie nodded.

'Isn't he a partner, Nigel?' Rhonda looked at her husband.

Nigel placed the last fork down. 'Set to take over, I shouldn't wonder, with Josiah on the way out.'

'He's retiring?' Hattie asked. Seth's arrival in Gillypuddle made more sense now. He'd told Hattie that the job had looked good and she'd wondered how a post in a small village like this had been so tempting, but she could see now that the idea of being able to take over the practice would have been a big lure.

'Almost retired now, so I hear. He lets Seth do most of the work. Some of the older clients don't quite trust the new guy yet and they won't let Josiah go without a fight, but that's only to be expected – they've had the same man for years and change doesn't come easy to some.'

'You mean like Rupert always coming to see you about his knee instead of going to the new GP?' Hattie asked with a grin.

'Yes. We're a funny bunch in Gillypuddle, aren't we? We don't like change very much.'

'People do tend to cling on to what they know,' Hattie agreed.

'He's rather good-looking,' Rhonda said with a dreamy expression. 'If you like that sort of thing, of course,' she added quickly after a sharp look from Nigel.

'Seth?' Hattie asked. 'He is. Shame he's taken.'

'Who told you that?' Rhonda asked. 'As far as I know he's not.'

'Melinda said so. She said her name's Eugenie or something – some clever clogs living in Oxford.'

'Oh, that's all water under the bridge,' Rhonda said.

'Are you sure?'

'Quite sure. Agatha Crook told me his girlfriend had taken a research post in Washington and he'd told her not to bother coming back. She told him she didn't much care for England anyway – too many skinheads – and away she went.'

'How on earth does Agatha know all that?'

'She heard it from Philip Stow.'

'How does Philip know?'

'Doesn't he play bowls with Josiah? I can't be certain, but I'm quite sure it's true.'

'He told her not to come back just because she wanted to do some research somewhere for a while?' Hattie asked doubtfully. 'Seems a bit harsh to me.'

'She was going to be away for more than a little while,' Rhonda said. 'Five years, so I heard. That is a long time to put a wedding off for.'

'They were getting married?'

'So I heard.'

Hattie sipped her coffee. It looked as if her mother had inadvertently explained another of Seth's cryptic clues. When Hattie had asked him why he'd come to Oxford, he'd told her a friend had taken him there and he used the word friend, rather than girlfriend, fiancée, partner…

Was this Eugenie woman the friend? It seemed like a safe bet. And if he was referring to her as a friend rather than something more significant, it looked as if she was out of the picture after all.

'The gossip in this village is ridiculous,' Nigel said, shaking his head as he went out to the kitchen. Hattie exchanged a grin with her mum.

'He's one to complain about gossip,' Rhonda said. 'Nobody's worse than him when he goes to the bridge meet.'

'We'll pretend we haven't noticed,' Hattie said.

'So,' Rhonda said with a mischievous look, 'if you were interested in the new vet, it looks as if the path is clear. Although, you will have to join the queue…'

'Oh yeah, behind Phyllis and Scary Mary who cleans the vicarage?'

'Oh, I'm sure his net's cast a little wider than just Gillypuddle,' Rhonda said mildly. 'For some of us, the world doesn't start and end in this village.'

'It doesn't for me either,' Hattie said, a slight note of offence creeping into her voice. 'I have been further afield, you know.'

'The world starts and ends at Sweet Briar Farm these days for you,' Nigel said, returning from the kitchen with a bowl of fresh leafy salad. 'We hardly see you. And all talk of education has gone out of the window since you moved up there.'

'I never promised that anything else was going to happen.' Hattie narrowed her eyes. 'Did you agree so readily to the move because you thought I'd never stick it out? Did you think I'd be back in a week with my tail between my legs begging to take up your plans?'

Rhonda shook her head. 'Don't be silly. We know better than that by now. Nobody can give any advice that you'd want to take.'

'Why do I need to take other people's advice? Why can't you let me get on with things? I like Sweet Briar and I know it may shock you but I like Jo too. She might be a moody cow, but she cares about those animals and she'll do anything for them. For instance, she spends every last penny she has on them.'

'How do you know all this when you say she never tells you anything?'

'I just do. I don't think she can even manage the vet's bills.'

'I'm sure Seth Bryson's pleased about that,' Nigel said caustically.

'Well, maybe he cares more about animals than money too,' Hattie fired back.

'I'm sure he does,' Nigel continued, his tone irritatingly level, 'but a business has to turn a profit or it ceases to be a business. In the case of a vet, he can be as fond of animals as you like, but he's got to make money or he won't be able to help any animals, no matter how much he wants to.'

'Does she owe him a lot of money?' Rhonda asked, and Hattie turned to her now, surprised by the tone of genuine concern in her voice, rather than the preaching note of her dad's. It instantly calmed Hattie's building temper.

'I don't honestly know,' she said. 'As Dad just said, Jo doesn't tell me a lot so it's all guesswork and conjecture, but I would imagine it's enough.'

Rhonda shook her head. 'You've got to admire her – I don't know how she keeps that place running.'

'That's what worries me,' Hattie said. 'I don't know how either.'

Rhonda studied her for a moment. 'It really does worry you, doesn't it?'

'She's a good person,' Hattie said, 'and she's doing a good thing. I don't know why she's so closed off to everyone – even me really – but the sanctuary matters to her for some reason – more than anything.'

'I think you're doing a good thing too.' Rhonda smiled. 'Doing your bit to help. I'm proud of you.'

Hattie's face lit up in a bemused smile. 'You are?'

'That's not to say that what you're doing now is what we would have chosen for you,' Nigel reminded her.

'I know that.'

'If it means so much to you perhaps I could pay Seth a visit,' Nigel said, 'find out what's going on. He might not tell me, but if I can talk to him, professional to professional, perhaps he will.'

'That's very kind of you, Dad, but I don't know what good it will do. Unless...' Hattie paused. 'Dad... say no if you want to but how would you feel about loaning me the money so I could pay Jo's bill?'

'I'd say it depends on how much it is. But how exactly are you proposing to pay me back in your current situation? You're hardly rolling in money yourself.'

'I know, but I'm working on plans to get the sanctuary earning. In fact, I already know what I'm going to do – I just need to get Jo to agree to it. If you didn't mind waiting a little while, we could pay you then.'

'I doubt she'd agree to anyone paying her bills for her,' Rhonda put in. 'Shouldn't you at least run this plan by her?'

'She probably wouldn't agree.'

'Then you probably shouldn't be doing it.'

'I'm trying to help her. She'll see that.'

Rhonda looked unconvinced but Nigel nodded.

'Leave it with me. I'll go to see Seth tomorrow morning.'

Hattie gave him a grateful smile, even though, at the back of her mind, there was a little voice telling her that Jo might not be quite as grateful for this intervention as she might hope. She decided that voice sounded better with a sock stuffed firmly into its mouth to muffle the noise. Jo *would* see in time that Hattie had the best interests of her and Sweet Briar at heart.

She was also tempted to go with her dad to see Seth in the morning for a bit of harmless flirting in light of the new information from her mum. But Jo would need her on the farm and, besides, to ask for the morning off at such short notice would require some sort of explanation, and Hattie was pretty sure she couldn't tell Jo about this yet. Her mother would have said that was because Hattie knew she shouldn't even be doing it, but if Jo wasn't willing to accept the help she so clearly needed then Hattie was going to have to find another way of giving it. In a way, she reasoned, it was just like when they hid the donkeys' medication in their sugar beet. They didn't want the medication but they needed it, so if a bit of subterfuge was necessary, where was the harm in that as long as the outcome was a good one?

Chapter Fourteen

Hattie smiled as Melinda's children fired questions at Jo, while Melinda just looked bemused:

How old is that one?

How many eggs do you get?

How fast can they run?

Why can't they fly?

Do they lie down when they go to sleep?

Are these the same chickens you get in nuggets?

Why do they scratch the floor?

Are those two fighting?

Which one's the cock-a-doodle-do?

Jo answered each question patiently and solemnly, as if each one mattered more than anything else in the world. As each child used their handful of feed, she gave them another, showing them how to scatter it evenly. Sunshine's attempts weren't too bad, Ocean arranged his on the floor in a sort of psychometric test pattern, while Rain only managed to dump hers straight on Peppa's head, leading to some very bad-tempered clucking.

Earlier there had been a chicken-naming ceremony. Hattie had overseen it at first, but it had drawn Jo in. She'd been determined to have nothing to do with the visit but, Hattie reasoned, who could ignore a family of adorable children trying to name a bunch of hens? Even Jo couldn't walk away from that. So now they had Peppa, Sam, Pat, Miffy, Paddington, Minnie, Daisy, Olga, Belle, Ariel, Elsa and Anna. It didn't seem to matter that they weren't all exclusively female names, and Hattie could definitely see a distinct trend.

'I swear they don't watch as much television as that list might suggest,' Melinda said behind a hand. Hattie laughed.

'If I had four kids they'd do nothing *but* watch television while I recovered in a dark room.'

'You know,' Melinda said, lowering her voice further still as they sat on the low stone wall of the orchard, watching Jo with the kids, the bright morning sun throwing leafy shadows on the carpet of grass between the trees, 'maybe you were right about her.'

Hattie grinned. 'I am right sometimes, aren't I?'

'Sometimes. I'm beginning to think you're a lost-soul magnet.'

Hattie threw her a sideways glance. 'What on earth does that mean?'

'Well,' Melinda continued, 'first of all you looked after Alphonse when nobody else would...'

'He paid me,' Hattie reminded her. 'And I needed the job when Bertrand left me high and dry so I had to put up with him if I wanted to eat.'

'I don't think any amount of money would have persuaded me to stick his moods out,' Melinda said. 'So that still makes it an act of mercy in my book. And now this. I'm beginning to think you're like that angel in that old film who comes down to earth to sort people's lives out when they're messed up.'

Hattie's laughter rang across the orchard. Jo and the kids all turned to see what the commotion was before they decided that, on balance, the chickens were still more interesting than whatever had tickled Hattie so much.

'Don't be daft,' she said once she was able to speak. 'I didn't exactly make Alphonse happy. I burnt his show down for a start.'

'Admittedly the burning-down thing might have blotted your copy book a bit, but I think he still actually cared a lot about you, and that was because you'd been there for him when he was lonely.'

'You mean when Raul left him?'

'I mean even after that. Why do you think he phoned the other week? He misses you because you did more than just work for him – you talked to him.'

Hattie turned back to watch Jo talking to Melinda's brood – or rather, listening to the crescendo of steadily growing noise and excited chatter that made getting her answers to their questions heard really quite impossible.

'I'm going to ask her tonight,' Hattie said. 'I think she'll say yes.'

'About the visitor thing?'

Hattie nodded. 'Look – she's fine with your lot. Admittedly there are some kids out there a million miles away from that type of good behaviour, but I can deal with those situations; Jo doesn't have to get involved at all. I'm going to suggest a trial, a month or so, see how it goes.'

'I think it's a good idea. She'd be nuts to say no – I honestly don't know why she's never done it before.'

'I suppose that would have involved interaction with lots of people, and we know she doesn't like that. But she has me now and I can take care of those things.'

Melinda nudged her with an affectionate smile. 'She's lucky to have you. Are you sure you don't want to come and be my nanny, Mary Poppins?'

Hattie grinned. 'I'm lucky to have this place.'

'You know, I'm still amazed at how you've settled. I never thought you'd stay.'

'I don't think anybody in Gillypuddle did. My parents said more or less the same thing.'

'Has your dad been to talk to you-know-who yet?'

'Yes.'

'And?'

'She does owe.'

'A lot?'

Hattie nodded, keeping one careful eye on Jo to make sure she wasn't catching any of this conversation. But Sunshine, Ocean and Rain were giggling and chatting so enthusiastically now that it was hardly likely.

'What are you going to do?' Melinda asked.

'I've already done it.'

Melinda stared at her. 'What's that?'

'Dad's settled it.'

Melinda sucked in her breath. 'She won't like it when she finds out.'

'I know. But then I can use it to persuade her that my visitor idea is a good one. She'll want to pay Dad back and she'll need money to do that, so…'

'Be careful it doesn't blow up in your face.'

'I am being careful.'

'But you're going to tell her about what you've done? You'll have to at some point.'

'I will – I'm choosing my moment.'

'So your moment won't be the same moment you put your ideas to her?'

'Um… I'm still thinking about that.'

Melinda shook her head. 'You're a braver woman than me.'

Hattie smiled but her stomach churned. The decision had been made in a split second of impulsive recklessness and it had plagued her ever since, despite her trying to pretend that she was perfectly at ease with it. Her dad had phoned her from Seth's practice and told her what he'd managed to find out, along with a figure for what Jo owed Seth, and she'd gone ahead and told her dad to settle it there and then. It was too late to change that now, but she'd had time to think over what she'd done and she was worried about Jo's reaction, despite what she'd have Melinda believe. Worse than that was the possibility of Jo finding out from someone other than Hattie. What if Seth himself mentioned it in passing? What if Jo called to actually pay it? What if she asked him to tally up what she owed and he told her there was nothing to pay and then told her why? Seth and Jo did necessarily have a lot of communication from week to week and that wasn't such a wild possibility.

There was only one thing for it – Hattie would have to go down to the practice and warn Seth; explain the situation and ask him to avoid discussion of Jo's bill with her if he could. It was going to sound odd, and maybe even a little dodgy, she supposed. On the plus side, at least she got to see him again.

Jo tossed a sack of hay onto the pile in the barn as if it weighed nothing. 'We're fine as we are.'

Hattie struggled with her sack but she wasn't going to be beaten, just like she wasn't going to be beaten on this. She was right and she just had to make Jo see that.

'We're not fine,' she said. 'Look at this place.'

'You don't like it you can leave,' Jo huffed.

'That's not what I mean and you know it. I just think we could do so much more here with more money – take more animals in, do better for the ones we've got.'

'The ones we've got are happy and well cared for. I do my best for them.'

'I know you do. I know you want the best for them, which is why I don't understand why this is such a problem. Visitors bring money and you can put that straight back into the sanctuary.'

'Visitors bring trouble.'

'Some might, granted. The odd one, maybe, but the majority of them will be animal lovers just like us.'

'My donkeys are not performing seals; they're creatures who've had hard lives. They deserve a little peace and kindness now. This place is called a sanctuary for a reason.'

Hattie swallowed an impatient sigh as Jo flipped another sack onto the pile. 'How much does all this hay cost?'

'I don't have to discuss my running costs with you.'

'And that's just one thing,' Hattie said, ignoring the dismissal. 'You can't even pay me more than minimum wage.'

'You're complaining now? I just said, if you don't like it—'

'I'm not complaining and I don't want to leave; I'm just saying. I'm trying to make you see that making the place earn a bit more money isn't a bad thing.'

'So that I can pay you a higher wage? I told you at the start what was on offer and you took the job. If you don't like it—'

'I know I can leave. But I don't want to leave. I like it here, Jo. I love it here. I feel like you've saved me like you saved the donkeys because I was lost, all at sea, and I didn't know what I wanted to do with my life. But now I know. I want to care for these donkeys like you do. You only want what's best and so do I. I just happen to think that this is what's best and I'm sorry if you don't agree and you don't want to hear it because I'm just going to keep on nagging until you say yes.' Hattie held Jo's disapproving gaze. 'You'd do it too if you thought it was going to help the donkeys.'

Jo rested her hands on her hips. 'It means that much to you?'

'Yes.'

Jo wiped a hand across her brow and studied Hattie. The look on her face was one Hattie hadn't seen before – at least not directed at her. Maybe she'd seen it directed at Norbert or Blue or Minty. It was almost tender. But then it passed like the clouds blowing in to smother the sun on a stormy day. A moment later, Jo shook her head and reached for another sack.

'Still no. I don't need folks tramping all over my land.'

Hattie let out a squeal of frustration. She hadn't wanted to lose her temper over this because she knew the moment she did, Jo would only dig her heels in deeper, but there was just no talking to the woman. As she stormed out of the barn, she half expected Jo to come after her – angry, apologetic – she didn't know which, but something at least. But as she marched up the hill to the high field, not really planning but letting her feet take her where they would, she quickly realised that Jo wasn't coming after her and probably never would. Maybe she just didn't care about Hattie after all. Maybe the friendship Hattie thought she'd seen just wasn't there. Hattie had been so certain that they'd been bonding over the past weeks, forming a connection, working together for a common goal in a way that was bound to form a team, and then a friendship, that before long Hattie would be able to reach across that icy chasm and touch Jo's humanity. But maybe Jo didn't want friendship as Hattie had imagined she must. Maybe she just wasn't like other people. Maybe she genuinely didn't care about being alone. Could anyone really be happy in such isolation?

All these weeks, Hattie had thought she was changing Jo, but what if it had been the other way around? What if Hattie had been assimilating into Jo's way of life and not vice versa? As the thought occurred to her, it startled her. After all, she'd left the bright lights of Paris for this and she ought to have felt more alien here at Sweet Briar than she did – Seth had even said so. The fact was, she didn't feel alien here – she loved it. So when she strove to talk Jo into opening Sweet Briar up to the world, maybe she wasn't trying to ensure the sanctuary's survival for Jo or the donkeys, maybe she was trying to save it for herself. She'd wanted to do something that mattered, something that had worth, and now that she'd found that thing she couldn't give it up. It made her feel so good and so useful. She'd never amounted to anything, never really felt she meant anything to anyone, and now that she did, she wanted to hold on to that feeling of worth. Now, she could think about Charlotte and not feel like the child who failed and she thought that, maybe, if her sister were here to see it, she'd think Hattie was worth something too.

At the top field, Norbert trotted over to greet her. She reached into her pocket for a treat but it was empty. She hated to let him down, but today the notion left her feeling more hollow and useless than ever. Now just about everyone was disappointed in her – even Norbert.

'Sorry, fella,' she said, scratching behind his ear. 'Looks like I forgot to stock up. I was kind of in a hurry.' He blew through his nose at her and she smiled sadly. 'At least you don't give me backchat.'

Across the field, Loki and Lola were braying at each other. Just the usual sibling rivalry then, Hattie thought. She turned back to Norbert and rubbed a hand over his neck. When Jo came up to the field, all the donkeys rushed to her. On a good day, maybe half of them would come to greet Hattie. On days like today, it was just Norbert. That was OK, she kept telling herself – she needed to earn their trust and they didn't give it easily. Jo had done that and of course they loved her. Jo didn't even have to try with them. She didn't have to be charming and sociable – she just had to care. The thing was, if they could look into Hattie's heart they'd see she cared too; it was just harder for her to get things right. She worried and doubted and second-guessed and she made the wrong choices – she didn't have Jo's composure and self-reliance. Hattie still thought she was right about her visitor plans, but Jo had the strength to stand her ground and say no whatever came her way, and Hattie wished she had a little of that in her.

Hattie looked out across the bay. The restless sea pushed and pulled under a grey sky. Even when the weather wasn't perfect, this view was. You could paint Sweet Briar in any palette you wanted – spring, autumn, storm or sun – and it would still be beautiful. She didn't want to lose this view but she could see a day when, perhaps, they might all lose it. Jo couldn't keep running it on fresh air, but it was beginning to look as if she'd never come around to Hattie's way of thinking. Perhaps, after their spat, she might even throw Hattie out. She couldn't deny that there was a small part of her that wondered if it might not be for the best. She was beginning to realise that she could never be content to watch Jo run Sweet Briar into the ground and do nothing.

When Hattie got back, Jo was standing at the stove stirring something in a pan. She didn't turn around as Hattie slipped in and closed the door softly behind her, though she must have heard her come in. Hattie decided to go up to her room, partly to get changed out of her grubby work clothes, but partly to stay out of Jo's way. She was just sneaking through the kitchen when Jo's voice stopped her.

'I don't want adverts all over the place,' she said. 'If they come, they come, and if they don't it won't bother me.'

Hattie turned around. Jo was still bent over the stove, intent on her pan.

'You can deal with them,' Jo continued. 'I haven't a clue what to charge but I trust you've thought of that – you seem to have been giving this a lot of thought.'

'I have,' Hattie said, trying to steady the beginnings of hope with a dollop of caution. Could this be the turning point? She didn't dare imagine it.

'A month,' Jo said.

'A month,' Hattie agreed. 'That's all I need – just to see how it goes. I won't let you down.'

'If you do, you'll be out.'

'I know,' Hattie said.

Jo gave a short nod and reached for the salt cellar from a shelf above the stove. But then she turned and glanced at Hattie. They had reached an understanding that didn't need to be spoken. Jo was trusting Hattie with a lot more than the future of Sweet Briar and Hattie realised that she couldn't screw it up. After all, she'd been here before: finally winning the trust of someone she'd been trying to wear down for months, finally winning a chance to prove herself only to cock it up marvellously. It had forced her to leave Paris, though, in the end, Paris hadn't meant that much to her – not like Sweet Briar and the donkeys did.

'I won't let you down,' Hattie repeated, and she hoped that was true.

Chapter Fifteen

She had three reasons to go into the village the next day, but Hattie shared only one of them with Jo. The first was to have a quiet word with Seth about the situation of Jo's bill. The second was to talk to a few of the local businesses about directing visitors up to the sanctuary. It wasn't advertising exactly, but Hattie decided to keep it quiet and low-key because she didn't want to risk Jo changing her mind. The third was to get her dad's help with creating a website for Sweet Briar. Her dad was the epitome of the silver surfer (though his silver hairs had parted company with his head many years before) and even Hattie had to admit that he was far more computer literate than she was. Before he'd retired he'd designed and built the website for the GP's surgery and it was better than any professional could have managed. It had to be, because the new GP was very particular and she was perfectly happy to continue using it.

The first call was Castle House Practice. Hattie had phoned ahead and made arrangements with a bemused-sounding Seth to go early, before the surgery opened for business. Although he'd sounded surprised, he'd agreed readily to the request.

At the entrance, Hattie took a moment to smooth her hair and then rang the bell. Thirty seconds later, Seth opened up.

'Good morning, Hattie.'

Hattie stepped in and found herself in the surgery reception. She'd never been in before – they'd had Peanut years before and her parents had taken care of all his health needs with no input from her or Charlotte. Since then they'd not had another pet even though Hattie had pushed for one many times. Her parents had said they were just too busy to have an animal around the place, but now Hattie realised that they were probably too tired from their demanding jobs to care for one, and once Peanut had gone they'd decided not to have another. The reception was a little on the chilly side, despite the season, the sun choosing to rise from a spot beyond the north-facing windows, and it smelt of antiseptic and old magazines.

'Thanks so much for seeing me.'

Without realising it, Hattie put another anxious hand to her hair and smoothed down the lengths. Melinda would have laughed to see how much effort Hattie had put in but Hattie didn't care – her friend would have been doing the same thing in her position. And Hattie's mother probably had a point – if Hattie was interested in Seth (and she couldn't deny that she was more than interested) then she'd probably have to join a lengthy queue. Or, better still, find a way of vaulting to the front of it.

Today, Hattie wore her hair down with loose curls pinned up at the sides, and she'd put on a little layer of the very expensive French foundation and blusher she'd treated herself to in Paris and that she would probably never be able to afford again once it had gone. She also had her floaty summer trousers on, which she never wore these days because they were perfectly useless around the farm but perfectly pretty on a day like today. There was no denying she'd made an effort. Anyway, she reasoned, only having herself to convince but doing it anyway, it did a girl good to make an effort from time to time. It was nice to feel nice. She'd spent the weeks since she'd moved into Sweet

Briar in farming clothes and she'd hardly recognised herself in the mirror that morning, but she'd liked what she saw. At least Jo had been busy with the chickens – she wouldn't have commented but Hattie was pretty sure she'd have some sort of opinion on Hattie's makeover and it probably wouldn't be encouraging.

'So…' Seth closed the front door and smiled expectantly at Hattie. Considering she'd put so much effort into her appearance he didn't seem to be taking a lot of notice. His tone was brisk, friendly, but strictly business. 'What can I do for you? Is there a problem at Sweet Briar?'

'Not exactly. I mean, yes, but it's not the animals.'

Hattie glanced past him to where the door to his consulting room stood open. There was a lot of ceramic and steel in there, and some very unfriendly-looking gadgets. She supposed everything had to be clinical and sterile, but it was a world away from the welcoming shabbiness of Sweet Briar Farm.

Seth dug his hands in his pockets. 'Can I get you a coffee or anything? It wouldn't take a minute.'

'Um…' Hattie paused. He smiled patiently, still waiting. Now that she was here, however, ready to explain herself, she couldn't help but feel that it was going to sound stupid. The whole daft situation that she had created was going to sound very stupid indeed. What had made perfect sense as she'd cooked it up and recruited her dad's help now made her seem… well, perhaps a little arrogant. At least, that might be how it looked to Seth.

'I need your help,' she blurted out finally.

'What's wrong?'

'Oh, nothing. It's just… well, it's Jo's bill.'

Seth frowned. 'I'm not sure I can discuss Jo's financial affairs with you. I know you work with her but—'

'I know the bill's been settled. My dad came to do it.'

'Your dad?' Seth looked confused, but then, he'd only been in Gillypuddle a matter of months and when he'd moved there Hattie had still been in Paris – and besides, he probably didn't have an encyclopaedic knowledge of everyone's connections yet. 'Your dad is Dr Rose?'

'Yes.'

'Oh.' At this, Seth looked even more confused. It was understandable and Hattie did feel very much to blame. 'I was under the impression that the payment was a donation that Jo was fully aware of. Are you telling me that's not the case?'

'I asked my dad to come and pay the bill. I'm going to pay him back as soon as I can. But Jo doesn't know we've done it.' Hattie felt the heat rise to her face. 'In fact,' she continued, deciding that it might as well all come out now, 'she kind of asked me not to interfere. Well, *told* me not to interfere… But I was worried,' she added quickly, seeing his expression darken, 'you know, that she might get into trouble for not paying it. Or that we might lose your services – and we definitely can't afford to do that.'

'I would never refuse to treat a sick animal regardless of an outstanding bill and I have absolute faith that Jo would have paid me eventually,' he said coldly.

'I know, I should have realised that. So, what I wanted to ask today is that you don't tell her that I've paid. Or rather, that my dad has.'

'You want me to *lie* to her?'

'Not exactly. I just don't want you to mention the bill at all.'

Seth shook his head. 'I can't do that. This whole situation is nothing to do with me. You need to be talking this through with Jo, not me.'

'But Jo doesn't like talking anything through! She doesn't like talking full stop! Trying to get a conversation about anything out of her is like trying to pull teeth.'

'She always seems perfectly reasonable to me.'

'Look, Sweet Briar will be making money soon and then she'll come down to pay you. All I'm asking is that you play along. Take the money from her and return it to my dad and she need never know.'

'What if she asks me about her account before then?'

'Then just tell her it's still outstanding.'

'A minute ago you wanted me to avoid discussing it with her at all.'

'Please…'

'I can't do that – sorry. My opinion hasn't changed – I don't think this is a situation I should be involved in. I'm afraid you're going to have to come clean with Jo.'

'You won't go and tell her, will you?'

'It's not my place but I think you ought to.'

'She'll hate me.'

'Quite possibly.'

Hattie's shoulders slumped, as if all the pride and optimism had been let out of her, leaving only a vacuum of uncertainty and worry behind. Why had she ever thought this was a good idea? Her impatience to fix what she thought needed fixing might well jeopardise the real progress she'd made with Jo on things that actually mattered. She ought to have seen the bigger picture more clearly before.

'What I can do,' Seth said, his expression softening as he witnessed Hattie's obvious shift to despondence, 'is refund the money your dad gave to me.'

'But then you wouldn't have your payment.'

'I also wouldn't have this extra thing to worry about. I don't want to be part of your wacky scheme but I don't want to cause tension between you and Jo either. It seems to me that you've done this for the right reasons, even if they're a little misguided. I was content to wait for Jo's payment before and I'm still content to wait now. If what you say is true and Sweet Briar is set to make money, then I expect I'll get paid soon enough.'

Hattie gave him a grateful smile. She couldn't say that she was entirely happy with the outcome of her visit but Seth's idea did seem like a sensible solution.

Seth went into his office and pulled a cheque from a desk drawer.

'I hadn't sent it to the bank yet anyway,' he said, walking back through and handing it to Hattie.

'Thank you.'

For all her scheming and plotting to catch Seth's attention in a romantic way, now all Hattie wanted to do was leave. She felt silly and she could only imagine that Seth thought she was silly too.

'I'm sorry to have taken up your time,' she said.

'It was no trouble at all.' Seth gave a little nod and smiled, and Hattie thought that maybe she saw something like playful amusement in his eyes, but she couldn't allow herself to dwell on it because she knew she'd blush from head to toe.

'So, I'll see you when you're next at Sweet Briar,' she said uncertainly.

'You will.'

'OK. Well, bye then.'

Hattie turned to leave. With her hand on the doorknob, his voice called her back. She turned to face him again.

'For what it's worth,' he said with that same playful look, 'it was a sweet idea. Even if it was a little screwy.'

Hattie grinned, and sure enough, her face started to burn. She dashed out so he wouldn't see, and as she let the door close behind her, she could have sworn she heard him chuckle softly.

*

Lance looked stressed. Hattie didn't think she'd ever seen Lance look stressed before. Mark was taking an afternoon off and Phyllis was on shift, taking up the slack so that Mark could rest as he was supposed to. It soon became apparent, however, that Phyllis was the reason Lance was stressed.

'Oh! Hello, Dottie!' she said brightly, turning with a broad smile as Hattie pushed open the door of the Willow Tree café. She looked as if she was clearing a table, but she also looked as if she couldn't quite decide which item to pick up first because she took up a teapot and then put it down, then did the same with a cup and saucer, before finally settling on a teaspoon. 'You're back from America then?'

Hattie smiled. Lance stood behind the counter. He rolled his eyes heavenward.

'Please tell me Medusa has sacked you,' he hissed as she approached the counter. 'That one's driving me mad – I'll be mad as a hatter if I have to deal with her for much longer.'

Hattie began to laugh, but Lance grabbed her wrist and fixed her with a pleading look. 'Seriously, the job's yours if you want it. Please tell me you can start right now!'

'You can't sack Phyllis,' Hattie said, trying to stifle more laughter. 'She's too nice.'

'Oh God, I know. Imagine her face – it'd be like telling your three-year-old you just shot Santa.'

'Where's Mark?'

'Lucky bugger's gone to get a reiki massage.'

'Maybe you could get some reiki massage to calm your nerves?'

'I'll need more than that to calm my nerves. Tell you what, another opening has just come up then. Apply. Please! I'll put you on shift every day. With a bit of luck she'll forget she works here and stop coming in.'

'You can't do that either,' Hattie said, her gaze wandering back to the table Phyllis was clearing, apparently picking up one item at a time to take through to the kitchen. She was well past retirement age but Hattie had always known her to be a sprightly and cheerful lady. In fact, since Rupert's wife had died, there'd been some in the village trying to throw him and Phyllis (whose husband had also passed on) together. Hattie would have liked to see it too, but it seemed that both Phyllis and Rupert were happier on their own.

'I'll pay you a million pounds an hour,' Lance said.

'She can't be *that* bad.'

The reply was an almighty crash from the kitchen.

Lance buried his face in his hands and let out a strangled cry. 'Give me strength!'

'Shouldn't you go and see what's happened?'

'I don't think I could bear it. Mark won't be the only one with heart trouble at this rate – mine's racing like an eighties drum machine!'

'Go and see if she's OK,' Hattie said with a smile. 'I can wait for my order.'

'So you're turning me down in my hour of need?'

'I'm afraid so.'

Phyllis tottered out of the kitchen wearing an apron that was far too large for her tiny frame and carrying what looked like strawberry milkshake.

'Don't worry – all under control,' she announced in a raspy voice before going to fetch another solo cup from a recently vacated table filled with cups. Lance shook his head.

'I'd offer to get you a drink but I don't think we could manage it without some kind of incident,' he said.

'Actually – that's OK. I've come to ask a favour.'

'Oh?'

'Sweet Briar Farm is opening to visitors, and I was wondering—'

Lance's mouth fell open in a most comical way, all thoughts of the one-woman disaster zone that was Phyllis clearly forgotten.

'Oh, sign me up!' he squeaked. 'I've always wanted to see what Hades looks like!'

'Lance!' Hattie scolded, but she couldn't help a grin.

'You can tell me off but I don't think you understand the significance, my love. You haven't been here for the last two years being shunned by that woman at every opportunity. Nobody has been allowed in there.'

'The vet has,' Hattie reminded him.

'Nobody who doesn't shove their hands up animals' bottoms for a living then. It'll be like the gates to North Korea opening.'

'I'm allowed in there,' Hattie said, starting to laugh again despite herself. She didn't entirely approve of Lance's comments, but she had to admit that he was funny.

'Yes, and you've been inducted into the cult now.'

'Lance – be serious.'

Lance smoothed a wicked expression into one of pure innocence. 'Go on then,' he said. 'What has this wonder got to do with me? You said you needed a favour. Are you looking for a sacrificial victim, because if you are I think I might know one – she's currently wrecking my kitchen…'

'I was wondering if you could give us a mention whenever you get tourists in. No need to shove it down anyone's throat but if they say they're looking for somewhere to visit, maybe you could big us up, send them our way.'

'And send all those poor innocent people to their doom?'

Hattie pretended to frown impatiently at him and he laughed.

'Alright – only because it's you. You're welcome to put posters up if you want; maybe leave some flyers with us.'

'I would but it's got to be low-key.'

Lance raised his eyebrows.

'I know,' Hattie said. 'Jo might be opening the doors but she hasn't quite decided if she likes the idea or not yet. I'm still trying to persuade her that it makes sense, and I'm hoping that a bit of money coming in might do that – we sure need it.'

'How much are you going to charge for entry?'

'I'm not. I was thinking more along the lines of voluntary donations but with a suggested amount – like they do in museums. It doesn't seem like quite such a capitalist venture then, does it?'

'I can't imagine her being very welcoming if anyone does go up – donations or not.'

'That's why I'll be taking care of the visitor side of things.'

Lance was thoughtful for a moment. 'What else are you doing with the place?' he asked.

'What do you mean? I don't think there's anything else we can do other than getting people up there.'

'What about sponsorship? You see the ads all the time, don't you – daytime telly's full of them. Three pounds a week for this cat or this dog.'

'Sponsor a donkey?' Hattie's face lit in a broad smile. 'That's brilliant!'

'I know,' Lance said, looking supremely pleased.

'How would I get the word out? We can't afford TV ads.'

Lance tapped the side of his nose. 'I think I might know someone who can help.'

'Who?'

'Let me ask him first and then I'll tell you.'

'OK, so now I'm going to be mad with curiosity until I find out.'

'I thought you might be. So, you're sure I can't tempt you to take that job, after all?'

Hattie was about to reply when there was another crash from the kitchen.

Lance made the sign of the cross over his chest. 'Lead me not into temptation,' he muttered, his gaze on the ceiling, and Hattie couldn't help but laugh again.

Chapter Sixteen

Hattie looked at the website her dad had designed. It looked good – nice and clear, well laid out, lovely photos of Sweet Briar Farm and the views along the coast, some adorable shots of the donkeys and chickens, and Hattie herself, looking as welcoming as possible as she hugged Norbert. Melinda had taken the last picture and, considering how many she'd had to snap before she managed to get one that included all of Hattie's head, it wasn't half bad really. Hattie had taken everything over to her dad a week ago and they'd spent the evening setting it up. He'd even managed to link it to a charity page so that people could donate to the upkeep of the donkeys online if they couldn't get to visit and wanted to help. Since then, they'd had a grand total of zero visitors and three donations – one was from Melinda (which was touching considering their own financial struggles), one from her mum and one from Rupert. It was hardly encouraging.

On the plus side, though, Hattie had never seen Jo look so happy. And by happy she meant not scowling. Hattie had to suppose that there was some kind of satisfying vindication in being right, because Jo had predicted that nobody would be interested in her donkey rescue centre. Hattie thought that a bit of her revelled in some martyred idea that the care of Sweet Briar was a labour of love for her to undertake alone, but Hattie could also see that it was no way to run a place like Sweet

Briar and she wasn't giving up yet. There was no denying the lack of visitors made Jo happy, however – whatever the reason was – and Hattie found it all massively frustrating. Surely somebody wanted to come? And preferably someone other than Melinda and her kids, who would have come every day if they'd been allowed. The fact that she couldn't do proper advertising was putting a serious spanner in the works.

In the meantime, Hattie carried on with the daily routine around the farm during the day, while in the evenings she tried to figure out how to get that extra publicity they needed, and what they could do to make themselves look more attractive to the paying public, while still respecting Jo's boundaries. She was still waiting for Lance to get back to her too about whatever this secret weapon was that he'd promised he had up his sleeve.

She was about to shut the lid on the laptop when her phone started to ring. It was almost as if she'd willed it by thinking about it, because she looked at the caller ID to see that it was Lance.

'Can you come to the café tomorrow?' he asked without preamble. 'There's someone I want you to meet.'

'Tomorrow? It's a bit short notice… Is this the person you were telling me about?'

'Yes. Tomorrow's the only day he can come.'

'Oh. Well in that case I'd better try. What time?'

'About noon?'

Hattie paused. 'I don't think Jo will go for that.'

'But this is for her! Can't you explain that to the evil hag?'

'Alright – I suppose I'll get there somehow. Who am I supposed to be meeting?'

'It's a secret but I think you'll be happy.'

'Will I? Is it the Duke of Sussex?'

'Better, my love.'

'Better than the Duke of Sussex? Now I'm interested.'

'Oh love, I've got to go – Phyllis has her hair stuck in the food processor…'

'But—'

'See you tomorrow. Wear something nice!'

The line went dead. Hattie looked at the screen as it went black. Then she pushed herself off the bed and went to her wardrobe. *Wear something nice?* Who was this person? And what was Lance's definition of something nice? She began to move along the hangers, pulling the odd item out thoughtfully. Sexy nice? Girly nice? Business nice? It was tempting to phone Lance back and ask him what he meant but he'd sounded as if he had his hands full and he was already doing her a favour in setting this meeting up – she didn't want to push her luck.

Just then, Jo's voice came from the bottom of the stairs.

'Dinner's ready!'

Hattie closed the wardrobe again. Decoding Lance's dress instructions would just have to wait.

She arrived at the Willow Tree as promised the next day at noon. She'd deliberated over her outfit for far too long the previous evening and, in the end, had thrown her hands into the air and decided that the first decent thing that her hand settled on in the morning was going to be what she wore. It turned out to be a fitted woollen top that she'd teamed with a short flared skirt and ankle boots. She didn't know if that was the sort of nice Lance was talking about but she was happy with her non-choice. As she walked into the café, Lance came bounding over.

'You managed to escape from Alcatraz then?'

Hattie's forehead crinkled into a vague frown. 'Perhaps you ought to stop it with the prison jokes now?'

Lance waved an airy hand. 'Oh, come on – you do think they're a bit funny.'

'I do,' Hattie said, 'but I wish I didn't and I don't like that I find them funny.'

Lance put an arm around her. 'I don't mean any harm, my love – you know that.'

'I suppose so,' Hattie said with a smile.

'If it makes you feel better you can poke fun at my pot belly and I won't mind a bit. It might even up the score – you know?'

Hattie's smile grew, despite herself. 'You don't even have a pot belly.'

'I wish,' Lance said. 'I used to have a six-pack before I started to run this place. Now it's more like a beer keg – all that leftover cake, you see.'

'Oh dear.' Hattie's gaze skimmed the café. Around half the tables had customers sitting at them. A few she recognised as locals, including Rupert, who was tucking into a toasted sandwich, and she'd have to try and grab a quick word with them if she could before she went back up to the farm. The air of the café was warm and sweet with the scent of sugar and cinnamon; the sun filtered through delicate net curtains at the window. There was no sign of Phyllis today – perhaps that was why Lance looked so much more relaxed than the last time she'd seen him.

'So where's this mystery guest?' she asked. 'You have no idea how much persuading it took for Jo to let me come down here today and I've had to promise to run anything by her if it concerns Sweet Briar. So it had better be worth the effort.'

'Oh, it will be,' Lance said. 'And I'm glad to see you've scrubbed up – you'll be glad you did too.'

'Will I? And it's definitely not the Duke of Sussex I'm meeting?'

'Come on,' Lance said with a grin as he grabbed Hattie by the hand and led her to a table by the window. Mark was sitting there with a man who was in his mid to late twenties. The man had shoulder-length hair the colour of ripe wheat, a good physique (from what Hattie could see) and he wore a powder-blue shirt – sleeves rolled up to the elbow – and a loose navy tie at his neck.

'Hattie!' Mark got up and gave her a brief kiss on the cheek. 'You escaped Medusa's clutches! You must tell us all about this valiant undertaking!'

Hattie rolled her eyes but she was smiling. 'Not you as well.' There was no real harm in Lance and Mark's banter and, though she'd told Lance off earlier, even Hattie had to admit that Jo wasn't exactly doing much to combat this type of attitude towards her. Then again, if she knew what people said about her, she probably wouldn't care anyway.

Mark gestured to the man at the table, who got up and offered his hand for Hattie to shake.

'You're the girl I've been hearing so much about,' he said as Hattie took it. His hand was warm and soft, but he had a firm and confident grip. And now that she could see him more closely, he also had the most incredible hazel eyes. It took her a second to realise that she was staring into them and she quickly tore her gaze away.

'Should I be worried that you've been hearing so much about me?' she asked with a half laugh.

'Not at all,' Lance answered for him. 'Owen is my second cousin – Mum's side. You're the perfect excuse to get him to come and visit because he never does.'

Owen looked apologetic but he was grinning.

'How's that?' Hattie asked.

'Because I also happen to work for the *Daily Voice*,' Owen said.

'You do?' Hattie turned to Lance. 'You never told me you had Fleet Street connections.'

'I'm telling you now,' Lance said. 'I thought maybe you and Owen could help each other.'

Owen reached for a business card from his shirt pocket and presented it to Hattie with a little flourish.

'Owen Schuster,' she read. She looked up. 'What's a features writer?'

'Otherwise known as a common or garden journalist,' he replied. 'Can I get you anything to drink?'

'Tea would be nice,' Hattie said.

'I'll bring a pot,' Lance said. 'I've got a feeling you're going to need one or two top-ups before the afternoon is out.'

'I've got things to be getting on with too,' Mark said. 'I'll leave you two alone to get acquainted.'

Hattie tried not to notice that something in Mark's statement was a little suspect. Acquainted? For what?

Owen gestured for Hattie to take a seat at his table as Lance and Mark both left them alone. 'So, Lance tells me you work at a donkey rescue centre.'

'Yes.'

'That sounds cool.'

'Does it? I'm sure it's not as cool as you think.'

'It's an unusual job.'

Hattie gave a vague smile, the gears of her brain slowly cranking into action. This had to be about the publicity for Sweet Briar, but surely a national newspaper like the *Daily Voice* wasn't interested? It was essentially a local-interest story at best – a non-story at worst. If the editor of the *Gillypuddle Newsletter* had been interested, maybe that would make a lot more sense. But for the *Daily Voice*, there had to be more interesting things going on in the world.

'Lance tells me you gave up a career in the Paris fashion industry to come and pursue the dream of rescuing defenceless animals to save them from the cruel lives they had before.'

Hattie bit back a laugh. His sentence sounded like it had been lifted straight out of one of his stories.

'Well,' she began, trying to smooth her features into something sensible, 'I'd left Paris anyway so—'

'But you *do* rescue donkeys?'

'Jo does. I just help really.'

'Who's Jo?'

'The woman who owns the farm.'

'Is that Medusa?'

Hattie nodded. Lance really needed to stop calling her that, though.

'And has she sacrificed a glamorous career to save donkeys?' he continued.

'I don't know – I've never really asked. She's not what you'd call open about her past. In fact, she's not open about very much at all.'

'Aren't you curious?'

'Sometimes,' Hattie admitted.

'Then why don't you ask?'

'I just don't feel as if I ought to. She's very private.'

Owen produced a tablet from a case on the table and swiped to unlock it. He started to type on the notes screen. 'I need an angle,' he said.

'Angle?'

'So I can feature your farm. Lance says you're trying to get people to come and visit.'

'Well, yes...'

'And you're potentially looking for sponsorship. How about local businesses – have you tried them?'

'No, I hadn't thought of that but that's a good idea—'

'We could certainly look at highlighting that.'

'You really want to put us in the paper?'

'I'm short of a story but to be frank, Hattie, no one cares about some nobody saving donkeys. There are people all over the country saving dogs and cats and donkeys and whatever and nobody cares. But people would care if you made it interesting. They'd care about someone who, for instance, gave up a glamorous life in Paris and money and fame to rescue donkeys.'

'But I wasn't famous and I didn't have any—'

'Let me worry about all that. If you want people to be interested and you want them to choose your farm over all the other attractions in the area then you've got to get a little creative.'

'But we're not really trying to compete with other attractions – we just need to get some money for the upkeep of the animals.'

'You've got more than just donkeys?'

'Jo rescued some hens that were destined for dog food.'

'Brilliant! See – already you're thinking like a journalist. Were the donkeys heading for the dog-food factory too?'

'I don't think so.'

'Could we say that they were?'

'I don't think Jo would like that.'

Owen was thoughtful for a moment, subtle calculations going on behind those brilliant hazel eyes. 'OK,' he said. 'Tell me about Paris. What's the journey? How did you end up there?'

Hattie shrugged. 'I just sort of went there.'

Owen leaned closer. 'But what took you? A burning ambition? An urge to follow your dreams? Had you always aspired to a life of wealth and fame?'

'I wasn't wealthy and I certainly wasn't famous. I sort of went with someone to visit and didn't come home. And then I sort of ended up with a job.'

'So how did that happen?'

'I was introduced to someone who needed help.'

'I'm going to need a bit more than that. Don't you want to tell me?'

'It's not that; it's just…'

'Someone broke your heart?' he asked with a look that was worryingly hopeful. 'Is there a tragic backstory here?'

'No,' Hattie said and she had to laugh. The idea of her life being like some glamorous soap opera was faintly ridiculous. Besides, she'd only just met Owen and she wasn't about to tell him all her darkest secrets. The last thing she wanted was her stupidity over Bertrand to be splashed all over the pages of a daily paper. 'This man offered me a job working for his design house and I took it. There was nothing more to it than that, I'm afraid.'

'Can I take your photo?' he asked.

'Sure… for the paper? Wouldn't it be better to get photos of the donkeys?'

'Yes, of course. But I want one of you too.' He winked. 'Maybe I won't delete this one from the camera roll when I've sent it to press, though.'

Hattie gave a self-conscious smile. Was he coming on to her? If he was he didn't mess about. He lifted the tablet and snapped a few shots of her.

'So what did you actually do in Paris?' he asked, putting the tablet back on the table.

'I was just a gofer really. I fetched and carried and ran errands. My background isn't in fashion at all. I was learning the trade though – at least, I was trying to. Just before I left I was getting much more involved in producing his shows.'

'Were you working for someone famous?'

'I wouldn't say he's exactly famous, but he does have very loyal clients.'

'I'll put junior partner at cutting-edge design house,' Owen muttered to himself as he typed, seeming to forget for a moment that Hattie could hear him.

'But I wasn't any of that,' Hattie protested. 'I was just a dogsbody. You won't make me sound like I'm something I'm not, will you?'

'Of course I won't. Tell me more about Paris. Who did you meet? Did your label dress any big stars?'

'Not really. Don't you want to hear about what we're doing with the donkeys?'

'All in good time. I want background first – got to have a bit of context.'

'Right. Well, I suppose we did have a few minor celebrities as clients, some musicians, that sort of thing.'

Owen started to type again. 'Rock stars and A-listers,' he said, looking at his screen.

'Seriously,' Hattie said, 'it's not like that at all.'

Owen looked up and smiled. His eyes really were… well, the only word Hattie could think of was beguiling. 'Trust me,' he said. 'You do trust me – don't you? I guarantee when this story goes to print you'll have visitors knocking down the doors to get in, but you've got to give people a bit of drama, fire their imaginations.'

'Yes, but—'

'I'm good at this. I promise I won't write anything that really upsets you.'

'Will I get to read it before it goes in the paper?'

'Generally we don't do that – tight turnaround times, you see.'

'Oh. Well, even if I don't mind what's in there, I'm a bit worried that Jo might not like it. I mean, I understand we have to have drama but…'

'I'm sure she'll see the benefits of running the story when your fortunes change. Anyway,' he continued, 'Lance tells me you're happy to be the face of…' He paused.

'Sweet Briar Farm,' Hattie reminded him.

'Right – Sweet Briar. So if you're happy then, I'll just feature you and your boss needn't worry. If she hates being in the spotlight then we can leave her out of it.' He looked at his tablet again, swiping to change the screen to a row of photos. Hattie recognised them as the ones he'd just taken of her. 'You know,' he said, 'our readers are going to love you.'

Hattie smoothed a self-conscious hand over her hair and gave a little laugh. Owen was definitely flirting. She felt she ought to be annoyed about this but she couldn't deny that she was flattered instead; he was good-looking and very charming. She looked up at the sound of a throat being cleared to see Lance standing at the table with a large teapot and cups on a tray. And was that a grin she could see him trying to hide?

'Please tell me he's behaving,' he said, putting the teapot on the table between Owen and Hattie. 'I'm sure you've already worked out that this one's a bit of a ladies' man.'

'Yes,' Hattie said, busying herself with pouring some tea in the hope that Lance might not notice her blushing.

'You flatter me with a bad-boy reputation that I want but totally don't deserve,' Owen said with a laugh. Hattie looked up and Owen winked at her again, addressing Lance while keeping his eyes fixed firmly on her. 'We're just trying to create an interesting backstory for you – aren't we?'

Hattie nodded uncertainly.

'And I was just getting somewhere,' Owen continued. 'So you can push off, Lance, and stop trying to interrupt the flow of my mojo. Genius doesn't come easy, you know – you can't turn it on and off like a tap.'

'Is that right?' Lance grinned. 'You don't change, do you? Always were a precocious little bugger.'

'Just telling it like it is.'

Lance fired a look of mock pity at Hattie. 'I'm so sorry to have subjected you to him. Can you ever forgive me?'

'Don't be silly,' Hattie said. She gave Owen a grateful smile. 'I'm sure it is a good idea to make the story sound as interesting as we can.'

She wasn't entirely sure this was true, but for now she'd have to indulge Owen's request to trust him. If it helped to get people and – perhaps more importantly – their wallets up to Sweet Briar, then it had to be worth a go, didn't it?

The interview had gone on for over an hour. Hattie hadn't planned on being out for so long and she still had to allow time to get back to the farm on top of that. Jo wasn't going to be very happy, even when Hattie explained why she'd been missing. In fact, explaining why she'd been gone for so much longer than she was meant to be would probably make Jo even more annoyed.

The teapot was empty now and Owen was packing his tablet away.

'It's been really great to talk to you,' he said.

Hattie drank the last of her tea and placed the cup back in the saucer. 'I appreciate you coming all this way to see me.'

Owen leaned forward and lowered his voice. 'Can I let you in on a secret?'

'What?' Hattie asked, unconsciously lowering her voice to match.

'I did sort of fancy a day by the seaside so it was no hardship. I've got to give my editor some excuse for my petrol expenses.'

Hattie laughed. 'Well, I'm glad I could be of assistance then.'

'Besides,' Owen continued, 'it's been good to catch up with Lance. I bet it's a good twelve months since we saw each other.'

'You're not that close then?'

'We were once but it's harder to keep in touch these days. Busy lives, you know? I'll bet none of us spends as much time with family as we'd like to.'

'That's true. Are you going back to London now?'

'I thought I might go and dip my feet in the sea first. It's a shame to come all this way and not get a little sand between my toes.'

'That sounds like a nice way to finish a day at work. I wish I could come.'

'Why can't you?'

'Jo'll be expecting me back. I'll have to run the four-minute mile as it is to avoid a roasting, without going for a paddle first.'

'If you don't mind me saying, I have to wonder why you bother. From what everyone here tells me, this Jo is hardly the most pleasant company and I can't imagine she's much of a boss.'

'She's not as bad as everyone thinks – you just have to get used to her.'

Owen paused for a moment. 'I suppose I'd better get that photo of your donkeys. It'd be better if I took one of you with them if we're going to do it properly. Do you think you could take me up there?'

'Won't the one on our website be OK?'

'Not professional enough, I'm afraid.'

'Oh. Well, if we're quick I think it would be OK,' Hattie said, though she couldn't say she was sure about that.

'I could drive us up – how's that? I could get you back quicker that way too.'

'Sounds good.'

Lance came over to clear their table and Hattie leaned over to kiss him on the cheek. 'Thanks, Lance; I owe you big time.'

'Me too,' Owen said, shaking his hand.

Lance straightened up and smiled at them both. 'My pleasure, Hattie. And Owen – you'd better not leave it so long next time. Better still, come and see me without the need for an excuse.'

'I'll do that,' Owen said, and although Hattie had found that in full journalist mode he could be a bit glib, she did believe the sincere look he wore now.

They left the Willow Tree, Lance and Mark waving them off, and Owen led Hattie to his car.

'It's a nice afternoon for toe dipping,' Hattie said.

'It's a nice afternoon for anything dipping,' Owen replied with a wicked grin. He unlocked the car and Hattie got in. She watched Owen get in beside her and wondered what other sort of dipping he might mean. Skinny dipping? She could imagine him doing that. Maybe by moonlight with a skinful of wine. She couldn't deny there was something about the idea that was appealing. She was attracted to wild streaks – it was why she'd been drawn to Bertrand – and she was almost certain Owen had the same unpredictability running through him. But as she looked at Owen she also felt that she'd got a fairly good measure of him, and she thought that he might just be the sort of man who was bound to bring trouble with him, no matter how charming or funny he seemed.

He turned to her and she tore away her gaze.

'You'll have to direct me,' he said, a note of amusement in his voice. She guessed that he'd noticed her looking. Considering how handsome he was, he was probably used to women looking at him.

'It's not that far,' Hattie said, trying not to look like she'd noticed that he'd noticed her looking. In fact, as he started the engine and pulled away from the Willow Tree, Hattie made an effort to stare very deliberately out of the window. When she dared to take a peek, his concentration was on the road ahead, but he was smiling to himself.

Jo was nowhere in the house when they got back to Sweet Briar. She was either up at the field where they were heading or in the orchard with the hens – not for a minute did Hattie consider that she might actually be out away from the farm, because it happened so rarely it was hardly likely at all. Hattie would have preferred to warn Jo that she was bringing Owen back to take photos, but as Jo didn't have a mobile phone (or if she did, Hattie had never seen any evidence of it), and she hadn't picked up on the landline when Hattie had tried to call on the journey back, it hadn't been possible. If she was up at the top field when Hattie and Owen arrived, there was a strong possibility she wouldn't like the unexpected visitor, but Hattie would just have to try and smooth things over as best she could. Who knew, maybe Owen's charm would persuade her to agree to a photo. Miracles did happen, or so they said.

After her fruitless search of the house, Hattie came back out to Owen, who was waiting with his car on the stones of the courtyard.

'No sign of her,' she said.

'Do you still want to go up?'

'Yeah, I think it would be OK. Want to walk it?' she asked, looking towards the path that wound up to the top field.

Owen followed her gaze. 'Is it far?'

'It's steep but it's not far. You look pretty fit to me.'

'So do you,' he said, and Hattie turned sharply to face him. He looked away, his face a picture of innocence which was far from convincing.

Hattie bit back a grin. She was fast learning that he was cocky, irritating, so obviously trouble... but he was frustratingly attractive. And he seemed a lot more interested than Seth, though, after their last meeting, she'd more or less given up on him anyway.

'Come on.' Hattie began to walk and he fell into step beside her. The afternoon was hazy and it felt as if the evening might bring rain, but it was still sultry right now. Hattie hoped that the changing weather wouldn't obscure the incredible view from the cliff top because she really wanted Owen to see that. The fields that bordered the path were strewn with daisies like sugar scattered over a cake, so many that they were almost more daisy than grass. Jo never brought the donkeys this far to graze so they were always filled with wildflowers but, even so, there still seemed to be more than the usual.

'It's funny,' Hattie said as they walked, 'I've spent the afternoon telling you all about my life but now that you're not writing it down I don't know what to say.'

'That's because I'm not prompting you. Told you I was good at my job – I was making you talk and you didn't even know it.'

Hattie gave him a sideways look. 'I can have a conversation with someone without prompts, you know.'

'Let's just say I take pride in my work and my ability to get people talking. Don't take that away from me.'

'You're not getting me to talk now.'

'What are you doing then?'

'Telling you that I don't know what to say.'

'Well,' he said, looking ahead and grinning, 'I'm off duty now, that's why.'

'You've got an answer for everything.'

'That's what Lance always says.'

'Why don't you tell me some stuff about you instead? I'll just listen.'

'Believe me, there's no story there.'

'There must be something. Tell me about your family, where you come from, what made you choose journalism…'

'OK,' he said slowly. 'I have one brother – Rhodri.'

'Another good Welsh name.'

'Thank you. No other siblings. The usual assortment of uncles and aunts and stuff. You know Lance, of course, second cousin on my mum's side.' He shrugged. 'That's it.'

Hattie nudged him. 'No it isn't.'

'God, you're so bossy! Are you sure it's Jo who's the tyrant and not you?'

'And that won't get you out of it.'

He grinned again. 'OK, journalism. I wanted to be a sports reporter and I wasn't really interested in anything else. Turns out the country only needs about ten sports reporters and they already have eleven, so I went into regular journalism.'

'And you like it?'

'Love it. I couldn't imagine doing anything else. I'm lucky I get to work on a national too – no two days are the same.'

'I'll bet they are at the *Gillypuddle Newsletter*. One year they ran a regular feature on the frequency of bin collections. For the whole year!'

Owen laughed. 'I don't suppose much happens here. I bet it's nice though. I know Lance loves it.'

'Trust me, you'd hate it.'

'Probably. Is it much further?'

'Tired already?'

'Hey, I'm a city boy – as you've just gone to great pains to remind me. It's not my fault there are no cliffs to climb in London.'

'There are gyms.'

'Nope... no clue what that word means.'

Hattie laughed.

'So,' he said, 'I'm just going to come straight out with it.'

'With what?'

'Do you have a boyfriend?'

'Um...'

'Don't tell me you haven't noticed my interest; I thought I'd been obvious enough.'

Hattie smiled. 'I like it – the direct method. Everyone knows where they stand.'

'What's the point in being any other way? I see what I like and I go for it.'

Hattie flushed. It could have been the damp heat on the path making her face suddenly burn – at least she wanted to pretend it was. She reached for something witty to say in return but her mind had gone blank.

'Oh!' she cried, far more excited than she ought to be, 'there's Jo!'

The owner of Sweet Briar Farm was striding down the path towards them.

'She must have just been to the field,' Hattie added. She waved, but Jo didn't wave back. 'Probably hasn't noticed us yet,' Hattie excused, although it was very obvious that she had.

Another minute saw their paths cross.

'You're back then,' Jo said to Hattie. Then she looked at Owen with the utmost suspicion. 'Who's this?'

'Oh, this is Owen. He's doing a story about the sanctuary for the paper.'

'What paper?' Jo asked.

'The *Daily Voice*,' Owen replied, seemingly unconcerned by Jo's cold manner. Perhaps he'd seen it all before – Hattie supposed he wasn't always welcomed everywhere he went, given his line of work.

Jo shook her head. 'Not happening.'

Hattie stared at her. 'Why not?'

'I said no adverts.'

'But this isn't an advert!'

'Sounds like it.'

'It's a personal-interest story!'

'To be honest,' Owen cut in, 'and I hope you don't mind this, but it's more about Hattie than the farm per se.'

Jo viewed him now with even deeper suspicion. 'Why's that?'

'Well,' he said, 'she's got quite a past and I think our readers would be interested in how she ended up here.'

Hattie noted that the distrust in Jo's expression cleared a little. Owen *was* good at his job. He'd been listening very closely to everything Hattie had told him about Jo and clearly taken it on board, and he'd played a blinder here by taking the spotlight off Jo when it was so obvious that she wouldn't want it. Maybe they'd get their story after all. Hattie couldn't help but notice that, as Jo looked back at her, there was also a measure of surprise on her face, as if she was somehow thrown by the idea that Hattie might have a past. Jo had never been inclined to ask about Hattie's life before she arrived at Sweet Briar and Hattie had taken that as a sign that she wasn't interested.

'I want to see it before you print,' Jo said finally.

'That means we can go ahead?' Hattie asked.

'No – it means I want to see it.'

Hattie was just about to repeat what Owen had told her about tight turnarounds and how difficult that might be when he spoke.

'Shouldn't be a problem.'

Hattie glanced at him but he didn't return her gaze. That was it – she had no choice but to go along with it now.

Jo gave a stiff nod. 'Where are you going now?'

'I want to get a couple of photos of Hattie with the donkeys,' Owen said.

Instead of addressing Owen, Jo looked at Hattie. 'Don't be long. Chicken coop doesn't clean itself.'

'Right.'

'Wow,' Owen said in a low voice as they watched her march off. 'That's some charisma there.'

'Thanks,' Hattie said.

'For what?'

'For not being put off by her.'

'Hey, I've done the death knock. It's going to take a lot more than someone like your boss to throw me off the scent of a story.'

'What's the death knock?' Hattie asked as they started to walk again.

'Don't ask. Let's just say it's one of the less pleasant aspects of the job.'

'Oh. So what are the more pleasant aspects then?'

He turned to her with a smile that made her knees want to buckle. It was sweet but bad, innocent but naughty, chaste but filthy, all at the same time, but most of all, it sparked something inside her that she knew probably shouldn't be there.

'Getting to meet girls like you.'

*

Hattie was sitting under a tree in the orchard. The only space in the house that was hers alone was her bedroom, and sometimes her bedroom, despite the efforts she'd made to brighten it up, still looked like a room where an old person had died. This evening felt like one of those times, so she'd wrapped herself in a big cardigan and found a quiet spot beneath the plum trees. She could hear the hens pecking and complaining in their coop and a chill breeze rolled across her, setting the hairs on her arms on end.

She looked at the business card in her hand. 'Call me,' Owen had said, and he'd looked like he meant it. He'd given her the special one, he'd told her, the one with the hotline to his desk printed on it, but also with his personal number listed too, and he said he didn't give that one to just anyone. Hattie couldn't decide if she believed him or even if she trusted him, but she couldn't deny that in a strange way it added to the attraction. He looked like he might be fun, and even though she'd been quite content to live up at Sweet Briar with the dour Jo, sometimes a girl needed a little fun.

She picked up her phone and dialled Melinda's number.

'Hey!' Melinda's voice was bright on the line. 'Where have you been hiding – I haven't heard from you in days. I was beginning to think Medusa had locked you up in her basement or turned you into pig feed or something.'

'We don't have any pigs.'

'Oh, don't be so clever. She could sell your remains for other people's pigs then. Perhaps she thought nobody would notice you were gone.'

'You're painting a lovely picture. Did I ever tell you that I wonder why I'm friends with you sometimes? I think now might be one of those times.'

'You shouldn't leave me for days on end without calling me then. You know my imagination goes crazy.'

'Sorry to disappoint you but I've been doing nothing more interesting than trying to get all this visitor stuff sorted.'

'Oh, of course. How's that going?'

'Good. I mean, we haven't actually had any visitors yet but Lance introduced me to his second cousin—'

'The journalist? He told me about that. How did it go? Is he going to run a story? Are you going to be famous? Can I tell people I know you or will I have to sign some sort of secrecy contract?'

'I'm pretty sure that won't be necessary.'

'Famous for fifteen minutes, eh?'

'More like fifteen seconds.'

'Lance said you seemed to get on well with his cousin,' Melinda said. Her tone was all innocence but Hattie knew her better than that. She couldn't help a smile as she looked down at Owen's business card.

'We did.'

'Ooooh. Do tell. Any developments in your relationship status I should know about?'

'Maybe. I don't know. I mean, I'm interested but something tells me he's trouble.'

'Aren't they your favourite type?'

'Maybe even more than I can handle.'

'So you like him?'

'I do.'

'More than our scrumptious vet?'

'I get the feeling he's not all that interested in me. I don't suppose you've heard any more about that girlfriend situation?'

'Would it make a difference if I had?'

'Maybe not. I'm just curious.'

'Well, I haven't. You want to know what I think?'

'Go on.'

'You say you like Lance's cousin…'

'Yes. I like him a little. I think I could get to like him a lot.'

'And he seems interested in you?'

'I think so. Unless he flirts like that with everyone he meets.'

'And you get more signals than you do from Seth?'

'It's hard to tell.'

'Hard to tell if there are more signals or whether Seth likes you at all?'

'Mel, you're tying me up in knots here!'

Melinda laughed. 'I don't really think there's an issue here. Go out with your journalist. He's related to Lance – he's bound to be a blast.'

'What if he's another Bertrand?'

'Does he seem like that?'

'I don't know. Bertrand didn't seem like that – if he had, maybe I wouldn't have gone to Paris with him.'

'Well, he might be but you're older and wiser now. You'd be able to spot the signs of another Bertrand and you'd be able to do the right thing now. Just don't let him take you to Paris.'

'I don't see him doing that to be honest,' Hattie said with a laugh. 'He seems more like the type to ask me to run away to Cardiff with him or something.'

'Oh, that's not nearly as sexy.'

'I know, but at least there are plenty of trains home.'

Melinda giggled. 'So, you're alright?'

'I'm fine. Busy.'

'The kids are asking about you non-stop.'

'Me specifically? Or the donkeys and the chickens?'

'A bit of all three honestly. They want to know when they can come again.'

'I'll have a word with Jo and let you know. Will that be OK?'

'Surely if you're open for business now I can come any time?'

'That's for paying customers. And they still can't come *any* time.'

'I'll pay.'

'No you won't. It's for other people to pay – you're my friend. Let me clear it with Jo and keep your money.'

Melinda clicked her tongue on the roof of her mouth to make a noise of disapproval. 'That's no way to run a business.'

'It's probably why we'll always be poor.'

'Undoubtedly.'

'Everything OK your end?'

'Apart from the fact I'm trying to drag up four kids?' Melinda laughed. 'Everything's absolutely fine. I'm going to hang up now.'

'Why?'

'Because if you're on the phone to me then you can't be on the phone to your journalist guy making plans for a hot date.'

'What makes you so sure I'm going to call him?'

'Oh, Hattie! You say you want this quiet life of do-gooding but I know you. From time to time you need a little adventure to keep you sane, and he sounds like he could be it.'

Hattie grinned. 'You *do* know me!'

Chapter Seventeen

Hattie had expected a meal in a nice restaurant, perhaps a trip to the cinema or a play if he was cultured – typical first-date territory. What she hadn't expected was a beer festival in a muddy field complete with naff tribute bands and speed-eating competitions. It was just another unexpected thing that made her suspect Owen had a wild, unpredictable streak, one that she knew she shouldn't like but did all the same.

She watched him amble across the damp, fusty tent from the bar with two bottles. The place had that peculiar smell of grass and sweat that always reminded her of summer fetes in the village when a sharp shower of unexpected rain would beat on the canvas and everyone would huddle inside, chatting until it stopped. He grinned at her, setting little fireworks of anticipation off in her tummy.

'What's this one?' she asked as he handed her a bottle. She turned it around to look at the label but by now her eyes were telling her she needed glasses, which was funny because she'd never needed them before.

'An Austrian blond beer with hints of raspberry,' he said. 'At least I think that's what the menu said.'

'How many's that we've tried so far? I've lost count.'

'Why are you keeping count?'

'So I know when to stop.'

'Don't be daft,' he said with a grin. 'Bottoms up!' He tipped the bottle to his lips and drank. Hattie took a sip of her own.

'It's nice.'

'It's not bad,' he agreed, looking at his bottle with approval.

This was the third tent they'd visited so far, all furnished with makeshift bars serving various imaginative brews. They'd yet to visit the food tent, which housed stalls of cheeses, cold meats, salads and sandwiches. There were smaller stalls dotted around the field between the tents, some slowly sinking into the mud of the field, offering barbequed meat, stone-baked pizzas and hot crêpes. But Hattie and Owen had yet to visit any of the snack vendors. Owen seemed intent on trying every single beer the place had to offer before he even considered food. Hattie, on the other hand, thought they'd better soon because if she didn't get something to soak up all this alcohol she'd be face first in the mud and she wouldn't be getting up again.

She couldn't deny she was having a good time, though. It might have been the alcohol, but after the austere silence of Sweet Briar Farm, the noise and bustle of the crowd here was a welcome change.

'I'm choosing the next beer,' she said.

'I thought you were going to let me pick for you. Don't you trust me?'

Hattie wagged a finger at him. 'No, I don't.'

He gave a look of mock offence. 'I asked you to trust me on the story and that turned out alright, didn't it?'

'Beer's a very different matter,' Hattie said. 'But the story was good – I'll give you that. A bunch of big fat lies but good lies.'

'It wasn't lies, it was creative writing. You know all those novels you like reading? They're all lies too. It's the same thing, only I start out with something that's a bit true and make it sexier. Not that I have to make you any sexier, of course.'

'Thank you,' Hattie said, and she couldn't tell if the heat in her face was from the drinking or his comment.

'Anyway, it was a great story – my editor loved it.'

'You can say it's great but I can't because I'm in it and that wouldn't be very modest.'

'I can say it because I wrote it and I don't care about being modest.'

Hattie giggled. One thing she was learning about Owen was that there was no filter when it came to singing his own praises. It should have been a real turn-off but it wasn't. She took another mouthful of beer. 'I can taste the raspberries now.'

'You look cute,' he said.

'Cute?'

'All drunk and silly.'

'I'm not drunk. And I'm silly all the time – I don't need to be drunk for that.'

'Kiss me.'

Hattie shook her head. 'I'm not that easy.'

'Bugger; I was hoping you would be. You do know the only reason I wrote that story was because I fancied you? I was all set to make some excuse to Lance and leave before you arrived but then you walked in and… well, I changed my mind.'

'I'm sure Jo would be thrilled to hear that,' Hattie said, but she was blushing again. She did want to kiss him – but she was trying very hard to keep some kind of respectable time limit on things. 'She was annoyed that she didn't get to see it before you printed it, you know.'

'There was no time – I did warn you that would probably happen. We don't usually let people see what's going to print beforehand anyway, even when there is.' He took another gulp of his beer. 'I don't know what she's complaining about anyway – it's done the job, hasn't it?'

'Sure. We've had more enquiries than we've ever had before.'

'How many's that?'

'About ten.'

'How many did you have before?' he asked, laughing.

'Zero.'

'Well, ten's not exactly going to fill Wembley Stadium but it's ten better than zero.'

'I suppose it will take time for people to find out about us and we're a bit out of the way really. People don't just pass by unless they're planning to drive their car off the cliff.' Hattie hiccoughed.

Owen looked thoughtful now as he tipped his bottle to his lips again. 'Maybe we should follow up – it might help you to stick in people's minds.'

'Not more of that cutting-edge label business,' Hattie said.

'We could do something on your boss. She's got to have some interesting backstory, right? Everyone's got something if you dig deep enough.'

'Spoken like a true journalist. Not that I know any other journalists...'

'So, what do you think?'

'No way. That would be the end of my plans for visitors if we so much as suggested it.'

'That's a real shame. It must be so frustrating that she's so disengaged when you're trying to help. You've got more patience than I have.'

'It's the animals I'm trying to help really. I mean, I want to help her but she doesn't care about that – she hates everyone. But the animals...' Hattie shrugged. 'I just want to do something good.'

Owen smiled. 'You really are the cutest thing...'

'I know.'

'So have you told her all this? How you feel? Your worries about what would happen to the donkeys if she went bankrupt?'

'I can't. For a start she doesn't let me talk. She just walks off if I start to ask something serious. She doesn't want to talk to me unless it's my turn to do the washing-up. And I'm not supposed to know about the vet's bill.'

'Maybe she just chooses not to pay that? Maybe the money situation isn't as bad as you think.'

Hattie shook her head. 'I can just tell. I mean, have you seen the state of the farmhouse?'

He studied her for a moment. 'I don't understand why you stay.'

'Honestly, sometimes neither do I. I feel like now I've thrown my lot in with her I have to stay. Plus, if I don't my dad gets to tell me he was right and I was wrong and I can't be having that.'

He laughed. 'Now that's a motivation I can understand.'

Hattie giggled. 'Is your dad always lecturing you?'

'He used to, but then I probably deserved it. He's not so bad these days.'

'My dad is. He's always telling me I'm going to amount to nothing. But I think I might be getting to the point where it's a bit too late to do anything about that now.'

'Is that really what he thinks?'

'It's OK – I'm used to it.'

'I don't think you're nothing,' he said. 'You're cute as hell and a little bit crazy…' He placed his bottle onto a nearby table and stepped closer. 'But you know what?' he added, his voice low and husky now. 'I find you insanely attractive.'

Before she'd had time to react his lips were pressed onto hers. He tasted of hops or malt or whatever it was that beer was made of and her head swam with drunkenness and craving. She kissed him back, a swell of desire rushing through her.

'Sorry,' he said with a grin as his lips left hers. 'Actually, who am I kidding? I'm not. I've been desperate to do that all afternoon.'

'Hmm,' was all Hattie could say in reply, still stunned by the kiss.

The sound of an electric guitar being tuned echoed across the grounds.

'Still want to see that Queen tribute act?' Owen asked, grabbing his beer again.

Hattie couldn't care less about a tribute act, Queen or otherwise. All she wanted was to feel his lips on hers again.

'Sounds like they're setting up now,' he added. He took her hand. 'Let's check them out and then we'd better feed you.'

'I think you'd better had,' Hattie agreed.

'You're hungry?'

'Only for you.'

'You're drunk.' He laughed. 'Maybe we should feed you first after all.'

'I'm not, but OK.'

He looked down at her and squeezed her hand. 'I'm having a great time.'

'Me too.'

'I still can't believe you said yes to me.'

'Really?'

'I don't know… I thought you were out of my league.'

'That's mad!' He'd seemed so confident, so assured that first day she'd met him it was hard to believe he'd harboured an ounce of uncertainty about anything. Maybe that Owen had all been an act. Maybe the real Owen was something very different. Right now, she wanted to find out the answer to that question more than anything.

'Why is it mad?' he asked. 'You're gorgeous.'

'Now who's drunk?' Hattie giggled.

He took her into his arms and kissed her again, and for one spectacular moment the rest of the world ceased to exist.

'Do you still think I've had too much to drink?' he asked softly.

Hattie opened her eyes. She didn't reply because she didn't want to break the spell she was under. Instead, she reached to pull him back and this time she took the lead, kissing him the way he'd kissed her, trying to make him feel what she'd just felt. When she was done, it was his turn to sway on the spot, lost to all but passion.

'Wow,' he said finally. 'Just… wow.'

Hattie looked into those hazel eyes as they smiled down at her and wished all the people around them would disappear so they could be alone.

'You're amazing,' he said, pulling her close again.

'I know,' Hattie laughed.

'And so modest.'

'Well, I am an incredibly glamorous member of the Paris elite,' she said with a giggle.

'Hey, if it worked…'

'Want to know what I think?'

'What's that?'

'I think there's two Owen Schusters. One is the spivvy reporter—'

'Hey!'

'And the other,' Hattie laughed, 'is a very sweet, very sexy, very handsome, total catch of the day.'

He moved in for another kiss. 'You got me,' he whispered. 'Just don't tell anyone; I've got a reputation to uphold.'

Chapter Eighteen

Hattie thought she might just be witnessing a miracle. Melinda was sitting across the table from her without a single small person hanging from one of her appendages. Stu had taken them all on a visit to his uncle in Weymouth where they planned to stay over. Poor uncle in Weymouth, Melinda had said, but it did mean that she got to have her first night off mothering duties in almost eight years. Hattie was thrilled that Melinda had chosen to spend those hard-earned hours with her.

On the table between them was a row of foil cartons containing the dishes they'd ordered from the curry house. They'd had to pay a small fortune for delivery from the next village but some sacrifices were worth making because these were the best curries in the south of England. At least, in Hattie's humble opinion. Curry had barely reached Gillypuddle yet anyway – Hattie suspected that many of the residents of their village were still blissfully unaware that someone had once brought a thing called a potato back from foreign climes, let alone curry.

Melinda peeled the lid from her korma, while Hattie opened the vindaloo she'd gone for.

'It's a good job you're not seeing Owen tonight,' Melinda said with a sideways glance at the fiery concoction Hattie was spooning onto her plate.

'I don't think I'll be able to see him for a week after eating this.'

'Let's hope it's worth it then.'

'Oh, it will be.'

'When are you seeing him next?'

'I'm not sure. He's got a lot on this week and he needed to be back in London so we didn't really fix up a day.'

'I don't think I'd be happy with leaving things hanging like that.'

'I think it's just the way his job is.'

'Other people must do that job and still manage to have a relationship.'

'But they probably don't live so far away from each other. This is practically a long-distance relationship.'

'But you do want to see him again?'

'God yes! We had a great time at the beer festival.'

'I can imagine,' Melinda said. 'I can't remember the last time I danced to a Queen tribute band in the pouring rain and ate dodgy hot dogs,' she added dryly.

'I'm not sure it's a feature of that many first dates to be honest,' Hattie agreed. 'That's why I liked it.'

'So it's no good me telling you that Seth Bryson is definitely single? I have it confirmed from the horse's mouth.'

Hattie dipped a poppadum into her vindaloo and munched on it. 'When did you talk to him?'

'I didn't; my mum did.'

'So you didn't have it from the horse's mouth?'

'Well, she had it from the horse's mouth and then I had it from her horse's mouth.'

Hattie swallowed her poppadum and grinned. 'You go wrong without children around you. All your intelligence must go with them.'

'I think Stu borrowed it to take them to his uncle's – God knows he hasn't got any of his own.'

'Awww, poor Stu. You love him really.'

'I must do. It's weird; I am missing them all already.'

'Well that doesn't insult me at all.'

'You know what I mean.' Melinda laughed as she helped herself to some naan bread.

'In that case, I suppose I'll have to get you drunk to take your mind off it.'

'I don't really fancy a drink.'

'What? You've got a whole night off and you don't fancy a drink? What's wrong with you?'

'Nothing.' Melinda put the lid back on her tub of leftover korma. Hattie studied her for a moment. And then she grinned.

'No!' she squealed. 'You're not…?'

'Maybe,' Melinda said, looking about as sheepish as it was possible to look.

'Oh my God!'

'It's no big deal.'

'No big deal? Baby number five and it's no big deal?' Hattie slapped her hands on the table in excitement. 'How far along?'

'About four weeks.'

'I bet Stu's thrilled.' Hattie paused. 'Or is he?'

'He'll be fine when I tell him,' Melinda said. 'It's not like we haven't done it before.'

'You haven't told him yet?'

'I only did the test this morning and I just haven't had the chance to sit him down.'

'Wow; I don't know whether to feel guilty or honoured that I know this before the daddy does. Are you happy?'

'Of course I am. But it starts to get a bit routine after number three.'

'It was planned?'

'About as planned as any of them.'

'Well, congratulations. What would you prefer? Boy or girl?'

'I don't mind.'

Hattie smiled. 'I'm chuffed for you.'

'That's all very boring now. Nobody else will be a bit shocked or pleased when I announce this one. Tell me about your date instead.'

Hattie gave a vague shrug, trying to play it cool, though the memory of Owen's lips still lay on hers. 'It was good.'

'That means you're almost definitely in love.'

'God no!' Hattie laughed. 'The man's trouble – you can smell it a mile away!'

Melinda raised her eyebrows. 'Don't forget that I know you better than anyone. Trouble is your favourite flavour of man.'

'Not since I grew up,' Hattie said. 'I remember now that the trouble flavour of man is what landed me in Paris in a right mess.'

'But that did end well eventually.'

'Sort of. For a while. Until I almost burned half of Paris down.'

'Well I think you should keep this one for a while. If only because he writes such great stories about you.'

'You've read it?'

'Are you kidding? I've cut it out to keep!' Melinda got up from table and dashed into the living room. A moment later she came back and smoothed the newspaper cutting out on the table.

FROM THE HIGH LIFE TO THE COUNTRY LIFE

Beneath the headline was a photo of Hattie looking windswept as she stood, grinning, next to Norbert. The body of the article went on to give a highly embellished and imaginative account of Hattie's time in Paris and how she came to be at Sweet Briar Farm.

'Honestly,' Melinda said as she reread the article, 'I had no idea my friend had been keeping her celebrity lifestyle a secret from me all this time.'

'Very funny. I did tell you it was a bit...'

'Dodgy?'

'Exaggerated. But if it works...' Hattie shrugged. 'It'll all be forgotten in a week and I doubt anyone's bothered to read it anyway apart from us.'

'Oh, I don't think so,' Melinda said. 'Haven't you been down to the Willow Tree recently?'

Hattie's face showed the merest hint of alarm. 'Not since I was in there with Owen...' she replied slowly. 'Why?'

'Let's just say you've been discussed in there. At some length.'

Hattie held in a groan. For some reason she hadn't really considered the people of Gillypuddle reading Owen's story. Most of them hardly took any notice of any news outside the village. Now she thought about it, though, it was obvious that Lance would be drawing people's attention to it. Did that mean her mum and dad had seen it too? She hadn't heard from them in a couple of days – not since the edition had gone out – and the *Daily Voice* was about as far from their sort of paper as you could get anyway; with a bit of luck, perhaps they hadn't. She wasn't sure what their reaction might be if they did. As long as they didn't venture into the Willow Tree until the story blew over, perhaps she'd get away with it.

'It's mostly Lance,' Melinda continued. 'You know how he is.'

'Basking in the reflected glow?' Hattie asked, and she couldn't help but grin. She wouldn't be surprised if she went in next time to see a shrine dedicated to her beside the tea urn.

'Something like that,' Melinda said. 'It *is* about the most exciting thing to happen in Gillypuddle since Mrs Lane's parakeet got loose.'

Hattie laughed. 'Does Lance know that I had a date with Owen?'

'Are you kidding?'

'Oh God!'

Melinda dug into the pot of mango chutney and put a blob onto the side of her plate. 'He's already choosing his wedding outfit. I've got a feeling him and Mark were hoping this might happen, you know. You know those two – they probably even tried to set it up. They love to matchmake – I'm surprised you didn't smell a rat when you went in that day.'

'I should have done, shouldn't I? To be fair to them, it was a good call.'

'You're taking it well,' Melinda said. 'You must like this Owen a lot; I'd be livid if they did it to me.'

Hattie tried to be annoyed with Lance and Mark for interfering but she couldn't. She'd had a great time with Owen and perhaps she had to give them credit for knowing a good match when they saw one. In fact, she ought to have a word with them – they could make a killing running a dating agency.

'What's the point in being livid now?'

What Hattie had said about Owen being trouble was true, but what she'd said to herself about not being interested in anything more lasting than a few weeks of fun wasn't. She liked Owen – she thought she might come to like him a lot. And maybe he wasn't such a wild card? She'd told him that she thought there might be two Owen Schusters and she still believed that. Which one would she get? Only time would tell.

Chapter Nineteen

The rain woke Hattie. She rolled over and looked at the clock by her bed. It was 4.30 a.m. and far too early to be getting up. She closed her eyes and tried to sleep again, but the wind heaved and tossed the rain against the window like gravel being hurled at the glass. She hadn't heard rain like this since she'd first arrived at Sweet Briar and it was faintly alarming – the glazing was old here in the farmhouse and she wouldn't have been completely shocked to see the window blow in with the force of it.

She lay in bed and listened for ten minutes, the room grainy and grey in the early-morning light, then she decided to get up and do something useful because there was no way she was going back to sleep while the storm continued to beat against the glass. The house was silent; Jo was probably still sleeping. Her room was at the back of the house and away from the sea view, so perhaps that sheltered it a little from the rain. Who knew, perhaps that was the real reason Jo had taken that room in the first place. Hattie decided to log into her borrowed laptop (quite honestly probably permanently borrowed at this point) to see if there'd been any action on the Sweet Briar website.

Grabbing her fluffy dressing gown from the old armchair by the window, she pulled the laptop from its storage bag and plonked herself back down on the bed, cross-legged, before switching it on.

And that was when she heard it. Another sound layered over the rain dashing against the windows, the unmistakable sounds of distress. Hattie sat and listened, motionless and straining to make it out. Then all was silent again and she relaxed. Perhaps she had been mistaken after all. Perhaps her senses had been playing tricks on her, and her agitation due to the weather wouldn't have helped with that. Perhaps it was the weather acting on something out in the farmyard – moving a water butt or a wheelbarrow, making some machinery squeak… something that she wouldn't have imagined would sound like a person moaning but did. Hattie tried to console herself with that thought but she couldn't deny she'd been rattled. She tried to shrug it off anyway and turned back to her laptop.

Then a scream tore through the silence of the house. Hattie leapt up and sprinted out onto the landing. There was another:

'NO! JENNY NO!'

Hattie raced to Jo's room and flung open the door. Jo was thrashing and moaning in her bed, sheets tangled around her like tourniquets. Even Hattie bursting in didn't wake her. Hattie ran to the bed – she had to wake her from whatever terrible nightmare had hold of her – but then she stopped short. She was in Jo's room and Jo was asleep and no matter what else was happening it suddenly felt like a boundary that Hattie shouldn't have crossed. It was just a nightmare. And everyone had nightmares from time to time. No matter how bad it looked to Hattie now, Jo would wake in time without Hattie's interference and she'd be fine once the dream had faded.

But then Jo called out again:

'JENNY!'

Hattie couldn't bear it. Whatever the consequences, whether Jo would even remember the dream when she woke, Hattie couldn't stand by and watch her go through this. She reached out to shake her, but before she'd got that far, Jo let out one last ear-splitting scream and then bolted upright.

Hattie froze. Jo stared at her, seeming to take a moment to focus, breathing hard. But then she spoke with her usual curt tone.

'You're in my room.'

'I'm sorry, I thought…' Hattie hesitated. Could she tell Jo what she'd just seen? Something about it felt deeply private, as if she'd just witnessed a snapshot of Jo's soul that she should never have seen. 'I thought I heard a noise,' she said finally. 'Downstairs. I came to wake you so you could come and check with me.'

Jo let out a resigned sigh and untangled the sheets from around her. She swung her legs over the side of the bed to poke her bare feet into a pair of work boots. Her hair hung limp around her face – Hattie had never seen it loose before; usually it was pulled back into a severe ponytail. This way it looked softer, made Jo seem younger and more vulnerable. It was funny, Hattie thought as they ran through the pretence of checking around downstairs for intruders, she didn't actually know how old Jo was. She'd taken a wild guess at mid-fifties, but seeing her now she wasn't so sure. Maybe Jo was much younger than that. And who had she been calling for in her sleep? Who was Jenny? Whoever it was, Jo had been terrified for her. How many times might Jo have been gripped by this nightmare before? How many times had it happened while Hattie slept on, oblivious down the corridor? It seemed silly that Hattie wouldn't have been woken by a scream like that, but maybe Jo didn't always scream? Maybe sometimes she didn't make a sound?

'Nothing's disturbed,' Jo said, shaking Hattie from her musings. She plodded over to the kettle. 'Might as well stay up now.'

'I'll get dressed then.'

Hattie's mind was racing – there was no way she was getting back to sleep now even if she wanted to.

The rain had stopped by the time Hattie began to clear the breakfast dishes away. Jo had been more taciturn and distant than ever during breakfast, but she also seemed vaguely uneasy too. Hattie wondered if the fading scenes of her early-morning nightmare were still playing through her mind. It would have been a safe bet – Jo had woken suddenly and hadn't been given time to pull herself together. Besides, Hattie had never seen anyone so distressed before and she was finding it hard to put it out of her own mind, so she couldn't imagine how shaken Jo might be. Hattie was becoming increasingly convinced that whatever had been playing out in Jo's unconscious was truly horrible.

'Jo…' she began tentatively as she washed the dishes and Jo wiped down the table. 'Is everything OK?'

Jo paused in her cleaning and looked up. 'Why wouldn't it be?'

'I don't know. I just thought… well, we rarely discuss how we're feeling.'

'You tell me every day,' Jo said, going back to her task.

'I just wondered… if there was something on your mind. I mean, if there was, you could tell me.'

'Apart from your incessant talking there's nothing wrong.'

'Well, yes…' Hattie gave a nervous laugh. Jo glanced up at the clock.

'Donkeys will need to go up.'

'Do you think the weather's fit?'

'Should be. They've got their shelter up there and if it turns really nasty we can bring them back down. That's if you haven't got anything better to do.'

'Me? Of course not!'

'I never know these days with your reporter and that woman with all those kids and your visits to the café every five minutes.'

'I am entitled to a life outside here,' Hattie replied, feeling a sudden need to defend herself. What she didn't add was that most of those trips had been to try and help turn the fortunes of Sweet Briar around. But what was the point? Jo would only have told her that Sweet Briar's fortunes didn't need turning around.

'I'm just saying I never know where you are.'

'I always tell you when I'm going out.'

'Which seems like all the time.'

'I go to do things for the sanctuary!' Hattie said, deciding to field the argument after all.

'I pay you to do things *at* the sanctuary, not away from it.'

'You barely pay me at all!' Hattie said and immediately regretted it. Jo held her in a stony gaze.

'You knew the terms – I've always been straight with you. You wanted to come.'

'I know that and I still want to be here, but you've got to stop shutting me out. If sometimes I want to go off into the village, have you ever considered that it might be because I'm lonely here with you? We ought to be friends by now but I barely know you.'

'There's nothing to know.'

'Maybe you could let me be the judge of that.'

'You're not here to be my friend.'

Tears stung Hattie's eyes but she held them back. 'OK,' she said slowly. 'So I'm here to help run the sanctuary but half the time you don't even let me do that. You make me clean the shed and feed the hens and walk the donkeys up and down.'

'That's all that wants doing.'

'It's not! There's a million other things – things I could do that would help this place be better – but you don't want to listen to my ideas!'

'What? Like your news story? I let you do that even though I didn't like it – what more do you want?'

'I want you to trust me! I want you to give these things a chance to work before you dismiss them. I want you to listen and discuss my ideas with me… properly. I want to feel like a part of this place, like it matters that I'm here, not just like a live-in slave!'

Jo rounded on her. 'Slave? Is that what you think? I do the same work as you; I treat you like I treat everyone else!'

Hattie wanted to say that the way Jo treated everyone else was the problem, because sometimes it felt to so many that she treated them only with contempt. But Jo's mind was so tightly closed that it probably wouldn't have changed anything. Hattie let out a sigh of defeat.

'I just wish I felt more welcome; that's all. I wish we could be friends. I know I'm not an equal partner in this place and I don't have any claim to your attention at all, but I wish you could see that I'm trying to help because I care.'

Jo regarded her carefully, silently. And then she looked as if she might say something. Maybe Hattie was finally getting through that emotional armour? But then she marched to the coat peg, pulled down her wax jacket and headed out into the grey morning, the back door slamming shut behind her.

There hadn't been much time to continue their discussion, and Jo had made it clear she didn't want to anyway. Instead, there had been chickens to worm, the coop to clean, repairs to the orchard fence where Jo suspected a fox had tried to get in, the barn to sweep and a consignment of hay to check through for mould. Hattie got on with it all without complaint, but she was plagued by a nagging doubt that there was so much that still needed to be said that she wouldn't be able to settle until it was. And she wondered, finally, whether everyone in Gillypuddle had been right about Jo and she, Hattie Rose, the lone voice of dissent, had got it very, very wrong. Had she been arrogant in her dismissal of everyone else's opinions, in her stubborn determination to prove that Jo Flint didn't have a heart of brick? She'd truly believed it and she still believed it now, but, in the end, did that count for anything? Could she continue to live like this, no matter how much she loved the donkeys and the views from the cliff top? In the end, could those things ever be enough?

The one bright spot of an otherwise miserable day was a call from Owen as she swept the barn. He'd be able to get away from London the following weekend and did she want to meet? After their argument this morning, Hattie didn't particularly care if Jo minded or not.

'I'd love to,' she said. 'Maybe I could even come to you.'

'In London?'

'Yeah – why not?'

'I'll come to you.'

'I fancy a trip to London.'

'But… won't you be needed at the farm?'

'I'm not going to have our date on the farm,' Hattie said with a laugh.

'Still… Better if I come to you.'

'There's not a lot to do around here.'

'Don't worry – I'll come up with something wild and romantic.'

'Maybe just the romantic bit this time. I don't think I've got the stomach for another beer festival.'

'Duly noted,' he said brightly. 'No beer.'

'I'm not saying no beer – just not quite as much as we downed that day.'

'Right. Some beer but not too much – got it. Any other instructions?'

'No. Other than that, feel free to surprise me.'

'Oh,' he said in a mischievous tone, 'I'll do that alright.'

'Should I be worried now?'

He laughed. 'Maybe a little.'

'In that case I'm already excited. See you Saturday then.'

Hattie ended the call and resumed her task, but she hadn't been going for longer than a couple of minutes before she heard the sound of an engine. She looked up at the open barn doors to see Seth's four-by-four pulling into the courtyard. Standing her brush against the wall, she went out to meet him.

'Jo called me,' he said. 'Something about Norbert.'

'What's wrong with him?'

'I thought you might be able to tell me. I just got a message on the answering service but she didn't say what it was.'

Hattie frowned. 'She hasn't said a word to me.' What she didn't add was that Jo had barely said a word to her all morning after their disagreement. Not that she said many more when relations were good. 'When did she phone?'

'Must have been early – before surgery began – but I didn't see my phone. Clients don't usually leave messages on there; they mostly leave them with the receptionist, so I don't always check. I came as soon as I could, though.'

Hattie tried to smother the anger and resentment that was building again. What was Jo's problem? Why hadn't she mentioned to Hattie that Norbert was ill – she knew Norbert was Hattie's favourite. Instead, she'd seen a problem and, rather than involving Hattie, she'd set her on a load of shitty tasks that would keep her out of the way, so that she wouldn't see any of the donkeys that day at all. Had Jo done that deliberately, with real malice? Hattie didn't want to believe that but it looked like the only answer right now. When had she noticed that Norbert was ill? Why wouldn't she at least mention that Seth was due to come and see him? Did that woman go out of her way to be mean-spirited and irritating or did it just come naturally?

Seth dug his hands in his pockets. 'Is she up at the field?'

'She's not down here so I'm guessing so.'

He nodded and began to walk back to his car. But then he turned around again. 'I saw your newspaper story, by the way.'

Hattie flushed. She didn't really know why, but possibly the last person, apart from her parents, that she wanted to see that story was Seth. 'You did?'

'Yes,' he said with a smile that she couldn't work out. Everyone said the Mona Lisa had an enigmatic smile and Hattie had never really known what that meant until now. 'It was very… illuminating. I had no idea you'd lived the high life in Paris.'

'Well…' Hattie began, but Seth's smile spread. It was a safe bet that someone in Gillypuddle had set the record straight on her behalf. She didn't know whether that made her feel less silly or more, though.

'But it was a good plug for the sanctuary,' he added.

'That was the idea,' Hattie replied. 'Although I can't say we've been inundated with visitors since.'

'It hasn't been any use at all?'

Hattie shrugged. 'A couple of enquiries but they didn't come. Some small donations on the sponsorship page – I suppose that's more than we would have had.'

'Do I detect a hint of disappointment?'

'I'd just expected more of a reaction.'

'You've had a reaction,' Seth said with a grin.

'I mean outside Gillypuddle,' Hattie said, and she had to laugh at the absurdity of the situation. 'It just all seems like a lot of effort for not very much return.'

'It's funny,' Seth said, studying her now with a strange look, 'I never had you down as a quitter.'

'I'm not – it's just…'

'For what it's worth I don't think you're appreciated as much as you ought to be.'

Did he mean Jo? Had he noticed how things were? Were they that obvious to people on the outside?

'And if you ever want to get a load off your chest,' he continued, 'my door is always open. It can be hard to keep pushing for something you believe in when the person you're trying to do it for keeps pushing it back at you. Believe me, I know.'

Hattie tried to reply but she didn't know what to say. It all seemed very cryptic, but, then again, perhaps it wasn't. Perhaps the answer to the conundrum was more obvious than she realised. *Believe me, I know.* Was he referring to his girlfriend? What had happened between them? Was that what he meant or was Hattie seeing a hidden meaning that just wasn't there?

'Anyway,' he said, 'I'd better go and take a look at Norbert.'

'I'll go with you. If you don't mind, that is. You know he means a lot to me too.'

'Be my guest. We'd better drive up; I'm a bit busy for leisurely walks today, even on your delightful farm.'

Hattie could have reminded him that it wasn't her farm but she was certain that Jo would take the first opportunity to remind everyone of that fact anyway. Instead, she followed him out to the car and climbed into the passenger seat.

It was such a short journey to the top field by car that it was hard to believe that Hattie and Jo spent hours walking the donkeys up and down every day. Hattie had to admit that, even so, those times were her favourite parts of her working day. The donkeys seemed to enjoy the exercise and, occasionally, Jo would even engage in a little small talk with Hattie – nothing important, perhaps a comment on the weather forecast or what funny thing one of the donkeys had done that day, but Hattie liked it. She was always hopeful that it would lead to something more meaningful but, of course, it never did.

As they bumped along, Seth turned to Hattie.

'Alright there?'

'Yes.'

'Are you sure about that? Something tells me you're not.'

'I'm just worried about Norbert.'

'I'm sure Jo would have mentioned it to you if she thought it was something serious.'

'I suppose so,' Hattie said. 'And I suppose he does have a habit of eating things he's not supposed to.'

'Exactly,' Seth agreed. 'Chances are he's done just that. I know Jo keeps any plants she thinks might be poisonous clear from the enclosure so I'm sure there won't be anything to worry about.'

Hattie could have pointed out that Jo wouldn't have phoned him first thing if there wasn't anything to worry about, but she appreciated that Seth was probably trying to put her at ease so she didn't.

'How long have you been in Gillypuddle?' she asked instead.

'About six months now. Are you happy to be back? Settling in again? It must be weird after Paris.'

'It's not so bad,' Hattie said. 'Things are a lot different than they were before I left though.'

'How's that?'

'Well, I'm not living with my parents for a start.'

'Oh, right. Your dad seems like a good man. Very smart. He used to be the GP?'

'That's how we ended up living here. He came to take the post before me and my sister were born and, after he retired, he and Mum decided to stay.'

'You have a sister? I didn't realise. Does she live here?'

'She died when she was eighteen.'

'Oh… I'm sorry.'

'You weren't to know. I don't suppose anyone's told you. People in this village gossip about just about everything but they don't ever mention that. I suppose they feel they can't, but it makes it seem sometimes like she never existed.' Hattie shook herself. 'Listen to me – as maudlin as they come today.'

'Maudlin?' He smiled. 'That's a good old-fashioned word. I don't think there's anything maudlin in remembering your sister.'

'I understand why people are scared to mention her, though. Mum and Dad have never got over her death.'

'What about you?' he asked gently. She turned to him. He was wearing such a look of tender concern that all she wanted to do was throw herself into his arms. It wasn't about sex appeal or attraction – though he had all of that – it was about finding someone who understood her. Something told her that Seth would be like that, that he'd understand her no matter how little she understood herself. His arms looked like a place she'd be safe.

'I think about her a lot,' Hattie said, tearing her gaze away and turning it onto the fields as they rolled by. 'I don't suppose our situation is any more special or difficult than anyone else's though; I don't think we deserve any special sympathy. Most people have sadness in their pasts once they've lived long enough. I'm sad about Charlotte, but I think we owe it to her to live where she couldn't, to make the most of our good fortune. I think she'd want us to do that too.'

'And you don't think your parents see it that way?' he said, instant understanding in his expression.

'Sometimes I don't think they do, no. Sometimes I think they still haven't let go of her.'

'Maybe they never will and maybe that's no crime.'

'You're right; it's not – I only lost my sister, but they lost their child. It's no wonder they see it differently than me.'

'I'm not trying to detract from your loss by saying that.'

'I know. Anyway,' she said, turning back to him, 'that's a long time ago and life goes on.'

'It does that.'

'Is there…' Hattie paused. She wanted to ask about his past, about the rumours she'd heard, but the moment had come and she couldn't. She didn't want to ruin this now, the understanding he'd shown her, the recognition of something deeper than just acquaintance made through his work. She thought, in time, he was someone who could be a good friend and she didn't want to jeopardise that by bringing up a bad memory that might become associated with this day and with Hattie herself. 'Jo moved to Gillypuddle shortly after I left for Paris,' she said instead.

'So I believe.'

'I don't know where she lived before; I don't think anyone does.'

'She seems very private.'

'So she's never told you?'

'No.'

'Or about how she got involved with the sanctuary here? Or how she paid for the farm?'

'No, but then it's really nothing to do with me.' He glanced at her. 'She's never told you any of this?'

'She doesn't tell me much at all.'

'I'm surprised at that. She thinks a lot of you.'

'She's got a funny way of showing it sometimes.'

'Maybe she just thinks she can ask of you what she can't ask of others. Sometimes that's the biggest compliment someone like her can give.'

'You mean that because she bosses me around and hardly says two pleasant words it's because she likes me? I'd hate to see her with someone she doesn't like then.'

Seth gave a soft chuckle. 'Trust me, she does.'

'What makes you say that?'

'You're here, aren't you? She lets you have access to her donkeys and not many people get that. She must think a lot of you.'

'I suppose,' Hattie said doubtfully.

'You two make a good team. Those donkeys are lucky to have found homes here.'

'I'm not very good at looking after them; there's so much I need to know that I haven't learned yet.'

'But you care and that's the most important thing. The knowledge and skill will follow in time.'

Seth slowed the car a few hundred yards from the paddock fencing and turned off the engine. Hattie wished the journey could have lasted a bit longer because she'd been enjoying their chat. It had been nice to talk to someone who was genuinely interested in Hattie's emotional well-being. Jo didn't care, Melinda was too busy to notice and her parents were too wrapped up in trying to push their own agenda. She felt like Seth would be someone who would always care. If the Gillypuddle gossip was right and his girlfriend really had left him to take up a research post in another country, then Hattie thought she might not be as clever as her education would suggest.

Jo was in the field when they got there, standing with Norbert, her face close to his and talking softly to him. The other donkeys were milling around close by, sometimes coming to take a closer look at Norbert before wandering away again, but they never strayed far when Jo was around. Only Blue stayed close, seeming jittery, as if he knew something was wrong. As Seth and Hattie came in through the gate, Jo looked up and watched as they walked across the field towards her. If she was irked to see Hattie had turned up she didn't show any signs of it; she was simply her distant self, although Hattie had to admit that that didn't really tell her anything about her boss's current mood.

'Hello, fella,' Seth said, rubbing a hand down Norbert's shaggy nose. 'What have you been up to now?'

Norbert did look under the weather. He'd always make a fuss of Hattie when he saw her, but today he simply stood in the middle of the field, barely reacting to her arrival at all. Seth turned to Jo.

'What do you know?'

Jo put her hands up to Norbert's neck and gave it a rub. 'You can see for yourself he's not as lively as he usually is. Doesn't seem hungry at all – I came up with a pocket full of sugar beet and he's not interested.'

'He seemed fine last night,' Hattie put in, and Jo looked coldly at her.

'How would you know? You weren't here last night.'

'I didn't leave for Melinda's house until after eight.'

'Then it wasn't last night you saw him.'

'So…' Seth interrupted, 'how long do you think this has been going on? Have you noticed anything before now?'

'I wondered if he didn't take a dip in form from time to time but I thought I was mistaken,' Jo said. 'I wish I'd called you now.'

'Sometimes it's hard to tell,' Seth said kindly. 'How are his stools?'

'I'm not sure. He's been with the others so it's difficult to know which are his.'

Seth rolled up his sleeves and began to feel around Norbert's abdomen.

'Anything?' Jo asked.

'Not sure.' He walked around to Norbert's head and looked into his eyes and ears. Then he peeled back Norbert's lips to look at his gums. The donkey barely flinched and usually he found anyone trying to prise his mouth open most offensive – Hattie knew this; she'd tried to rescue inappropriate foodstuffs from his mouth often enough.

'Colic?' Jo asked.

'Could be.'

'Like babies get?' Hattie put in, and Jo shot her such a withering look that Hattie felt a sudden rush of anger, something she'd never felt for Jo before, even at her most exasperating moments. But Hattie was doing her best and it was constantly being thrown back in her face – surely Jo could see that eventually it would wear down any goodwill Hattie had for her? She'd successfully alienated the rest of the village. Was she actively trying to do the same with Hattie?

'Not quite,' Seth said patiently. Perhaps he'd seen something of Hattie's mood in her expression because his tone was far more conciliatory. 'It's more serious than that in donkeys. It could be symptomatic of a big underlying problem and we need to get to the bottom of what that is.'

'What sort of problems?'

'It could be any number of things – I'd need to take a proper look to establish what's going on. I might even need to hospitalise him.' He looked at Jo. 'Happy for me to do that?'

'I'd be happier if you could treat him here,' she said.

'I'll do what I can, but it might be too big and complicated in the end.'

She gave a grim nod. 'Do what you have to.'

They all knew that what Seth was really asking was could Jo afford to hospitalise Norbert? And they all knew that the answer to that was a big fat no.

'I'll get my kit,' Seth said.

Hattie watched him walk to his car. She turned to Jo, but Jo was watching him too and she didn't even look at Hattie, though she must have been able to feel her eyes on her. So Hattie turned to Norbert, standing very still in the field, and she rubbed a hand along the scruffy teddy-bear fur of his neck while she tried very hard not to cry.

Chapter Twenty

Hattie knew when she wasn't needed and, though she was worried about Norbert, she decided that Seth would be able to do his job better with Jo's assistance. So she went to finish the list of chores Jo had given her that morning and when she'd done those she decided to wash the bed linen. The rain of the morning had cleared completely and now, although it wasn't exactly a heatwave, it would dry her washing nicely.

She was hanging the sheets on a line at the far end of the courtyard when she noticed Seth's car drive past the gate and away from the farm. She'd half hoped he might pull in and let her know how Norbert was, but she supposed that he would have expected Jo to do that and he probably had other patients to get to. Feeling a little let down anyway, she turned back to the washing line. Jo would probably stay up in the field for a while yet so she might as well keep busy for now. Later, she decided, they would have to talk about the argument they'd had that morning, whether Jo liked it or not. It wasn't healthy to let it fester and they needed to clear the air.

She'd just turned back to the washing when her phone rang. She dug into her jeans pocket.

'Dad?'

It was rare for Hattie's father to call out of the blue, even rarer during the daytime.

'What's wrong?' she asked.

'Nothing's wrong? I can't call you unless something's wrong?'

Hattie smiled. 'Of course not.'

'I just wondered if you'd checked the charity page we set up together for Sweet Briar?'

'I meant to this morning but I haven't had time. Why?'

'I think you should look when you can; I think you'll be pleasantly surprised.'

'There's been more donations?'

'Yes.'

'That's brilliant! How many? Are they decent amounts? Are we finally on our way?'

'I'd say you are,' Nigel said with a chuckle. 'Go and look when you have a minute. There's one in particular that you'll be very pleased with.'

'Will I?'

'Oh yes.'

'Is it big?'

'Fairly.' Nigel chuckled again and Hattie could tell by his playful tone that he was trying not to spoil what might be a nice surprise.

'Oh, how much?'

'I'm not telling you; go and look!'

'I will!'

But then a thought occurred to her. 'Dad…' she said sternly. 'This donation… it doesn't have anything to do with you, does it?'

'Why would you think that?'

'Well, why were you checking the page? You didn't need to.'

'I was just curious.'

'Are you sure? I don't recall you ever being just curious about anything.'

'Maybe you don't know me as well as you think. I get curious. It was curiosity that made me study medicine.'

'Alright then, you haven't been curious since 1965.'

'Cheeky!'

Hattie laughed. 'So this donation has absolutely nothing to do with you?'

'I still don't know why you'd think it would be down to me.'

'I don't know… to make me feel better about what a terrible failure it's been so far?'

'I'm not silly enough to think that I could sneak that past you. I can assure you that it's nothing to do with me.'

'Hmm. Well, in that case, thank you for letting me know about it – I'll take a look later.'

'Oh, and your mother says I need to ask when you're coming to see us. She says she wants to know about that journalist fellow.'

'Journalist? How did…' Hattie let out an exasperated sigh. 'Melinda?'

'She might have mentioned it when we saw her in the village yesterday.'

'I'm sorry I didn't tell you, Dad. It's just that I've only had one date with him so it didn't seem worth mentioning yet.'

'That's what I told your mother. You'll come down anyway?'

'I'll try. Can I get back to you on the arrangements? I'm kind of up to my eyes in it right now but I promise to try to get over soon.'

'I hope you keep that promise. Your mother says we saw more of you when you lived in Paris.'

'I don't think that's true.' Hattie laughed. 'I'll try to make it one evening this week then.'

'That's good – I'll tell her.' Nigel paused, and in the pause Hattie heard uncertainty. 'Is everything still going well for you?' he asked finally. 'Your mother got the impression from Melinda that you might have some regrets about your move up to Sweet Briar, and—'

'It's fine, Dad,' Hattie said. She wasn't about to tell him what had happened that day, or how wretched she'd felt since, otherwise he'd be driving up there, bundling her into his car and locking her in her old bedroom at home until she agreed not to go back. She knew he would have acted from love but she still wanted to make her own decisions, no matter how wrong they might turn out to be or how much he disagreed with them.

'But if there was anything...' he continued.

'I'd tell you,' Hattie said. 'Dad...' she added, another thought occurring to her, 'do you know much about Jo from before she arrived in Gillypuddle?'

'Nobody does,' he said. 'I think that, and her harsh ways, is what makes everyone so suspicious. Why do you ask?'

'Oh, no reason – just curious,' she said brightly. 'So I'll call you about coming over.'

'Good – don't forget.'

'I won't. Bye, Dad. Thanks for calling.'

'And don't forget to look at your page later.'

'I won't.'

Hattie put her phone away. She'd finish what she was doing, go to see how Norbert was and check if Jo wanted any help bringing the donkeys down to bed, and then she'd look at the page. And maybe she'd start to do a bit of digging too. Why didn't anyone know about Jo's past? Why was she so secretive; what did she have to hide? And who was Jenny?

Jo had cooked roast chicken and potatoes. It was Hattie's favourite dish – at least, her favourite from Jo's very traditional repertoire – and

Jo knew this because Hattie had told her. Hattie also knew that Jo hadn't intended to cook roast chicken for this evening's meal because she'd taken minced beef out of the freezer to thaw the night before. And when Hattie went snooping after they'd washed up she found the minced beef cooked and cooling, presumably ready to use the following day instead. Hattie wondered if the chicken was Jo's way of apologising.

'Chicken's from the farm shop before you ask,' Jo said, plonking the plate down in front of Hattie.

'Do you think Norbert will be alright?' Hattie asked as she cut into a crisp roast potato.

'Seth'll do his best.' Jo sat across from her with her own dinner and reached for the salt.

'I suppose so. He didn't say what's caused him to get colic? He said it was a symptom, right?'

'He doesn't know yet. Tests will be back soon enough.'

Hattie nodded and began to eat again. They were silent for a minute or two, the only sound that of cutlery scraping against china. But then Hattie spoke again.

'Jo… is it somehow my fault that Norbert's ill? Did I do something wrong? Have I done something I shouldn't have done or not done something I should? Did I not check his feed properly for mould? I feel like maybe I haven't looked after him properly—'

'If there's a blame it lies with both of us. We've both looked after him. It might be nobody's fault. Sometimes it's just how things are.'

'I can't stop thinking about it.'

Jo looked up from her meal and Hattie was startled to see something like tenderness in her expression.

'I'm sure it's nothing you've done,' she said. 'Don't blame yourself.'

Hattie nodded again and Jo turned back to her dinner.

'I shouldn't have been short with you today,' Jo said without looking up. 'I forget that just because Sweet Briar is my whole life it shouldn't have to be yours.'

'I do love it here, though.'

'I'm sure you do but there's more to life than this.' Jo chewed solemnly on a slice of chicken but then she looked up again. 'Did you like your life in Paris?'

'Paris?'

Hattie was floored. Was Jo actually interested in her? Interested further than delegating the next chore?

'I suppose so. I don't really think about it much now, though.'

'You don't want to go back there?'

'Oh, no. That's all out of my system now.'

'So you're not leaving me yet?'

Yet? It sounded as if Jo had decided that Hattie's leaving was inevitable. Perhaps she would one day, but Jo's choice of words made it sound as if she thought she'd already lost Hattie.

'Not at all,' Hattie said.

Jo didn't reply. She looked down at her plate again, all her concentration on sawing at a potato.

'My dad says there's some activity on the donation page we set up for the sanctuary,' Hattie continued, more for something to say than because she thought Jo would get excited about it. 'I haven't had a minute to check yet, but my dad seems to think we'll be pleased when we look.'

Jo sprinkled more salt on her dinner. 'It was a good idea. I appreciate everything you're doing for this place.'

'Well, it benefits me too,' Hattie said modestly. Now she knew she was dreaming. Any moment now she was going to wake up and the old Jo who never thanked or praised her was going to be shouting her down for breakfast.

The room became silent again apart from the sounds of them finishing their meal. After a few minutes more, Jo shovelled the last forkful into her mouth and got up, still chewing, to put her plate in the sink.

'Checking on the animals,' she said, grabbing her coat from the hook on the wall and heading out. Hattie was pretty sure that there was one animal in particular that Jo really wanted to check on. She'd have offered to go with her but she also got the impression that Jo would rather go alone. Instead, Hattie finished her own meal in silence and tried to figure out what the hell had just happened.

When she was done, she added her own plate to the dishes soaking in the sink, washed them quickly and then headed upstairs to get out her laptop. While it was booting up, Hattie wandered to her bedroom window. The sun was low in the sky, not quite set but hovering just above the ribbon of sea beyond the headland, clouds rolling by to obscure it every now and again. The day had ended more brightly than it had begun in more ways than one.

Who is Jenny?

The thought came to her again now as she cast her mind back to the terrible rain of the morning and how it had woken her just in time to witness Jo's nightmare. Jo being so nice to her this evening had made Hattie more curious than ever. What had made her do that? Were the nightmare and Jo's change of heart connected? Was Jenny the key? Was Jenny the reason Jo hated being around people?

Hattie shook herself and turned from the window to see her homepage had appeared on the screen of her laptop. She logged into Sweet Briar's website and clicked onto the donation page. There had actually been half a dozen since she'd last checked – mostly small amounts: five, ten pounds. No fortune by anyone's standard but progress. But then her eyes widened as they settled on the one her dad must have meant. She sucked in a breath. It was far, far more than any of the others, probably a good few months' salary for someone. They could do a lot with that. They could... It was enough... Hattie thought for a moment.

They could pay Seth.

Hattie grabbed her phone and dialled her dad's number.

'Twice in one day,' he said as he picked up. 'I'm honoured.'

'Dad, you promise you didn't make this donation?' she asked.

'I said it wasn't me. Honestly, why would I do that?'

'Because it's a rounded-up version of the amount we owe Seth Bryson and only you, me, Seth and Jo know how much that is. As neither Jo nor me have enough money to make this sort of donation and the coincidence is too huge, that makes me think—'

'Have you considered it might be a coincidence?' her dad asked with that amused tone again. 'Stranger things have happened.'

'Dad...'

'Hattie – I'm not one for false modesty or acting the unsung hero; you know that. If I'm telling you I didn't make the donation then I didn't.'

'But then who did?'

'If I were you I'd stop worrying about where it came from and go and pay Seth... *again*.'

Hattie was thoughtful for a moment as she studied the screen, her dad's joke washing over her. Anon, the tag said. An anonymous donation for almost exactly the amount they desperately needed to pay their biggest debt? Who would do that? No matter what her dad said, she couldn't just let it slide and she couldn't believe that it was a coincidence.

Seth? Could Seth have done it to help them out? His way of wiping the slate clean for them? Jo would never accept help from him willingly but this might work. But why would Seth do that? Surely he needed to be paid no matter how much he might want to strike off the debt for them?

No, Hattie decided. Seth had been to see them that day and he was caring for Norbert still, so that would mean the cost was continuing to build. This amount would have settled the bill as it had been but probably not as it was now. Maybe it was just a coincidence, after all? Maybe somebody out there did just really like donkeys that much.

'Is there anything else?' Nigel asked. Hattie shook her head slowly.

'Sorry, Dad. I didn't mean to go all kamikaze on you.'

'Congratulations. It looks as if your idea is working out after all.'

'It does, doesn't it? With lots of help, of course.'

'You're welcome.'

Hattie smiled now. 'Thanks, Dad. Bye.'

She ended the call and put her phone on the bed. She really wanted to tell Jo about this and she wanted Jo to be happy, but Jo was so unpredictable right now that she wasn't sure the result of that conversation would be the one she expected. Then again, they did need the money – at least, Sweet Briar did – and surely her employer could be pragmatic about it if only for the sake of her precious sanctuary? What did it matter where the money came from? Though if that were true, why did Hattie feel uneasy about it? She couldn't honestly expect Jo to be comfortable with it if even she herself wasn't.

She needed to talk to Jo, and the sooner the better. Grabbing the laptop, she headed downstairs to find her.

When Hattie got to the kitchen, Jo was hanging her coat up.

'How is he?' Hattie asked.

'Quiet,' Jo said. 'About the same.'

'You're worried?'

Jo went to the sink to wash her hands. 'You washed the dishes,' she said.

'Jo, I need you to see this.'

'In a minute… stove needs wiping down.'

'I think you should see it now.'

If Jo was surprised at Hattie's tone she didn't show it. She came over and looked at where Hattie was pointing on the screen of her laptop.

'What's that?' she asked.

'Someone's given it to us.'

'What?'

'It's a donation for the sanctuary.'

Jo stared at the screen. She looked vaguely horrified. Hattie had expected many reactions but that wasn't one of them. And then Jo shook her head forcefully.

'Send it back.'

'What do you mean, send it back?'

'Send it back.'

'I can't.' Hattie looked up at Jo. 'Why would we do that anyway? We could do a lot with this, couldn't we?'

'I said send it back!'

'I don't know how to.'

'Then tell them to take it back!'

'It's anonymous! How can I tell them to take it back when I don't know who they are?'

Jo opened her mouth to argue, but then it seemed Hattie's argument had finally sunk in and she closed it again. She shook her head, looking at the screen. 'I don't understand it,' she said after a moment. 'Why would someone give us that much?'

'I wondered that,' Hattie replied. 'But they have and they obviously wanted us to use it. We could do a lot with that money, couldn't we? I mean, we could... say... pay the vet's bills...? Norbert's treatment might cost a lot,' she added quickly, 'and then there's Speedy's leg and all the worming we did for the chickens when they arrived...'

Hattie stopped as Jo stared at her.

'I mean, it was just a suggestion,' Hattie finished lamely, wondering if she'd already said too much.

'I knew that newspaper business would be trouble,' Jo said, picking the teapot up from the table and taking it to the sink to empty out the old teabags.

'But it's brilliant, isn't it? Doesn't it help? That's what the donation page was set up for, after all, and we can't really complain about a donation that generous, can we?'

'That amount of money,' Jo said, swilling the teapot under the tap, her voice irritatingly level again. The few seconds of actual reaction, of actual emotion had gone, replaced by that cold, distant Jo once more. 'There's bound to be a catch.'

'Well maybe somebody just wanted to be nice!' Hattie slammed the lid down on the laptop. 'It's not that unheard of, you know!'

The sound of Jo running the tap faded as Hattie went back to her room, frustrated and angry. She'd really believed they'd connected tonight, that they were finally coming to a new understanding, that Jo was finally beginning to realise that Hattie was on her side, that not everyone was out to get her, but Jo was just as stubborn as ever. So much for progress.

Chapter Twenty-One

The next morning was bright and clear. When Hattie came downstairs Jo was making a pan of hearty porridge. Hattie sat at the table without a word, gazing out of the window at a sky that was blue as cornflowers, wondering what to say. She looked around as Jo placed a bowl in front of her and sat down with her own breakfast.

'Thanks,' Hattie said, but Jo simply picked up her spoon and began to eat. Hattie had struggled to fall asleep the night before and she'd started to wonder whether she'd been a bit short-tempered and unfair to Jo – after all, it wasn't her fault that she struggled with people, and Hattie wondered if she hated the way she was as much as others did. It had to be a lonely existence; at least, Hattie thought so.

'Have you been out to the stables this morning?' she asked finally, guessing that Jo would have and it was at least something they could communicate about.

Jo nodded as she sunk her spoon into the bowl of oats in front of her.

'And?' Hattie pressed.

'He seemed brighter.'

Hattie heaved a silent sigh of relief. If Norbert was through the worst of it then that was one less thing to worry about. 'He'll be OK then?'

'We'll know soon enough – Seth's coming over later.'

'Right. Should we take Norbert up to the field this morning?'

'Perhaps not. We can leave Blue down here with him if he's staying in the stable a while – parting them will only make Norbert worse. Donkeys are sensitive to that sort of thing.'

'Want me to take the others?'

'See to the chickens – I'll do it.'

Hattie turned to her own breakfast again. It was stodgy and wholesome and another very traditional dish that Jo seemed to get just right. It was a shame she wasn't so skilled when it came to making Hattie feel like a real part of the farm.

After breakfast Hattie went to see Norbert before going to do the chores Jo had delegated to her. He was standing in his stall, those gentle old eyes looking dolefully out at her.

'Morning, mister…' she said, running a hand down his shaggy nose. 'What have you been chewing on now?'

He gave her a nudge of recognition but he wasn't himself at all. Hattie's eyes filled with tears but she sniffed them back. Didn't Jo say that Seth was coming to see him and Jo thought he was on the mend? So what was there to cry about?

She put her face close to his neck. 'Don't worry – Seth will have you good as new in no time.'

'I can only hope.'

Hattie's head whipped up to see Seth standing in the doorway. Hastily she dried her eyes.

'I didn't see you arrive.'

'Stealthy like a ninja,' he said with a tight smile. 'I thought I'd better come and check on him before surgery starts rather than leave it all morning, in case the poor guy's in pain.'

'You think he is?'

'Probably,' Seth replied with a grim nod.

'Have you managed to figure out what's causing it yet?' Hattie asked, not wanting to dwell on the possibility and feeling powerless to do anything about it.

'There's a list of possible reasons as long as my arm. I can rule some of them out fairly confidently with a good physical examination, but some are going to have to wait for test results, and, unfortunately…' he rolled up his shirt sleeves and stepped into Norbert's enclosure, 'the lab's got a backlog so they haven't got anything for me yet.'

'When will they have them?'

'Monday possibly. I've asked them to process as urgent. I can't say I'm pleased about the delay, and all I can do in the meantime is keep Norbert comfortable and stable. If I think it will help I might hospitalise him over the weekend. I need to chat to Jo about that.' He pulled a stethoscope from his bag and pressed it to Norbert's belly.

'His heart's there?' Hattie asked with a frown.

'No.' Seth smiled. 'I'm listening to his stomach to see what sort of sounds it's making.'

'Oh.' Hattie watched him work for a moment, keeping as quiet as she could.

'Is Jo around?' he asked, putting the stethoscope away again.

'She's transferring the others up to the field,' Hattie said. 'Except for Blue…' She nodded at the donkey in the next stall.

'Norbert's best pal?'

Hattie nodded.

'Probably wise,' Seth said, looking satisfied with the arrangement. 'Although I'm afraid I might have to part them later anyway. Jo will have to keep an eye on Blue to make sure he doesn't show signs of distress. Norbert will be OK – I'll have him on medication.'

'We'll do our best for Blue,' Hattie said.

Seth shoved his hands into his pockets and held Hattie in an approving gaze. 'I know you will,' he said gently.

'Seth… can I ask you something? It's going to sound a bit… well, maybe it will sound a bit silly.'

'Ask away. I'm sure it's not.'

'Well, it's just that we got a donation recently on the charity page of our new website and it just so happens to be around the amount we owe you.'

'I didn't know you had a charity page. Good idea.'

'Didn't you?' Hattie replied. She'd been certain that she had mentioned it but was now doubting herself.

'It's a stroke of luck for you, getting a good donation. But I'm not going to press you for the money if that's what you're thinking. That's why you're telling me? If you've got more immediate uses for the money then I completely understand. I said I could wait – you don't need to worry that I won't treat Norbert just because you have a little outstanding balance.'

It was a big outstanding balance, Hattie thought, and if he thought it was small what kind of amounts must others run up? But she gave a hesitant smile. It certainly didn't look as if Seth knew anything about their mystery donor. Either that or he'd missed his true vocation as an actor. So if it wasn't Seth and it wasn't her dad, then who did give them the money? Was it really just a happy coincidence, after all?

'Does that clear it up?' he asked.

'Um, yes… but I expect Jo will want to pay you when she can. I have to process the money and transfer it into our account and I'm not quite sure how to do that yet. It might take a few days.'

'Whenever you're ready.'

'Thanks.'

Hattie looked at Norbert. They'd got this massive donation, but all the money in the world was no good if they couldn't help him.

'I'll do what I can,' Seth said, perhaps following her train of thought.

'I know – I just hate to see him like this.'

'He's a tough old character so that's a good start.'

Hattie nodded.

'Right,' he said, springing into action again, 'I'd better finish my examination and then I'd better talk to Jo.'

Hattie hadn't much felt like going out on a date, but when she'd told Melinda that she was thinking of cancelling her plans with Owen, her friend told her in no uncertain terms that she was to do no such thing. Melinda was sure that Hattie needed something to take her mind off Norbert, who had been taken away from Sweet Briar for more tests and to try to get his symptoms under control. Blue was already beginning to pine for his best friend, and Hattie was often greeted with the heartbreaking sight of him wandering the field like a lost soul or staring out to sea as if expecting to find Norbert there. Jo seemed to be more closed than ever before, and Hattie was now attuned to listening out for her violent nightmares which meant, as a consequence, now heard them nightly. Hattie had to admit that she was physically and emotionally drained and, if she felt like this, then she had to consider that Jo must be feeling ten times worse, and Jo wasn't lucky enough to have a hot journalist boyfriend to take her out and cheer her up. On reflection, she decided that Melinda had a point – blowing off Owen was a bit like looking a very handsome gift horse in the mouth.

So she kept her date and Owen turned up on that Saturday morning as arranged to collect her from the farm. Jo hadn't expressed any opposition to the plans when Hattie had informed her of them, but then, relations between the two of them were so frosty and strained with all the added external stresses that they were barely speaking anyway. Hattie was fed up, and the only thing stopping her from packing up and heading back to her parents' house now was that she felt Jo needed her – or, rather, the donkeys did, because Jo was at Seth's practice checking on Norbert almost as often as she was at the farm.

Hattie hadn't known what to wear for her date, as the pile of discarded clothes still lying on her bed attested. In the end, she'd gone for simple and basic with her best jeans and an embroidered cotton blouse.

'Where are we going?' she asked as she got in the car and Owen leaned over to give her an unexpectedly shy kiss. She glanced up to see Jo at her own bedroom window, watching them.

'It's a surprise,' Owen said. 'No amount of questioning will get the information out of me yet.'

'It's still a surprise? How long do you think you can keep this up?'

'Until you guess it.'

'Well, have I at least dressed appropriately? At least you can tell me that. If we're mud-wrestling I'd rather put something less white on.'

'No mud-wrestling.' He grinned. 'You'll do just fine.'

'Wow – *you'll do*? Two dates and already complacency has set in!'

'OK, what I meant to say is that you look gorgeous.'

'That's better.' Hattie grinned.

'Ready?'

'I'd say yes but I have no idea as I don't know where I'm going.'

Owen gave a grin of his own as he pulled out of the courtyard. Hattie looked back to see that Jo was still watching at her window like some unhinged antagonist from a cheap thriller.

'So, how's your week been?' he asked as they emerged onto the road that led away from the farm.

'Not the best if I'm honest. Norbert is still really ill. I know I'm not supposed to have favourites but he kind of is.'

'I'm sorry,' Owen said, though he didn't sound like he really got how Hattie was feeling. She supposed it was difficult when you weren't close to the donkeys like she'd become. 'You still don't know if he's going to be OK?'

'Not yet, no. The vet had to take him to hospital and he's keeping him there for the weekend.'

'Donkeys have hospitals?'

'It's just like us needing specialist treatment, isn't it? We'd go to hospital, so why not them?'

'It just seems like a weird idea. I suppose it makes sense when you really think about it.' He glanced at Hattie. 'You're cut up about it, aren't you?'

'I'm fond of him. Jo is too – we're both worried.'

'I can't imagine her being moved by anything.'

'You're not alone there. She gives that impression but, don't forget, she runs that place from her own pocket – at least she has done up till now – and she gives up a lot to take care of those donkeys, so she must have some compassion in her.'

'That's true.'

'It's honestly the only reason I take her bullshit,' Hattie said, a note of bitterness creeping into her tone. 'I'd have left anyone else by now if they treated me the way she does.'

Owen turned to her with a look of surprise before focusing on the road again. 'I thought you loved it there. It *has* been a tough week.'

Hattie sighed. 'Sorry – I shouldn't be ranting about this to you. We've just had a few disagreements and we're not exactly seeing eye to eye at the moment.'

'She must take a lot of work to get on with, even for someone as easy-going as you.'

'She does.'

'You know…' Owen continued thoughtfully, 'I can't help feeling there's something about her I ought to know.'

'What do you mean?'

'The first time I saw her something about her rang a bell, but I can't quite place it no matter how hard I try. Trust me, I will though.'

'That's strange. If you do remember what it is I'd love to know. I've lived there for weeks now and I still know absolutely nothing about her. I don't even know where she lived before she came to Gillypuddle, where she was born, whether she has family… it's crazy. I don't even know how old she is! How does that work? She could be anyone and I wouldn't have a clue!'

'Think you might be living with an axe murderer?'

'I could be!'

'Don't you think she'd have done the deed by now?'

'Maybe she's waiting for a special moon – the equinox or something.'

Owen laughed out loud. Hattie liked his laugh – it was fearless, irreverent. It didn't care what anyone thought.

'Maybe I should rescue you like a knight in shining armour and take you to my flat in London that is most definitely big enough for two.'

Hattie gave him a sideways look. 'Wouldn't I cramp your style?'

'Probably, but for you I could suffer.'

'Seriously though, it does bother me that I know so little of Jo.'

Hattie wondered whether she ought to mention the nightmares. They troubled her, but did she know Owen well enough to talk to him about it? It still felt inappropriate enough that Hattie should know about them, let alone anyone else, but she was convinced now that they were a clue to Jo's past. Hattie had heard the name again coming from Jo's room during her more restless nights, a couple of times now, always with the same fear and urgency: Jenny. She had to be someone significant, but who? If Owen's intuition was right and he really did know something about Jo that currently evaded him, perhaps that information might help to trigger something more?

'If it really bothers you, how about I see what I can dig up?' he said.

'Like spy on her?'

'Not spy, exactly. Just see if we have anything in our archives. I can do a search with her name easily enough.'

In light of her thoughts on the subject it was tempting, but Hattie shook her head. It didn't feel right to pry, no matter how frustrating the gaps in her knowledge of Jo's life were.

'I don't think so; it doesn't seem right somehow.'

'You're saying it's a little bit unsavoury?'

Hattie gave a sheepish smile. 'Sort of. Sorry.'

'Well,' Owen said, slowing for a red light, 'it's your loss. You're the one losing sleep over this thing. But if you don't want to know...'

His flippant statement was more accurate than he could know. Hattie was losing sleep. Maybe not entirely because of Jo, but it certainly wasn't helping. She wanted a reason to understand Jo's moods, she wanted a reason to forgive her when she was being awkward, a reason to like her, to tolerate the brusqueness, because she wanted to believe that everything she'd thought about Jo, about a good soul buried deep within the thorny exterior, was true. Again and again, Hattie came back to the same conclusion: anyone who sacrificed so much to care for defenceless animals couldn't be all bad.

'It's good of you to offer,' she said. 'And I do appreciate it but honestly, I think it's better to keep persevering with her the straight, old-fashioned way.'

Owen smiled. 'OK – I won't do anything if you don't want me to.'

'Thanks.'

Hattie turned to the window. The coast was behind them and she could tell they were moving inland now. The scenery became flatter, with fields of wheat and yellow rapeseed blocked out across the landscape like a giant chequerboard.

'So, exactly where are you taking me?' she asked.

'Don't think if you keep asking you'll trip me up,' he said with a laugh. 'I told you it's a surprise.'

'Can't I even get a little clue?'

'No, because then you might guess and ruin the surprise.'

'Spoilsport.'

'No, that's you.' He laughed. 'Wait and see!'

'I can't. I'm impatient – ask my dad. In fact, ask anyone who knows me.'

'I don't think I'll ask your dad just yet, if it's all the same to you.'

'Scaredy cat.'

'Of your dad? Hell yeah! Of any girl's dad! All guys are scared of their girlfriends' dads.'

'My dad's a softy even when he pretends to be strict.'

'To you, maybe. To me he's licensed to kill.'

Hattie giggled. 'So you're still not going to tell me where we're going, even if I threaten to get my dad on you?'

'Nope. Not on pain of death.'

'Aren't you worried I'll hate it?'

'Nope.'

'Confidence, eh? I like it.'

Owen grinned and Hattie turned back to the windows, looking for clues in the road signs.

An hour later, they ran into a queue of traffic. Owen drummed on the steering wheel in time to the song on the radio as they inched forward. He didn't seem overly concerned at the development.

'It's weird that we should run into this suddenly,' Hattie said.

'Not really.'

'But the road's been clear and there aren't any roadworks that I know of. It's not even a very main road – this one is always quiet whenever I've been down it.'

'It wouldn't be today.'

'You expected this?'

'Yeah.'

Hattie wondered why he hadn't avoided the route if he'd expected to run into traffic but she didn't say so because she didn't want to sound as if she was complaining. She was happy just being out with him, even if they were sitting in traffic together. She looked out of the window instead. There were fields and farmhouses, the odd bit of scrubland and distant forests. Nothing to queue in traffic for.

They moved another half mile, crawling in much the same way, and then Hattie saw a large, colourful sign and she burst out laughing.

'Monster truck rally! Please don't tell me that's where we're going!'

Owen grinned. 'Well, I did tell you I'd give you something totally unexpected.'

'What! That's seriously our date?'

'You don't like it?' he asked, sounding less sure of himself now.

'I've no idea! It's not something I've ever considered doing.'

'Trust me, it's more fun than you might imagine.'

'You've been to one before?'

'My dad used to bring me.'

'Well, you definitely had a very different upbringing to me,' Hattie said with a laugh. 'You wouldn't have got my dad within ten miles of one of these – his idea of a wild time is watching back-to-back episodes of *Countryfile*.'

'It's honestly not that wild,' Owen said. 'Not like I imagine they would be in the States – it's all quite British and civilised here.'

'Well, I definitely can't complain that you don't surprise me,' Hattie said. 'First a beer festival and now this; I can only wonder how you're going to keep your roll going. What's the next date going to be? A zero-gravity flight or something?'

'You know, that's not a bad idea,' Owen said with a grin.

They continued to move with the traffic until, at long last, they made it through the entrance and parked up. Owen got them past the ticket booth while Hattie took a look around, marvelling at how huge the crowd was. The place was buzzing: gangs of teenage boys, families with young children, fathers with sons and grandfathers with grandsons, dads with daughters who looked surprisingly more enthusiastic than them. As they made their way to the arena Hattie noted rows of kiosks selling everything from alcohol and fast food to souvenir programmes and merchandise.

'Want a hat?' Owen asked with an impish grin, nodding towards a stand that sold peaked caps with the logo of the rally emblazoned on the front.

'Do you know what, maybe I'll pass on that,' Hattie said.

The day was turning into a warm one and Hattie peeled off her cardigan and tied it around her waist, glad now that she'd opted for the more casual choice of clothes rather than the tiny dress and heels she'd almost settled on. Owen reached for her hand. She smiled up at him and he bent to give her a quick kiss.

They emerged into the main space of the arena. It was vast, and looked like perhaps during the rest of the year it made up an extensive part of a farmer's land. Not that Hattie was any expert. There were low stands placed around the central space, standing room in front cordoned off at a safe distance and another stand close to the action labelled 'VIP and Press Area'. Owen started to lead Hattie there.

'This is us?' Hattie asked, looking up at the stand. 'Did you have to pay a lot for these tickets?'

'Actually,' he said a little sheepishly, 'I thought I'd kill two birds with one stone. I thought I'd write a piece about the rally as I was coming anyway so I contacted the organisers and… well, there has to be some perks in anyone's job, doesn't there?'

Hattie wasn't a naturally suspicious person but even she was beginning to get the sneaky feeling that this day and the VIP tickets might actually be a press freebie. Part of her felt she ought to be annoyed at the idea, but part of her liked Owen so much she didn't want to dwell on the possibility, which would take the shine off her day out. And after the week she'd had at Sweet Briar she felt like she'd earned this day a hundred times over, no matter where it came from. So she said nothing about it and followed Owen to their seats, feeling slightly conspicuous as the people in the cheap seats watched them make their way to the press box.

Up there was better quality seating and a small, manned bar area. Owen left Hattie to get comfortable while he went to get drinks. As she watched him go, she wondered why she wasn't more put out by the idea of him bringing her here as part of a job, but that didn't stop her snapping a photo of her seat and sending it to Melinda with the caption: *Finally living the high life! VIP area at a monster truck rally – talk about classy, lol!*

Keeping her phone to hand, she waited for a moment to see if Melinda would respond, but as Owen returned with a Pimm's for her and beer for himself (the only one, he promised, and the drive back was hours away, plenty of time for it to pass through his system), she decided to tuck her phone away and settle down. As she did, the public-address system announced that the show was about to start.

Hattie was forced to admit she'd enjoyed herself more than she could have imagined had someone suggested a show like this to her. Of course, it was as loud and brash as she'd expected it to be, with blasting music, revving engines, fireworks, pyrotechnics and general whooping and hollering, but it was good-natured, mindless fun. She'd never been a petrolhead, but even she'd been impressed by some of the outlandish vehicles and highly advanced driving skills they'd seen. Owen was clearly having the time of his life and, as Hattie hadn't seen him make a single note throughout the event, she had to wonder how on earth he was planning to write about it.

As the last show ended and the crowds began to file out of the stadium, Hattie and Owen joined them, slowly making their way back to his car. The air had cooled and, despite the heat of so many people around them, Hattie pulled her cardigan back on. Owen reached for her hand again. All afternoon he'd been tactile and attentive – little touches, affectionate looks – but he'd been modest and respectful when it came to anything more. Perhaps he was mindful of where they'd been sitting and his professional appearance. But when they got back to the car and locked themselves in, he reached for her and pressed his lips urgently to hers.

'God, I've been so desperate to do that,' he said.

'Well…' Hattie began slowly with a dreamy look that she couldn't hide, 'maybe you ought to think about that next time you decide to take me on a free trip.'

He gave her a sheepish smile.

She smiled now too. 'I suppose I ought to be thankful you didn't take me on a death knock,' she added.

'You looked it up?' he asked.

'Yes, and it sounds just as horrible as the name would suggest.'

'Luckily I don't have to do them these days. Monster trucks are about as traumatic as it gets.'

'I'm glad.' It was her turn to instigate a kiss, and when they finished she raised a questioning eyebrow. 'Tell me honestly – was the beer festival a press freebie too?'

'You think this was a freebie?'

Hattie's eyebrows went even higher and he laughed. 'OK, caught red-handed. But the beer festival wasn't – I just really like beer enough to pay for that.'

Hattie giggled and she let him kiss her again. Then he leaned back in his seat and studied her. 'You are *so* cute. Lance did me a solid when he introduced me to you.'

Mentioning Lance brought back to mind life at Gillypuddle and the responsibilities that were waiting back there for Hattie.

'I should probably get back,' she said, wanting anything but a trip back to the depressing interior of Sweet Briar Farm. For a while, she'd been able to forget all the worries that existed within those walls, but now she was reminded forcefully of them.

'Do you have to?' Owen asked. 'We're having so much fun.'

'Don't you have to get back too? Your journey is a lot longer than mine.'

'Yeah, you're probably right,' he said, his reluctance obvious in his voice. He turned the key to start the car engine. 'But maybe it wouldn't add too much time to the journey home if we stopped off somewhere for supper?' he added. 'I don't know when I'll be able to see you again and I'd like to make the most of today.'

'You make it sound as if you're going off to war,' she said with a laugh. 'Your schedule can't be *that* bad, surely?'

'More like unpredictable,' he said. 'That's the real problem.'

As they pulled out of the car park, Hattie remembered to check her phone. Melinda had replied, expressing insane jealousy over Hattie's temporary VIP status but rather less approval of the monster-truck aspect of the date. What she actually said was that if a man took her to see trucks she'd push him under one of them. Even Stu her mechanic husband knew better than that.

There were also a couple of missed calls from the landline at Sweet Briar. Hattie dialled the number to see what Jo wanted, although she probably wanted nothing more than to show her annoyance at Hattie's absence and to demand to know what time she would be back. Hattie wasn't in the mood for it, but she supposed that she had to call and find out anyway.

There was no answer. Perhaps Jo was out seeing to the donkeys or hens. The thought of it made Hattie feel a little guilty that she wasn't there to help, even though she didn't want to feel that way. And, she reasoned to herself, trying to feel better, it wasn't as if Jo was a stranger to managing alone – she had done it all before Hattie had moved in.

'Do you mind if we skip that supper and head straight back?' she asked, putting her phone away. She looked up as Owen glanced briefly at her before turning back to the road. He looked disappointed but he didn't argue.

'Sorry,' she added. 'But I've been missing for most of the day and I think Jo might need me.'

'It's a weekend,' he said. 'Everyone deserves a weekend off.'

'You don't always; you were working today.'

'You don't ever as far as I can tell.'

'Yes, but the donkeys don't know it's the weekend, do they? They still need to be cared for, no matter what day it is.'

'Can I speak plainly?' he asked after a pause. He didn't wait for a reply. 'I think Jo relies too heavily on you. Just because that place is her life she can't expect it to be the same for you.'

'It's kind of what I signed up for.'

'Nobody should have to sign up for that. She can't ask that much of you or anyone else. You need other things in your life or you'll burn out.'

'Other things like you?' Hattie asked with a half-smile.

'Like anything,' he said. But then he added: 'Yeah. Maybe a bit like me.'

Hattie let out a sigh. 'You're right – I know. It's just hard to make her see it.'

'But you have to; you have to sit her down and talk to her. If she keeps pushing you, she won't have you at all.'

'I know that too, but right now isn't the best time to have that discussion.'

'Maybe not, but I don't think any time will be the right one.'

'I guess not.'

'Do it anyway, whether the time is right or not. If you don't, I guarantee something will snap.'

Hattie looked out at the landscape flashing by, the fields of wheat and rapeseed burnished by the low sun. Maybe Owen was right. No – Owen *was* right. But a conversation like that wasn't going to be easy to have with Jo, who barely wanted to talk on a good day and certainly wasn't very interested these days. And with so much else to worry about, it only felt like an unwelcome and selfish distraction from what really mattered. She'd talk to Jo, but the time had to be right, and now wasn't it.

Chapter Twenty-Two

Owen had left her with a long, lingering kiss. She could have sat in the car for hours with him, making out like some teenager in an American movie, but she couldn't know if Jo was watching, just as she had been from her window before they'd left, and the idea was more than a little off-putting. So she bid him a reluctant goodbye with a final kiss, and he promised to call her the minute he knew when he was next free.

Once he'd driven away, she looked for Jo. The donkeys were already fastened in for the night, as were the chickens. Around this time of the evening the kitchen would usually still be full of the smells of whatever Jo had cooked for dinner, but tonight it was cold and clean and didn't smell of anything but old stone and waxed wood. Hattie even went into Jo's room, concerned that maybe Jo had taken to her bed feeling unwell. But there was no sign of her there either. Hattie checked the garage and the car was gone. It seemed the farm had been deserted and, knowing Jo as she did, that fact in itself was a cause for concern. Annoyingly, Jo's absolute refusal to own a mobile meant that Hattie couldn't phone her either. If it had been anyone willing to embrace the twenty-first century, it was possible that Hattie would have been able to locate them with a lot less fuss and worry.

Puzzled and concerned, but really unable to do very much but wait around and hope that Jo would return soon, perhaps having ventured out for some kind of emergency supplies or something, Hattie decided to call Seth to see how Norbert was. Seth had given her and Jo his private number so they could call any time if they were worried. Hopefully, there would be good news and Norbert would be improving.

It rang for a while and Hattie was just about to give up when Seth finally answered.

'Hi, Seth, it's Hattie. I hope you don't mind me calling at this time on a Saturday, but I was wondering how Norbert was.'

'Ah,' Seth said, and the tone of his voice in that short exclamation was enough to tell Hattie that she needed to brace herself. 'Um… Hattie, it's not good news, I'm afraid.'

'What's happened?'

'We've had the scan results back early. Norbert has a sizeable tumour – it's the cause of his problems.'

'A tumour? Like cancer?' Hattie asked incredulously. Somehow the idea that an animal could get cancer just like a human had simply never occurred to her, and the idea of that being the root of Norbert's malady had similarly never crossed her mind.

'I'm afraid so. It's really quite advanced. Jo's here with him now. She says she tried to contact you but…'

'I couldn't hear my phone,' Hattie said. 'I was somewhere a bit noisy. Jo's with him now? What does that mean? She's locked up the farm and everything and she'd never leave…'

There was only one possible reason that Jo would lock everything up at the farm and venture out, and Hattie knew now that she should have realised that straight away. 'Oh no…'

'We have to do the kindest thing for him,' Seth said.

Surely Seth didn't mean what Hattie thought he meant? Surely he wasn't talking about the unthinkable? 'Can't he be cured? There must be something you can do. Isn't there some operation to get rid of it? Chemo? My dad always—'

'I'm sorry,' Seth said gently. 'Listen, this is not a conversation to have over the phone. If you want to come down now I'll talk you through everything.'

'But I can't get to you!' Hattie said, blinking back tears. 'Jo's taken the car! You're not doing it today, are you?'

'I wouldn't usually do this sort of thing on a weekend but he really is suffering and I don't see any point in delaying it.'

'But you can't!'

'It's not fair to keep him hanging on as he is,' Seth said, his voice full of sympathy.

'But I need to see him! You can't do it just like that – I have to see him first!'

'I'm sorry but it's for the best. Is there no way you can get here? I can wait for you before I do anything.'

'I...' Hattie hurriedly weighed up her options. Maybe Owen would come back for her? But it didn't seem like the sort of thing she could ask of him at this stage in their relationship. Her dad? Yes, her dad would do it; he'd come.

'Please wait,' she said. 'I'll get there as soon as I can.'

Hattie ended the call and dialled her parents' house. Her dad picked up on the third ring, as if the universe had willed him to be there in her hour of need.

'Oh Dad...' she sobbed. 'I need you!'

Seth had left the gate open so that Hattie and her dad could drive straight into the section of his practice that housed the inpatients. Jo came out of the hospital block as Hattie headed towards it. She showed no sign of emotion – for all anyone could tell she'd been checking on the contents of the barn at Sweet Briar. Only the fact that she was here at all gave any clue to how upset she was.

Hattie's dad had wanted to come in with her but she'd sent him away. This was her task and she needed to do it; she needed to be there for Jo whatever happened, and Jo wasn't going to open up if Nigel was there. Hattie needed her to feel free to talk if she was going to be able to support her. So he'd driven away with the instruction to call him if she needed him again. Hattie was certain she wouldn't because she imagined that she'd be travelling back to the farm with Jo once Norbert had…

She didn't want to think about that because it hurt too much, even though she knew that very soon she'd have to.

'How is he?' she asked, running to Jo.

'Didn't Seth tell you?'

'Well, yes, but…'

Jo shook her head. 'I'll see you back at the farm.'

Hattie stared at her. 'You're not staying?'

Had they already done it? But Seth had promised to wait. Why would Jo leave now?

'I've said goodbye. The others need me now; I've got to keep an eye on Blue especially in case he gets distressed.'

'So you're not going to be with him when…?'

Jo looked at her and Hattie wished she could work out what was going on behind those eyes. She shook her head.

'That's for you to do,' she said before walking to her car.

Hattie stared after her. What did that mean? Was Jo doing her a kindness or leaving her with a dirty job? Was she asking Hattie to do this because she couldn't bear to see Norbert's end, or because she thought Hattie would want to be the one to see him through his last moments?

Jo was already through the gates and away and it looked as though Hattie was going to have to work all that out for herself. But whatever Jo's reasons, Hattie had also been handed the solemn responsibility of being with Norbert as Seth sent him to sleep. She wasn't sure now whether she could do it. She could barely find the strength to go in and see him now that she was here, let alone watch as Seth did what he needed to do.

As she was thinking of all this, Seth came out. He looked calm but weary. Hattie wondered whether he ever got used to making this decision about an animal, even though he must be called on to make it time and time again.

'Are you alright?' he asked.

Hattie nodded, unable to speak. Seeing him now reminded her of why they were there and for a moment she was overwhelmed.

'Jo said you'd want to do this,' he continued gently. 'She said you'd been closest to him since you arrived. But if you're not sure then you don't have to—'

'Yes,' Hattie said, forcing her tears back. 'I have, I suppose, but…'

'I understand if it's too much for you.'

'I don't know,' Hattie said, breaking down again. 'I'd feel terrible leaving him alone to face this, but I don't know if I'm strong enough… Jo should have done it; she'd have been better… not so pathetic.'

'It's no weakness if you can't; it just shows that you care, that's all. It shows that you loved him.'

'I do!' Hattie said, hating the way Seth was talking about Norbert in the past tense already. 'And you're sure there's nothing that can be done? There has to be something. If it's just money I can ask my dad—'

'It's not money,' Seth said. 'He's suffering, and no amount of money can change that. If it was just money I'd come to some arrangement with you. I would never see you struggle; what you both do up there for these animals is too important to make it about money.'

Hattie nodded. What Seth had said struck a chord with her, and she realised that, despite his denial, he just had to be the mysterious donor who'd given them enough money to pay his bill. He'd have maybe thought that, having not paid their bill, they'd be too scared to ask for his help – and he would always want to put the animals first. The idea only made her sadder, though, and she began to cry again, tears soaking into her shirt. She was still wearing her date clothes and she could still smell Owen's cologne on them. How could a day turn like this in a matter of seconds?

'We should go in,' Seth said. 'The nurse is waiting for us.'

Hattie followed him in. Norbert looked older and sadder than she'd ever seen him, and he barely registered her arrival. She didn't want to admit that Seth might be right about this but she had to trust him that leaving Norbert like this wasn't kind.

'Oh…!' she cried, and went to him, pressing her face to the teddy-bear fur of his neck and weeping into it.

'Hattie…' Seth said gently, his hand on her arm to guide her away. 'It's time.'

'Goodnight, Norbert,' she whispered into the donkey's ear. 'Don't be scared – I'm here…'

But then she looked into his old eyes and she couldn't do it; she couldn't stay.

'I'm sorry,' she whimpered, and then ran, sobbing, out into the evening.

*

Seth found her sitting on an ornamental bench in the quadrangle of the surgery's Victorian gardens.

'Did you do it?' she asked, trying to steady her voice as she looked at a wall of climbing roses, wild and wayward, laden with pink blooms on thorny branches. Her dad would have been itching to prune them.

'Yes.' He sat next to her on the bench. 'He wouldn't have known anything of it, if that helps.'

'It does. I'm sorry.'

'For what?'

'For being so pathetic. I feel just awful that I didn't stay with him.'

'It doesn't matter.'

'It does. Jo trusted me to do that much and I let her down.'

'You're being too hard on yourself. There aren't many who'd be able to stay – trust me; I see it all the time.'

'You won't tell Jo, will you?'

'Not if you'd rather I didn't.'

'Thanks.' Hattie looked up at him. 'How do you do your job? Doesn't it break your heart every time you have to do this?'

'Of course it does. I trained as a vet to save animals at all costs. But sometimes that's not the kindest thing, and doing the kindest thing is more important. Sometimes ending their pain is saving them. I don't like it, but shying away from what needs to be done doesn't help the animal in question, so I just have to take my responsibility seriously and do it.'

'I couldn't do it.'

'I know. But that doesn't make you weaker than me, if that's what you're thinking. It makes you sweet and compassionate. It makes you the kind of person the world should have more of.'

At another time, maybe Hattie would have been comforted, or even flattered by his words. But now, they only caused her to sob again.

'Hey…' Seth put an arm around her and she buried her face in his shirt. When she finally managed to stop crying she sat back.

'Oh God!' she said, mortified. 'I got mascara all over your shirt! I'm so sorry!'

'It's just a shirt,' he said. And he smiled with such tenderness that Hattie couldn't help what she did next.

Chapter Twenty-Three

Every time she thought about it she burned with shame. Seth had been so sweet, so chivalrous and understanding, and they had both excused it as an extreme reaction to the stress of the day. But in the back of her mind, Hattie couldn't ignore the voice that was telling her that even though her actions had been spontaneous and utterly inappropriate, she'd kissed Seth and she'd liked it. No – she'd *loved* it. Not only that, and no matter what they'd said, Seth had kissed her back. He'd gently pushed her away eventually, but there had been a delay, one charged moment before he had, something she was finding hard to put out of her mind.

Hattie had made her excuses and raced out, her emotions pulled in directions that she didn't think were even possible. Although she'd told her dad she wouldn't need him, she phoned him as she started to walk home and her own personal knight had come out to rescue her. Anything to get away from Seth and what she'd done. At least she'd been able to explain away her strange mood on what had happened to Norbert so her dad hadn't asked too many questions.

He'd dropped her at the farmhouse. There was a low light on in the kitchen, but when Hattie went in, Jo was nowhere to be seen. She went out to the stables. Her hunch had been right; Jo was fussing Blue there.

'Is it done?' Jo asked, not turning as Hattie approached.

'Yes.' It was all Hattie could say without her voice cracking.

Jo gave a solemn nod but said no more on it.

Hattie stood at her side and reached to scrub behind Blue's ear. He barely reacted and it was obvious he wasn't himself. They were silent while Hattie composed herself.

'Will Blue be alright?' she asked finally.

'He's lost without his mate,' Jo said. She looked at Hattie now. 'I don't know. Donkeys get attached… they don't do well when they're separated. Might be as well to take Blue down and let him have a sniff at Norbert so he understands what's happened.'

Hattie stared at her. 'You mean, let him see Norbert… well… as he is now?'

'I'll see what Seth says,' Jo replied quietly. 'See whether he thinks it's a good idea or not.'

Hattie looked back at Blue, silent and sad. It seemed a strange thing to do, but she was sure that Jo and Seth knew better than her. She just hoped Blue would be OK. Jo was putting a brave face on things, but Hattie knew that Norbert's loss had been hard – to lose another donkey would be utterly devastating and Jo had already told her about how vulnerable a distressed donkey could be.

Jo went to talk to Seth the next morning. Hattie agreed to stay at the farm until she got back but decided she'd then go and visit her parents, whose support and counsel she desperately needed.

It might have been healthy and sensible for Hattie to talk to Seth at some point too. But as the days went by, she was unable to bring herself to contact him or mention it, and it seemed from his silence on the matter that neither could he. Not that she'd been given much of an opportunity to talk to him because Jo's obsession with the donkeys had gone into overdrive since they'd lost Norbert. Determined that they weren't going to lose another one, she monitored them more closely and rigorously than ever. When Hattie went to feed them Jo had to check every morsel before it hit the trough; when they came down at night, she looked each one carefully over, and she did the same in the mornings before they went up to the field. She rang Seth for advice almost every day about some imagined sign or symptom she thought she'd seen.

She'd finally got her way over the visitors too, and Hattie's dreams of opening Sweet Briar up to the public had been shelved. Jo had decided that nobody could be trusted around her precious donkeys and there was no telling what danger random members of the public wandering across the farm might put them in. Hattie had begged for the donation page at least to stay live, though with little pay-off for anyone giving money, she expected the income from that to dry up soon enough anyway.

Blue suffered – as they'd expected without his best friend to keep him company – but he improved steadily as time went on. As for the others, they were as well as ever and probably the best cared for donkeys in Dorset. Hattie imagined there were millionaires with lower relative living standards.

The extra attention on the donkeys had provided Jo with even more of an excuse to ignore any other conversation with Hattie too. They worked more closely than they had ever done and yet, Hattie had never felt more distant from her. And at the end of the day when Hattie finally fell into bed, if Jo was still having her nightmares, Hattie was too exhausted to let them wake her.

It was Friday of the week after Norbert had been put to sleep. Jo had gone out but hadn't told Hattie where, so Hattie had taken her lunchtime sandwiches out into the orchard where she could watch the hens cluck and fuss and wonder how much easier life might be if she were a chicken and the only thing she had to worry about was getting to the feed before everyone else did. Jo had plated up the leftovers of a beef joint the night before and Hattie was currently enjoying a slice on a hunk of home-baked bread along with a tub of salad. It was the most peaceful she'd felt all week and she was hopeful that the weeks to come would calm down a little so she could feel like this more often.

She'd called Owen briefly on the Sunday after they'd lost Norbert and told him all about it, and while he'd made sympathetic noises, Hattie could tell that he didn't really understand why she was upset. He hadn't used the phrase: *It's only a donkey*, but Hattie could tell that it was running through his mind. She supposed that if you didn't live with them and see them every day then perhaps it was hard to understand how close you became to them.

He'd told her that he still didn't know when he'd next be free and that his editor had given him a stack of leads a mile high to follow up on, but as soon as he could see a free day in his schedule she'd be the first to know. Hattie couldn't deny that it had left her feeling a little more than second best, and she wondered if this was the life anyone who chose a journalist had to endure. Long term, though she really liked Owen, she could see a day when never knowing when she might see him next would get a little wearing. It hadn't helped that Seth was still on her mind too, and the guilt she'd felt as she talked to Owen made her squirm. In a way, she also had to admit that perhaps it was her own guilt that was making her judge him so harshly. If ever she needed to see him to remind herself that he was the one she wanted and that she shouldn't be having the thoughts she was having about another man, it was now.

They hadn't spoken since, though he had sent her a text every night to see how she was. Her answers were polite and not very meaningful, because how could she encapsulate all that she felt and all that she wanted to say in a text?

Hattie had phoned Melinda too, and although they hadn't been able to meet up, Melinda had been her patient and supportive best. But Hattie, as much as she loved Melinda and trusted the advice that came from her friend's heart, couldn't even bring herself to tell her what had happened with Seth in the quadrangle that day. She didn't know how she was supposed to talk to anyone about it, though she desperately wanted to.

She'd just finished her salad and set the tub to one side when she heard voices in the courtyard. Quickly gathering up the rest of her lunch, she headed out to see who it was.

Jo had returned, and she was cradling a polished wooden box. She was talking to Seth. Either they'd come to the farm together for some reason, or else Jo had arrived by coincidence at the same time as he had arrived. Hattie wondered if Jo had called him yet again about some fictional symptom in one of the donkeys, but this time the complaint must have had enough of a ring of truth to bring him out. If she had, she hadn't told Hattie, but then, she rarely told her anything these days. Their relationship felt like a marriage that had broken down but the couple had been forced to continue sharing the house; only Hattie and Jo didn't even have the wedding day to recall with fondness.

As Seth and Jo became aware of her presence they both turned to her.

'Norbert,' Jo said, nodding at the box. 'I've brought him home.'

'Oh,' Hattie said, unable to think of any other response. Once again, the sight of Seth brought so many emotions, and the sight of Norbert's remains a thousand others to confuse them even further.

'Hi, Seth…' Hattie said, feeling the need to somehow acknowledge him, although the sudden tension in the air was doing a very good job of that. Was he feeling as confused as she was? Did he long to reach out and touch her as she did him? Had he even thought of her at all after their kiss? Jo looked from one to the other, suddenly astute. Had she guessed, or was that in Hattie's imagination? If she had, what must she think of Hattie when she'd watched Owen come and go?

'Tea?' Jo said, looking at Seth.

'That would be wonderful,' Seth said.

Jo glanced at Hattie. 'There'll be plenty in the pot for you too if you've got nothing better to do.'

Hattie followed them both into the kitchen, warm sunlight swapped for cool shade. While Jo busied herself making the tea, Hattie sat across the table from Seth and reflected on how hard it was to see him sitting there and to know that she mustn't even breathe a word of what she really wanted to do. It wasn't fair, and she had to put it out of her mind – it wasn't fair to Seth, it wasn't fair to Owen and it wasn't fair to Hattie herself. She liked Owen and he liked her, and he'd got there first and that was that.

'Want me to do anything?' Hattie asked.

'Not especially,' Jo replied as she poured hot water into the teapot. 'Unless you want to get some fruit cake out of the pantry.' She turned to look at Seth. 'You'll eat some fruit cake, won't you?'

Seth seemed to jump at her voice, as if he'd been caught doing something he shouldn't, and as he replied that, yes, he'd love some cake, Hattie could have sworn she saw him look her way with guilt in his expression. Puzzled, unreasonably hopeful for things that couldn't and perhaps shouldn't be, she went to the pantry to find the tin full of homemade cake.

When she came back, Jo was already at the table talking to Seth with the teapot surreally sitting next to Norbert in front of them.

'Cake,' Hattie said, hovering with the tin and not quite sure where to put it down. Somehow, the idea of placing fruit cake next to Norbert on the table didn't seem right. But Jo took it from her and prised it unceremoniously open before dropping it down in front of Seth.

'Thank you,' Seth said, peering into the tin. 'This looks good.'

Hattie got the impression that he couldn't have cared less about the cake. She couldn't say why, but it just felt as if he was going through the motions when it came to the pleasantries.

'It is,' Jo said, and in any other situation Hattie would have laughed at her reply. 'So, what can we do for you, Seth?' she continued. 'Is it about the bill because Hattie's got that in hand…' Jo glanced at her. 'At least she's told me she has.'

'I have,' Hattie said. 'The money's being processed and it will be in our bank account in a few days.'

'As soon as it clears I'll send you a cheque, Seth,' Jo said.

'Although,' Hattie added, 'it won't be enough to pay everything we owe, as you know. It'll only clear the balance we had before Norbert…'

Hattie stopped as she saw Jo stare at her. What had she…?

Shit! She'd given away that she'd known how much Seth's debt was. Would Jo put two and two together? Was that why her features were even darker than usual?

'Oh, I'm quite sure it will clear the bill,' Seth said, helping himself to tea from the pot. 'And if it doesn't, as I've always said, I can wait.'

Hattie stared at him. Why would he have said that? Surely there would be more to pay now that they had Norbert's extra treatment to add on. 'Hopefully more donations will come in over time and we'll be able to pay whatever we owe whenever we owe it,' she said, trying to collect herself.

'Bearing in mind that we're always going to need veterinary care, we're never going to be clear,' Jo reminded her.

'But if we continue to get steady donations…' Hattie insisted.

Jo pursed her lips, her gaze going to Norbert's box.

'Would you like me to put that somewhere safe?' Hattie asked.

'I'll do it later,' Jo said. She turned back to Seth. 'So if it's not about the bill, what is it?'

'I was passing. I thought I'd look in and see how Blue's bearing up.'

Jo gave him as close to a smile as Hattie had ever seen. 'That's good of you,' she said. 'I could take you up there after we've had our tea.'

'Or I could do it,' Hattie put in, but then blushed uncontrollably as Jo gave her another flinty stare worthy of her surname. 'I mean,' she added, 'if you were busy, because I know you have a lot to do.'

'That's very kind of you,' Seth said to Hattie.

'I could even take you right now,' she added.

Jo dragged a spare mug across the table and filled it up from the pot. 'Let him drink his tea and then I'll take him.'

Hattie fell silent. She looked at the cake tin on the table and wished she could ram it onto Jo's stupid miserable head. This was the first real opportunity she'd had to talk to Seth and Jo was taking that away. They might not even discuss what happened between them – maybe Seth wouldn't want to – but they certainly would never discuss it left in Jo's hands. It might have been an arrogant thought, but Hattie half wondered whether Seth's 'just passing' visit might not have been an excuse to come and talk to her about it. Perhaps he felt the need to clear the air as much as she did. She could only hope that it mattered that much to him.

Later, just after Seth had drained his cup and proclaimed himself full of cake, Jo led him outside. Hattie wasn't going to be beaten, though. If they were going up to the top field, then she was going with them.

She wasn't sure how it was going to help her cause, but sitting in the kitchen waiting for them to come back was even more useless. Jo marched off, not waiting to see who was keeping up with her, as was her way, so she didn't even notice Hattie following behind. In a second Hattie had caught up with Seth and they walked together in Jo's wake. He didn't waste any time taking advantage of the situation, and Hattie's suspicions were confirmed.

'I wanted to talk to you about…' His voice was almost a whisper.

'What happened?' Hattie whispered back.

'It was very unprofessional of me—'

'God, it was completely my fault – you did nothing wrong.'

'Well, I'm glad to hear that you think so, but I'm afraid I did. The thing is… I can't stop thinking about it, and as you sort of began proceedings I thought… maybe you might feel the same way…'

Hattie's heart began to race.

'I've been thinking about it too,' she said. 'I just feel so bad for what I did.'

'You feel bad?'

'I shouldn't have done it.'

'But…'

'And your girlfriend?' Hattie asked.

'Eugenie? You know about her?'

'Seth, we live in Gillypuddle. Everyone knows about her.'

'Oh,' Seth said, looking deflated. If he'd been clinging to any hope that he might have some semblance of a private life now that he lived in Dorset's nosiest village, it looked as if it had just been well and truly prised from his grasp. 'That's over now.'

'It's just… I heard… So it's over?'

'Have people been gossiping about me?' he asked incredulously.

'Like I said, this is Gillypuddle…'

'Right. It doesn't matter. Eugenie and I are definitely over and she's gone to Washington. There are no hard feelings and I don't still love her if that's what you're worried about.'

'That's good,' Hattie replied, uncertain what else she was expected to say.

'So what do you think?' he asked. 'About us? I know I'm a little older than you, but that doesn't mean anything, right? At least, it doesn't to me if it doesn't to you.'

Hattie shook her head. 'We shouldn't have done it. I mean, *I* shouldn't have done it. I don't know why I did but it was wrong.'

'So… what did it mean for you, then?' Seth asked. 'Why did you do it?'

'It was just… like I said at the time…' she said miserably, realising now that she couldn't take this any further without being completely honest about Owen, and not even knowing how she felt about Owen or Seth. Who did she want? Was this worth jeopardising what she might have with Owen one day? If Owen could see her here now, how would that make him feel? It wasn't fair and he didn't deserve it. 'It was the moment. I needed something and you…'

She looked away. His step quickened and he no longer seemed as if he wanted to walk with her.

'I'm seeing someone,' she blurted out. 'I'm not proud of it and you must think I have no morals whatsoever, but when it comes to it, no matter how I feel about you, that's the facts about it.'

'Well,' he said coldly. 'Thank you for putting me straight.'

Jo turned to look and for the first time noticed Hattie.

'It doesn't need all three of us,' she called, and Hattie knew exactly which of the three was the expendable one. She turned around and walked back the way she'd come. She'd waited almost a week to talk to Seth and, in the end, he'd reached out, and this, apparently, was the best she could do once the opportunity had come. *Must try harder, Hattie,* she thought, and gave herself a D minus.

Hattie watched Seth's car pull away from the farm. He hadn't sought her out to say goodbye, but she supposed she couldn't expect him to. She'd led him on – at least that was how it must have looked – and though she could never have foreseen these consequences, she could imagine why he might be angry and hurt. Truly, though, even as she'd kissed him and afterwards longed for him, she'd never imagined that he might feel the same even if she'd wished it. She had to let it go now, though, and she had to remember that Owen was the one she wanted and needed. Owen was closer to her age, they had great chemistry, and, most importantly, had been there first. Maybe if she could talk to him it would remind her of why she'd made that choice, why that choice was the right and proper one, and she'd feel better about it all.

Her thoughts were interrupted by the sound of Jo's voice behind her.

'Who told you about my account with the vet?'

Hattie spun to face her. 'What do you mean?'

'Has he been discussing it with you?'

'Of course not!'

'Then how do you know so much?'

'I don't!'

'It didn't sound that way in the kitchen.'

Hattie hesitated. 'I suppose you must have told me at some point. I don't remember now.'

'I'd know if I'd done that and I haven't. You've been snooping around.'

'Of course I haven't—'

'Don't lie to me! I don't know who's told you but keep your nose out of my affairs!'

'But they're *our* affairs; that's the thing. I live here too!'

'As a guest at my pleasure.'

'So you make all your guests work ridiculous hours?' Hattie fired back.

'I've told you before, if you don't like it you can go.'

'Maybe I will! Let's see how you manage then!'

Jo stared at her. 'I've managed before and I'd do it again,' she said coldly. 'So if that's how you feel, then pack.'

'You're sacking me?' Hattie asked incredulously.

'I'm relieving you of your obligations. It's up to you whether you leave or not.'

Jo turned to go inside.

'So that's it?' Hattie called after her. 'After all I've done for you, that's it?'

Jo didn't look round.

'No wonder everyone in the village hates you and now I know they're right!' Hattie shouted, tears filling her eyes.

Jo simply let the door close behind her as she went into the house.

It was then that her phone rang. She pulled it out of her pocket to see Owen's name flash up. Talk about timing.

'Hey…' she sniffed. 'How are you?'

'I'm good. But you sound… Are you OK? I know you were cut up about that donkey thing—'

'I'm fine. Something and nothing. What I'm really interested in right now is when you're coming to take me away from all this.'

'All what?'

'It's a saying, isn't it?'

'I've no idea.'

Hattie shook her head. 'Never mind. Please say you're calling to tell me you're free.'

'Not as such. But… how would you feel about coming to London? To my offices?'

'Would I be allowed?'

'I could swing it; I'll just say we're doing a follow-up piece on your story.'

'For a *date*?' Hattie asked.

'There's something I want to show you.'

'Well, can you tell me over the phone?'

'I could but it's quite complicated and it's probably easier for you to see it.'

'Can you send me a photo of whatever it is?' Hattie asked, her recent argument with Jo leaving her feeling unreasonably impatient with just about everyone, including poor Owen, who'd done nothing to deserve it. 'I really don't have time to come to London.'

'Well, it's in our archives so that's kind of hard to do…'

Hattie narrowed her eyes. 'You didn't…'

'I know you told me not to look but I couldn't leave it alone. Blame it on my journalism genes – if there's a question, I have to know the answer.'

'And you found the answer?' Hattie asked, forgetting that she was supposed to be annoyed with him.

'Yes.'

'Should I be worried?'

'About what I've found? Not unless you're planning to go out on a boat with her.'

Hattie's eyes widened. 'A boat?'

'Like I said, it's probably easier for you to see what I've found – there's quite a lot and you'd be able to draw your own conclusions from it. And then maybe afterwards we could grab dinner somewhere…?'

'Owen… I'm sorry, I can't come to London right now – there's just too much going on here.'

'You don't want to know about this stuff?' he asked incredulously.

'Well, yes, but…'

'Listen, don't worry about it. I'll come to you and tell you what I know.'

'When?'

'Um… let me get back to you on that, OK?'

'Right. I'll see you soon then.'

'You sure will,' Owen said with a smile in his voice.

Hattie ended the call and put her phone away. She had things to do in the house, though she hardly wanted to go in there now when she knew Jo was in there, but things that needed doing still needed doing whether they'd had an argument or not. And maybe it would be a chance to clear the air. Hattie wondered whether she ought to come clean about her dig into Jo's financial affairs and her motives for doing that. Maybe Jo would understand that Hattie was only doing it with the best interests of Sweet Briar at heart. Maybe they could start again if Hattie could explain and apologise. And who knew, maybe Jo would apologise – there had to be a first time for everything, she thought wryly. For her part, Hattie was sick of being at loggerheads with Jo; she just wanted them to get along as they had done when Hattie had first arrived at the farm and she'd thrown herself into the work and getting to know the donkeys. Those days seemed so far in her past now, even though she'd only been there for a couple of months.

With a heavy feeling, Hattie went inside. Jo was in the kitchen scrubbing the cooker top. By now, Hattie would have expected to see some evidence of what they'd be eating for their evening meal as Jo began to prepare the ingredients – maybe grinding her own beef or marinating some chicken – but today the worktops were clear. Perhaps they were having something quick and easy if Jo wasn't in the mood to cook – and if she wasn't, Hattie could hardly blame her because she herself was barely in the mood to do anything.

'Haven't you gone yet?' Jo asked without looking up.

Hattie stopped in the doorway. 'You're serious?'

Jo looked up now and held her in an icy stare. 'Why would I say it if I wasn't? If you need time to arrange transport then you can have until the end of the day.'

'But what about the donkeys?'

'I can manage.'

'But Jo—'

'End of today.'

Hattie continued to stare as Jo returned to her cleaning. But then she marched across the kitchen and out towards the stairs, letting the door slam behind her, and thumped up to her room. It made her sound like an unreasonable teenager but Hattie didn't care. If Jo wanted her gone then she'd go, leave her wallowing in her own misery. Clearly she enjoyed being hated by everyone, so why wouldn't Hattie want to oblige by hating her too?

Chapter Twenty-Four

Nigel came to collect her from the farm later that day. Hattie had wondered how long it would take him to issue *the I told you so* speech but it hadn't happened so far and she had to be surprised about that, because she'd been back at home for a full twelve hours now. Her parents had asked what had happened and Hattie had told them – most of it anyway. She'd put her belongings back into her bedroom cupboards, had a long bath, changed into crisp cotton pyjamas and it was like she'd never been away.

It was actually Rhonda who broached the subject of Jo with Hattie over supper the following evening.

'Dreadful woman,' she said as she placed a bowl of nachos and cheese on the table. 'I could never understand what possessed you to go there, let alone stay there as long as you did. If you were that desperate to do good then you could have done something medical – your father could have helped you there.'

'I didn't want to study, though.'

'You wouldn't have had to study much – you could have done something voluntary with a little training.'

'I suppose I'll have to get another job,' Hattie said, ignoring her mum's not-so-subtle steering. Maybe Hattie would consider volunteering for someone like St John Ambulance or the Red Cross, but she didn't want to do that at the detriment of earning her own living. She was twenty-six now – no age to be living on her parents' retirement income with them. Do that and she might as well sit back and wait for her own old age to speed towards her.

'I'll bet Lance would have you,' Rhonda said.

'Doesn't he still have Phyllis working for him?'

'I think he's so fed up with her breaking things he'd sack her in a heartbeat if you wanted to work there,' Rhonda said briskly.

'That hardly seems fair,' Hattie replied.

'I don't think you'll find much else in Gillypuddle.'

'There must be something else. There are more businesses than just the Willow Tree.'

'Not many,' Rhonda reminded her as she took a seat at the table.

'I suppose I'll have to look further afield then,' Hattie said. 'Where's Dad? Isn't he joining us?'

'He's gone to see Rupert about his leg; he said to start without him and he'd be back shortly.'

Hattie reached for a handful of nachos, piled high with gooey cheese and guacamole, and began to pick at it. If she hadn't been so tempted to meddle when she'd first arrived at Sweet Briar then right now she'd be sharing something solid and homemade at the scrubbed wooden table of Jo's kitchen. Did Hattie feel regret for that? Was she sorry that she'd had to leave? Would she miss it? All day she'd been too busy to ask herself the question but now it came to her and she didn't know how she felt. She'd miss the donkeys, that was for sure, going into the stable in the morning and seeing their silly faces, as pleased to see her as if they were a bunch of waggy-tailed dogs. And she'd miss that view from her window of the bay stretching before her.

Would she miss Jo? Maybe she'd miss aspects of her life with Jo rather than Jo herself, who had proved, in the end, to be as truculent as everyone had warned her she would be. Mostly, though, the thing that stung was that Hattie felt like a failure again, just as she had when she'd first come home from Paris. Here she was again, back in the family home, unable to make it on her own, Charlotte's smile from every wall of the house reminding her that Charlotte was the good girl, the one who was meant to be someone, while Hattie was stuck in this twilight zone where she couldn't seem to make it no matter what she did. Maybe her dad had been right all along – maybe she should have trained for some kind of meaningful vocation. But maybe it was too late for any of that now.

There was one thing that her new-found freedom meant – she could go and visit Owen in London now. Tomorrow, when she'd pulled herself together and her mood might be brighter, she'd call him to arrange it.

Owen met her at Waterloo station. He didn't have time to drive and fetch her but that was OK; she'd needed a change of scenery and a bit of adventure, and although it was only a train journey, Hattie had enjoyed it. It made her realise just how isolated and insular life was at Sweet Briar, because sitting on the train to Waterloo had made her feel like some kind of intrepid explorer, which was ironic when she considered that she'd certainly been no stranger to travel in the past. Owen was waiting at the gates to the platform looking relaxed and handsome in casual trousers and a stonewashed denim jacket.

'Good journey?' he asked.

Hattie nodded. She waited for him to kiss her but he didn't; he simply nodded for her to follow him to the station exit. 'I'll get us a cab – it'll be quicker than the Tube.'

'Oh, right,' Hattie replied, wondering why he seemed a little preoccupied. He was cheerful enough but not quite himself. Perhaps it was down to the fact that she was visiting on a work day and he had that on his mind. Yes, that was it – she was seeing too much into it because she was feeling fragile right now.

The cab journey to Owen's offices reminded her of how exciting the world could be too. She'd been so settled at Sweet Briar that she'd forgotten how much she loved the bustle of a big city. Perhaps she'd been too settled; perhaps a few more years would have seen her become as dour and antisocial as Jo.

And it would do her good to engage with the big bad world of the capital – who knew, maybe it would shake things up enough that she'd start to see a future outside Gillypuddle again? There were no jobs in her village, but there were thousands in London. She'd be close to Owen and she'd be far away from Jo and Seth – all good things in her book. She'd be sad to leave Melinda and her parents behind again, and all the other amazing people in Gillypuddle, but it wasn't like they'd cease to exist the moment she left, and she could go back to visit far more easily from here than she could from Paris.

'You know,' she said to Owen as they passed the Houses of Parliament, 'maybe I *could* get used to living in London.'

'Wow… that's a big and sudden statement. It would be a far cry from Gillypuddle.'

'Yes, but don't forget I lived that high life in Paris,' Hattie said with a grin.

'So you did,' he said, smiling. 'But I thought you wanted to leave all that behind and settle in the country doing *things that matter*…'

'Well, I can do things that matter just as easily in the city, can't I? Besides, all that do-gooding just ends in disaster, doesn't it?'

'I'm sure it doesn't always. Maybe next time don't set up home with a sociopath and things might turn out differently.'

Hattie tried to smile but Owen's joke had hit a nerve. It had done nothing to make her feel any better, nor had it alleviated any of the lingering unease she felt about leaving Jo to continue living alone as she had done before. Even though she'd been forced to go, and even though Jo absolutely deserved what she got, Hattie didn't want to think of her feeling abandoned and she still couldn't quite believe that this was what Jo really wanted. After all, she'd invited Hattie to live with her in the first place because she'd needed live-in help, but Hattie had always suspected that it was also because she was lonely, even if she didn't consciously realise that herself.

Half an hour later saw them step into the reception of the *Daily Voice*. It had a surprisingly unassuming frontage, and if Hattie hadn't known what the building housed, it would have taken some detective work to find out. The reception consisted of a long desk with a young man and a young woman sitting side by side. They both nodded to Owen as he led Hattie across the marble-floored atrium and they regarded her with not a little curiosity.

'Probably amazed I've persuaded a girl to be seen in public with me,' Owen joked in a low voice as he noticed it too.

'I thought maybe it was because I wasn't supposed to be here.'

'You're with me – that's OK.' He pressed to call the lift and the doors opened. They stepped in and Owen selected the floor.

'Are we going to your office?' Hattie asked.

'We're going to the archive,' he said.

'I'm not going to see your office at all?'

'What do you want to see that for? There's nothing interesting going on in there.'

'But isn't that where all the magic happens?'

Owen grinned and tapped the side of his head. '*This* is where all the magic happens.'

A moment later the lift came to a halt and they got out. This floor wasn't as Hattie might have imagined at all. Somehow, the idea of an archive brought to mind dusty libraries filled with ancient tomes, but this was a bright, white corridor with open-plan offices lining either side. Owen walked through with Hattie. Some people sitting at the desks looked up briefly but didn't seem all that interested. Some were talking on phones and others were poring over scanned newspaper articles on large screens.

'This one will do,' Owen said. He led Hattie to an empty desk and pulled a spare seat over for her to sit while he took the main one himself and logged on to the computer sitting there. A moment later he gave a grunt of satisfaction and turned the screen for Hattie to see better.

'There… that story, top left.'

As she read the scanned page, Hattie pulled in a sharp breath.

Owen had found Jenny.

Chapter Twenty-Five

Owen had taken Hattie straight to lunch after showing her his discovery. They were sitting now in a little Greek place – furnished with rough wooden tables and painted the traditional brilliant blue and white of the many *tavernas* Hattie had seen while holidaying in Santorini with her parents as a girl. It brought to mind kind owners who fussed over her and Charlotte and brought them sweet treats to finish their meals, declaring them on the house for such beautiful children.

'It's so sad,' Hattie said as she pierced a plump black olive with a cocktail stick and popped it into her mouth. 'It certainly explains why she's the way she is.'

'Does it?' Owen asked. 'I wouldn't go that far.'

'But it must be so hard for her.'

'You're being too nice about it. Remember what she did to you.'

'I know, but…'

Owen shook his head and helped himself to an olive from the dish they were sharing. 'I knew there was something the moment I saw her; I just didn't know what. It must have happened when I first started to work at the *Voice* so I wouldn't have taken as much notice as I would have done if the story had broken now. I'm telling you, if something like this happened now I'd be all over it.'

'Do you think I should go and see her?' Hattie asked.

'And do what?'

'Talk to her about it – tell her it's OK.'

'She killed her sister!'

'She didn't – she was cleared! Her sister died and that's different. Owen…' Hattie took a deep breath. 'My sister died too. So I know how it feels and I could help her.'

Owen looked up, shock in his features. 'God, I'm sorry; I didn't know that. If I'd known I never would have shown you the story—'

'It was a long time ago. I'm not telling you because I want sympathy or I want you to feel bad about what you did; I'm telling you because it means Jo and me have something huge in common and if I can make her see that, I can patch things up with her.'

'I get that, but you really want to help her after all she's done? Surely you're ready to throw in the towel by now? She's made it clear what she wants.'

'I have to try.'

'She'll throw it back in your face like she always does.'

'I want to try.'

'Hattie – I love your compassion and kindness and God knows the world needs more people like you…' Owen said, and Hattie was reminded of what Seth had said just before she'd kissed him. For a split second the scene replayed in her head and she shook it away, filled with guilt and shame. 'But some people are just lost causes and that's that. How do you know she wasn't exactly like she is now when her sister was alive? How do you know it was her sister's death that changed things?'

'Because *my* sister's death changed things, that's why. When you lose someone that close to you, it changes you. My life is split into two parts – with Charlotte and after Charlotte – and I'm a different girl in this half than I was before. I wasn't even there when my sister died but I still felt the trauma of the way she passed. Jo witnessed her sister's death – that's got to have hit hard.'

'Some would say she caused it,' Owen put in but Hattie ignored it.

The conversation was halted as a waiter came to the table with their starters. He placed them down with a flourish and left them again. Perhaps the interruption had been timely because Hattie could feel herself getting frustrated with Owen's attitude. He sounded like everyone in Gillypuddle did when it came to Jo. Was Hattie's intuition really that off? Could she really be so wrong about Jo? She wondered if anyone there knew about Jenny. It seemed unlikely, because if they had it wouldn't have taken long to get around the village. Would it help people to understand her more if they *did* know? What if Hattie told people? Would Jo be shown forgiveness or would it make things worse?

Owen's mobile rang. He snatched it from his jacket pocket, looked at the display and then shoved it back again.

'Aren't you going to answer that?' Hattie asked.

'It can wait.'

'What if it's a major scoop and you miss out on the Reporting Today reporter of the year award or something?'

Owen laughed. 'I'm pretty sure you just made that award up. It's not, and I can call them back later.'

Hattie shrugged, and though something about his reaction didn't sit right with her, she had bigger things to think about.

'So what should I do?' she asked.

'About what?' Owen cut into his stuffed vine leaves.

'About Jo!'

Owen put down his knife and fork and looked steadily at Hattie. 'I think you should leave it alone. She doesn't want you; she doesn't want anyone. So stop beating yourself up about her and get on with the rest of your life.'

Hattie found her dad pruning the roses. It was his favourite variety – Bathsheba – and he'd always loved them for their scent. Hattie could hardly bear it as the smell brought Seth's lips back to her mind. God, she wished she could stop thinking about that man, especially now after the way they'd left things. The irony was, she didn't even need to see him now that she no longer worked for Jo, but part of her still wanted to, no matter how painful the meeting might be. Many times she'd thought about somehow engineering it, passing close to the practice in the hopes of bumping into him on the way in or out, hanging around the Willow Tree more often so that she might be there if he called for a take-out coffee... It was silly, of course, because he'd most likely avoid any kind of actual conversation with her anyway and that might make her even sadder about everything.

Nigel had stopped and listened, his head glistening with perspiration under the midday sun, as Hattie explained to him what she'd learned about Jo and the dilemma of whether she ought to go and tell her what she knew in the hopes it might draw Jo into some kind of meaningful dialogue, get her to finally open up.

'I honestly don't see it changing anything,' he said in a measured tone once Hattie had finished. 'I always tended to find that if people didn't seek help in the first instance then they probably wouldn't ever. The first step to any rehabilitation is that the patient has to want it. I'm sorry to say that it looks to me like she doesn't.'

Hattie was thoughtful for a moment. Her dad had the experience and he was probably right. *Her dad had the experience...*

'What if you went to see her?' she said brightly as the solution occurred to her.

'Would this be as a concerned member of the local community, annoyed father or as GP? Because I'm sorry to say, I'm not particularly concerned, I am an annoyed father – though you won't let me go and give her a piece of my mind for sacking you – and I'm no longer a GP.'

'What about the new GP?'

'She's not going to bowl up there for no reason. Unless Jo makes an appointment to see her, the new GP can't do anything... Hattie, you know this,' he concluded, his voice showing the first signs of waning patience. 'Why are you persisting with this woman? As far as I can see she's done you a huge favour – now you can get on and do something proper with your life.'

'Ignore all that – what about as one human being to another? Doesn't that at least bother you – that she's suffering up there alone?'

'Who's to say she's suffering? She seems perfectly content to me and, don't forget, she could have company any time she wanted. She had you and she threw you out. I wouldn't worry yourself; she's probably advertising for a new assistant as we speak.'

'But, Dad...' Hattie began, and then her shoulders slumped in defeat. Nigel retrieved the secateurs from his basket and turned back to the rose bush.

'If you ask me, it ought to be a case of once bitten twice shy. You enlisted my help to interfere in her affairs before and look how that ended. Forget about it, Hattie. Spend your time and energy on more useful pursuits.'

Hattie wanted to say something more, but what? Her dad had thrown himself back into his pruning and it seemed that the matter – for him at least – was now closed. Maybe he was right – maybe she ought to just leave well alone now. Jo had made her choice and she'd chosen to reject help or support. Hattie had to admit that her dad was probably right about Jo wanting help anyway; she wasn't asking for it and who was Hattie to decide that she needed it anyway? Maybe she'd received counselling in the past, maybe she'd got it just after her sister's death. Maybe the Jo everyone saw now *was* the fixed Jo, not the broken one. Maybe solitude was just in her nature. It didn't matter now, because it looked as if Hattie was just going to have to let it be.

'Watch out!' Lance cried.

Hattie sidestepped a large puddle of what might be hot chocolate, though it was hard to tell. Lance came rushing over to the front door of the Willow Tree with a mop and bucket.

'Run, Hattie, run for your life!' he cried.

'Phyllis is on shift?' Hattie asked with a wry smile.

'Oh, yes,' he said, mopping up the spillage. 'What gave it away?'

'The unchecked panic in your eyes?'

'That and the fact there's more food up the walls and on the floor than there is on customers' plates?'

'Yes,' Hattie laughed. 'I don't suppose you've got time to make me a latte then?'

'Always, my love. Find a seat; I'll be right over.'

'There's no rush,' Hattie called as he scooted off with the mop and bucket. 'I'm waiting for Melinda to get here anyway.'

'Right, my love,' Lance said. 'I'll get the toys out for her little ones.'

'Thanks, Lance.'

Phyllis came out of the kitchen and smiled at Hattie.

'Hello, Dottie.'

'Hi, Phyllis,' Hattie said. 'Still enjoying your job?'

'Oh, I love it here!' Phyllis gushed. 'Gets me out of the house every now and again, otherwise it's just me and the walls and they're no company at all, are they?'

'I don't imagine they are,' Hattie agreed. Phyllis rushed off to answer a yell from Lance in the back. She might be driving the proprietors of the Willow Tree insane, but Hattie could never deliberately try to take Phyllis's job away from her. She didn't really think that Lance and Mark would want to do that either – everyone in Gillypuddle was very fond of her, despite her clumsiness.

Hattie looked up at the sudden commotion at the door. It involved a lot of high-pitched squealing and crying. Melinda was coming in and her kids weren't happy. Hattie couldn't remember the last time she'd seen them acting up like that, but they were bickering like a bag of ferrets and Melinda looked frazzled.

'Look… there's your Auntie Hattie,' she said wearily. Sunshine and Ocean ran to Hattie's table, pushing and shoving each other as they went. Rain followed, looking as if she'd been crying, while Daffodil wailed in her pushchair.

'Welcome to my world,' Melinda said as she dropped into a chair, looking rather less perky than usual.

'Morning sickness kicked in?' Hattie asked.

'With a vengeance. I should imagine that means another boy – never had a bit of it with any of the girls.'

'I'll bet Stu's happy.'

'It'll certainly help to even the score,' Melinda said with a quick grin.

'I'm going to the counter to order,' Hattie said. 'Want me to get something for you?'

'Just a green tea,' she said. Hattie raised a questioning brow.

'Only thing that won't have me throwing up,' Melinda added in reply.

Hattie went to the counter, where Phyllis served her. God only knew whether they'd get what they'd asked for. As Hattie sat down, Lance came over with lollipops for the kids.

'Can we go to the toy corner?' Ocean asked.

'As long as you don't try to murder each other you can go to the moon for me,' Melinda said.

'Bad day?' Lance asked with a sympathetic grimace.

'I've had better. See if you can get them to be more civilised than I can today.'

'Kids are always more civilised with other people than they are with their mothers,' Lance said airily. 'Come on, kids.' He looked at Daffodil in her pushchair. 'Someone's tired.'

Melinda looked and heaved a sigh of relief as she noted Daffodil's eyes starting to close. 'Thank the heavens and all the angels,' she said. 'It's a shame they don't all nap during the day now. Why can't they make every day a school day – there ought to be a law about it.'

Hattie laughed. 'When would you cuddle and love them if they were at school all the time?'

'When they're asleep.'

Lance took the rest of the kids to play and Melinda looked at Hattie.

'So, you're back in the land of the living?'

'Yes – looks like it.'

'And that's the end of your adventure up on the hill?'

'Seems that way. Jo's made it pretty clear she's had enough of me.'

'Witch,' Melinda said savagely.

Hattie sighed. 'Maybe I deserved it.'

Melinda clicked her tongue on the roof of her mouth as if she might disagree but said nothing. Hattie had been over all the details of who said and did what with her on the phone, and Melinda had already made her feelings clear on where the blame lay. The only thing Hattie had kept back was what she'd learned about Jo's sister, Jenny. It wasn't that she didn't trust Melinda to keep it quiet, but she didn't think she could cope with her disapproval. What if she viewed the event in just the same way as Owen and her dad had? As if it was somehow karma, something Jo had deserved, and something that didn't deserve anyone's pity?

Phyllis came over with two cups and Hattie was happy to see that they looked close to what they'd ordered, though Phyllis didn't manage to get away without spilling a drop of Melinda's tea.

'Oops!' she said with a raspy chuckle.

'I ought to demand a refund,' Melinda said in a low voice when she'd gone. 'There's hardly any tea left in here.'

'She's doing her best,' Hattie said.

'I wish you'd got the job here.'

'I realise now it wouldn't have solved anything. I came home looking for a direction and I'm still doing that. It wouldn't have mattered whether I'd found a job here or at Sweet Briar.'

'The kids are sad that they can't go up there anymore to see the donkeys.'

'To be honest, I actually think that's one thing Jo will miss about closing the gates to Sweet Briar again. Even though she'd never say it, I think she quite liked seeing your kids.'

'I got that impression too,' Melinda agreed. 'So, what are you going to do now?'

'I don't know.' Hattie took a sip of her latte. Lance had definitely not made this one and she wondered whether Melinda might have a point about refunds after all because she'd tasted better. 'When I went to see Owen I did half wonder about heading to London.'

'To see if the streets really are paved with gold, Dick Whittington?'

'To see if there's a future there. I don't know... I have fashion experience – sort of. And I quite enjoyed it. Maybe my CV would get me something in the industry in London.'

'If you want to work in fashion what's the point of going to London? You said Alphonse was desperate to have you back and you loved Paris. Why not give him a call? Not that I want you to run away to Paris again, of course, but if you're thinking of leaving Gillypuddle anyway, it makes more sense than London does.'

'But Owen is in London.'

'Ah! So this might be going in a serious direction?'

'It might be... Mel... if I tell you something you absolutely have to keep it to yourself. You cannot breathe a word of it to anyone.'

'You know I won't, but if it's that important perhaps you shouldn't tell me. Under torture – or gas and air – there's no telling what secrets I might let out.'

'It's just...' Hattie lowered her voice. Perhaps she shouldn't even be having this conversation here, of all places, where Owen's second cousin Lance might hear it, but Hattie would explode if she didn't tell someone and Melinda was as good a confidante as she could think of. 'Seth and I... we sort of... well, we had a moment...'

'What?' Melinda's eyes were wide. 'But I thought you were madly in love with Owen!'

'Not madly in love. I mean, I like him...'

'Please tell me this hasn't turned into a huge mess.'

'Seth asked me out. At least, that's what I think he was trying to do. He's not actually very good at it – though in the circumstances I don't blame him. I had to tell him about Owen.'

'Why would you do that?'

'It wouldn't have been right to lie about it, would it? What if he'd found out about Owen from somewhere else? Here, for instance? You know how gossip travels in this village.'

'I suppose so. Does that mean you have to choose?'

'I think Seth sort of made the choice for me. Once I'd told him he wanted nothing else to do with me.'

'But if you'd been free to choose in your own time, would you have gone for Seth or Owen?'

Hattie was silent for a moment as she took another sip of her latte, instantly wishing that she hadn't bothered.

'I don't know,' she said finally. 'That's the problem, I wish I did. I really like Owen, but when I'm with him I think about Seth. In fact, I think about Seth all the time and it makes me feel so guilty because I think Owen likes me a lot. But then I have a great time with Owen – really great; he doesn't feel like hard work like Seth sometimes does.'

'Wow,' Melinda said, 'you really have made a mess.'

'Thanks. What do you think I should do?'

'I don't think you should be taking my advice for a start. There's only one voice to listen to and it's in here…' Melinda placed a hand on her chest. 'You have to listen to your heart, even though I admit that sounds like a corny lyric from a nineties power ballad.'

'But what if my heart doesn't even know the right answer?'

'Then…' Melinda shrugged. 'I hear Paris is nice at this time of the year…'

Hattie gave her a rueful smile. 'The old running-away tactic. Admittedly it's served me well in the past.'

'Your dad's happy that you're not living up at Sweet Briar now anyway. I take it he's not started the education offensive yet, otherwise you'd have been ranting about it by now.'

'I think he's given up on that. I think he's finally accepted that Charlotte was the achiever of the family. Me… I just seem to drift.'

'You don't! You stuck months up there on the hill with Medusa and nobody else would have done. You raised money for her even when she didn't want it—'

'Hardly – I'm convinced the only big donation we had was from Seth to pay his own bill so I wouldn't call that successful fundraising.'

'*And* you brought people to her door…' Melinda continued with a frown that told Hattie to shut up and listen, 'to make her life better, even though she didn't realise that's what they were doing. I wouldn't call that underachieving. You achieve, Hattie. You just have a different idea of what needs achieving than Charlotte would have done.'

Hattie's smile was warm and grateful. 'What would I do without you?'

'Oh, I'm sure you'd be just fine,' Melinda said with a shrug. They looked up as Lance sauntered past the table with a tray full of sandwiches.

'I'm coming back your way in a minute,' he said. 'I want to know all about how Hattie is getting on with my cousin. Mark wants to know if we have to buy hats yet…'

Hattie looked at Melinda. That was all she needed right now.

Chapter Twenty-Six

Hattie woke shortly after four in the morning. For a moment she was vaguely surprised to find herself not in the dingy bedroom at Sweet Briar, but back in the clean and cosy surroundings of her bedroom at home. She'd dreamt about Charlotte again, the third time that week, and her dreams hadn't been that frequent for a long time. While she'd accepted long ago that life went on, Hattie still missed her sister, and though mostly it was the constant dull ache of absence, sometimes she felt the pain more keenly. Perhaps learning of Jo's loss had lent her own a new potency because, every now and again, she'd stop and remember and the sorrow would steal her breath.

Their circumstances were so different, their lives and personalities, what drove them and what they craved, and yet Hattie felt that she was connected to Jo, whether Jo or she liked it or not, by this one defining fact of their lives. There was this one thing that bound them and made them the same. Hattie didn't have all the facts about Jenny's death – what Owen had managed to find out touched only on the basics of the accident and subsequent inquest that had cleared Jo of wrongdoing – but it was clear that it had been very different from the way in which Hattie had lost Charlotte. Still, Hattie couldn't shake the continuing urge to reach out to Jo, despite what reception she might expect, despite how everyone warned her not to. She didn't even know why she should feel this way; she only knew that she did.

'You can't help everyone,' Nigel said with a tone of exasperation as they sat at breakfast a few hours later. 'I keep telling you this. You can't help someone who doesn't want to be helped.'

'Your dad has a point,' Rhonda put in.

'You needed help after Charlotte; you had counselling…' Hattie began, but instantly clammed up at the look on both her parents' faces.

'That was different,' Rhonda said briskly.

'I know, but…'

'I don't want to hear it again,' Nigel said. 'It's none of our business.'

'She lives in Gillypuddle – of course it's our business!' Hattie insisted. 'She's one of us!'

'She's made it quite clear that she doesn't want to be,' Rhonda said. 'I'm afraid I have to agree with your father.'

'She won't talk to me if I go up.' Hattie reached for the teapot as Rhonda put a plate of toast in front of her.

Rhonda rolled her eyes. 'Then don't go up.'

Hattie poured some tea, tight-lipped now. What was the point in talking to her parents about this? They didn't want her to make peace with Jo anyway – they'd much rather things stayed this way so they could persuade her to pursue a career that was far more agreeable to them. Maybe Hattie was a perpetual meddler, maybe it was an aspect of her personality she couldn't control, but she couldn't leave things with Jo as they were; she had to try and let her know that there was someone out there who understood. If nothing else, it was what Charlotte would have wanted her to do.

*

It was mid-morning when Hattie started out on the walk to Sweet Briar Farm. Summer was breathing its last and the breeze that chased her up the cliff path was fresher than it had been of late. It felt like a long time since she'd first made this walk to see if Jo would give her a job; so much had happened in such a short space of time.

Hattie's hand shook as she pushed open the gates to the courtyard. It was silly to feel this much trepidation and yet she couldn't help it. How would Jo receive her? Would she even listen, or would Hattie be sent away before she'd even opened her mouth? And there was a moment, too, when Hattie wondered if she wasn't quite mad for even attempting this.

The courtyard was silent and still. Hattie could just make out the grumbling clucks of the hens in the orchard and the distant bray of a donkey carrying down from their field up the hill. She missed the donkeys – at least that was one warm welcome she might get if she went up to see them. She called out for Jo.

'Hello! Jo, it's me… Hattie!'

There was no reply.

It was easiest to check the orchard first, then maybe the field, and then the house last, because going into the house really did feel like trespassing when she wasn't expected or invited, and Hattie would only do that if she really had to. Hattie went through and crossed into the shadow of the neat rows of plum trees. Jo wasn't at the chicken coop and she wasn't tending to the trees. Hattie checked the vegetable garden. The soil was freshly turned in places and she guessed that Jo had harvested something, but she couldn't tell what. Despite the signs of recent activity, there was no Jo here either.

Hattie was about to make her way up to the top field when she heard a scream from the open window of Jo's bedroom. She looked at her watch. Jo was sleeping now? It hardly seemed likely at this time of the day – Jo was always up at the crack of dawn – but there was no mistaking the sound of her recurring nightmare; Hattie had heard it often enough.

She hesitated. To go up there would undoubtedly be breaking some sacred unwritten Jo rule. Not to mention that, technically, it was probably close to breaking and entering (though she could perhaps scratch the breaking bit if Jo's old habit of never locking her doors still persisted). Jo could easily ring the police and she'd be within her rights to. But then there was another, lesser scream, but no less rattling, and Hattie blew out a breath.

'For God's sake!'

She went inside. The usual order of Jo's kitchen had given way to unwashed pots piled in the sink and leftover food still sitting on plates by the bin. A ginger tabby cat sat amongst the debris, eyeing Hattie with some suspicion.

A cat? Clearly, Jo hadn't finished taking in waifs and strays when she'd rescued her chickens. The cat looked a bit older than a kitten. Hattie wondered how Jo was managing to keep it away from the hens – perhaps she wasn't letting it out of the house, though Hattie couldn't imagine that.

Leaving the cat as a puzzle for another day, Hattie moved through the house and up to Jo's room. For a moment she waited, ear pressed against the wood of the door. All was quiet now.

And then the bedroom door was flung open, knocking Hattie off balance and back towards the stairs, almost sending her down them. Jo stormed out in a nightie, hair wild and face full of fury, a length of pipe held menacingly above her head.

'You!' she cried. 'You nearly gave me a heart attack – I thought you were robbing me! What do you mean by coming here? Didn't you understand what I said last time?'

'I know, I just want to talk—'

'No more talking! All you ever did was talk and I was stupid enough to listen!'

'But—'

'Get out! I don't want you here!'

'But, Jo—'

'Are you deaf? I said—'

'I know about Jenny!' Hattie cried.

Jo lowered her arm, her face now white. 'What did you say?'

'I know about Jenny,' Hattie repeated, her eyes darting to the length of pipe Jo was still holding and hoping that she'd never really planned to use it.

'My sister, Jenny…?' Jo asked.

Hattie nodded. 'I know it wasn't your fault.'

'Nobody said it was.'

'But I think you do. I think you blame yourself.'

'I was cleared.'

'I know.'

'Not my fault.'

'I know that too. It was an electrical fault on the boat. The fire… you couldn't have done anything about it. It said so on the inquest report – right? You were out at sea, you'd gone off course, it was dark…'

'We'd gone out in my uncle's boat,' Jo said slowly, her eyes looking at a spot in the past. 'He'd told us it needed checking over and I said I'd do it and we'd take it out.'

'And you checked it over?'

'I was too quick. It looked fine…'

'But there was a fault you hadn't seen?'

'She was supposed to be getting married. She was moving away… this was… a last trip on the boat – just me and her – for old times.'

'What happened?'

'I survived.'

'It was five years ago, Jo. You can't spend your life feeling bad about it. You can't really believe that you ought to be punished forever because you made it out and she didn't?'

Jo stared into space. 'I couldn't help her... it was dark... the water, the fire... the boat was sinking and I held onto something. I couldn't see Jenny... I thought she'd got something to hold onto too...'

'It's not your fault.'

Jo snapped back to the room and scowled at Hattie. 'How would you know? You can't possibly understand.'

'I lost my sister,' Hattie said.

Jo looked at her now, as if she'd never seen her before.

'She died when I was thirteen,' Hattie continued.

'That doesn't change anything,' Jo said, but Hattie could tell that it did.

'It was sudden,' Hattie said. 'I couldn't do anything to save her – none of us could.'

'Was it your fault?'

'No, but—'

'Then it's not the same at all. I should have checked that engine!' Jo prodded herself in the chest. 'I should have found that fault! It's because of me she died. It's because of me—'

'You couldn't have known!'

'What would you know? What would anyone else know? Everyone blamed me and they were right! Nobody would talk to me, nobody wanted to know me... I spent so long trying to make it right with my family but they didn't want to know and they were right to shun me – it was my fault!'

'*Everyone* blamed you?'

'Why do you think I came here?' Jo asked. 'Why do you think I came to a place where nobody knows me, where nobody wants to know me? They don't want to know me here just the same as they didn't at home, but I was OK, because at least nobody here knew *what* I'd done… but then you come today and act like you know everything and all you've done it make it worse.'

'I had no idea…' Hattie said in a small voice.

'I should never have invited you into my home,' Jo said savagely. 'I should have managed, like I always did.'

'You don't look like someone who's managing now,' Hattie said. 'And I don't think you were before. I want to help, Jo, I can—'

'I don't want your help! Why can't you understand that I don't want you meddling, bringing outsiders in! I don't want to be reminded of Jenny. Why did you have to come back? Why couldn't you have left it alone?'

'I didn't mean to make things worse. I found out and I thought… well, I thought we both went through the same thing and if I'd had someone else when my sister died then… maybe things would have been different for me too.'

'You're saying the way I live is wrong?'

'Of course not!' Hattie let out a sigh. 'I just want to help.'

'Who told you?' Jo asked quietly. 'How did you find out?'

'Owen.'

Jo shook her head, a silent question.

'My boyfriend.'

'The journalist,' Jo said stiffly. 'I might have known.'

'He wasn't trying to cause trouble.'

'It's his business to cause trouble.'

'Owen's not like that.'

'Owen is *exactly* like that. These people thrive on the misery of others. They wouldn't leave me alone… knocking on my door, hounding my parents, making everything worse!'

The death knock, Hattie thought vaguely; the thing that Owen had hated doing as a new journalist. *Owen's not like the rest*, she thought. She had to believe that, but… hadn't there been just a little too much glee in his discovery of Jo's past? Hadn't there been just a little less compassion than there ought to have been?

'So…' Jo said, cutting into Hattie's thoughts, 'is that it? Have you said what you came to say?'

'No… I mean, yes, but—'

'Then you'll kindly leave.'

'Can I at least go and see the donkeys?'

'No. You had your chance.'

Hattie's eyes swam with tears. She sniffed them back and, for the first time, noticed that Jo was crying too. Hattie had wanted to breach the defences of Jo's heart, to reach inside and bring the real Jo out into the sun, but not like this. What had she done?

'I'm sorry…' she said.

'I don't need your sorry,' Jo replied, rubbing a hand over her eyes. 'I don't want to hear it; I just want to be left in peace – is that too much to ask?'

Hattie shook her head. 'No,' she said in a tiny voice. She turned to take the stairs, feeling Jo's eyes on her back.

Well, Hattie, you've played a blinder, once again.

Chapter Twenty-Seven

Hattie dialled Owen's number. When it went to the answering service, she took a breath to leave a message but then hung up. What was the point? How could she say the things that filled her head to a machine? Pulling out the business card he'd given to her, she dialled the number for his desk phone.

'Hello?'

It was a man's voice but not Owen's.

'Oh… is Owen there?'

'Not right now, he's out on a story. Can I help you?'

She began to pace up and down the bedroom floor. She really needed to speak to him about Jo. She wanted to know if he could find out anything else, anything that might help – though she had no idea how anything would help now.

'No… thank you,' she said, frustrated but ultimately stuck.

'He'll probably be back briefly around five if you wanted to try him then. Only for an hour, though; I know he's got arrangements to pick someone up from the airport shortly afterwards.'

'Oh,' Hattie replied, suddenly thrown. The airport? It wasn't as if he had to tell her every detail of his life or what he did on a daily basis when he was in London, but picking someone up from the airport would be quite significant, wouldn't it? You picked people up from the airport when they were important to you, didn't you? He'd never mentioned anyone significant flying in. 'Who?'

'I really don't think it's my place to say.'

'Of course,' Hattie said. 'You don't know me from Adam. It's just… well, I'm his girlfriend and I really need to speak to him so I was wondering how long he might be.'

'His girlfriend?' The man sounded confused. 'But aren't you on the flight right now?'

'No, I'm at home.'

'So you need me to tell him not to come to the airport? Hold on, let me leave a message on his desk…'

Hattie's mind raced as she tried to process what she'd just been told. What flight? What was going on? She heard the receiver being put down and footsteps, and then he came back.

'So, tell me again…'

Suddenly filled with panic as she worked it out, Hattie ended the call. Owen was picking up a girlfriend from the airport, but it wasn't her. How stupid was she? How could she have missed the signs? Why on earth would she think that someone as charming and handsome as Owen would be available? God, she was an idiot! Of course Owen had a girlfriend waiting for him at the airport. He probably had one in every town he visited.

Her mobile rang and her blood boiled as she saw his name flash up. He must have just seen he'd missed her call.

'Hey,' he said breezily as she picked up. 'Sorry; I was just doing some piece about the new Japanese wood-carving collection at the British Museum, and I was stuck with the curator – couldn't get to you, didn't want to seem rude or anything, but I did see your call come through. Did you want me for anything in particular or just to tell me how sexy I am?'

'I don't suppose you have time to speak to me right now, do you?' Hattie asked coldly. 'I imagine traffic will be bad on the way to the airport at this time of the day.'

There was a moment's silence on the line.

'Who told you?' he said finally.

'I have absolutely no idea, but I think he's definitely more confused than either of us.'

'Hattie, let me explain—'

'Seriously? You're even going to give this a go? Come on then, I can't wait to hear it.'

'Neeve is… well, it's complicated. She lives in Dublin—'

'Oh, so that makes it alright? She doesn't live in England so… what? You have an open relationship? You're allowed to date other people as long as they don't get in the way when she comes home? Is this why you didn't always have weekends free?'

'I'm not getting this across very well. I'm trying to break up with her. I've wanted to break it off ever since you and me started dating but… well, the timing's always off.'

'Well, it's off now alright!'

'You don't understand – she needs careful handling.'

'And I don't? I can be handled any damn way you like?'

'No, Hattie… please… I promise I'll do it this weekend and then we can be together – properly.'

'How very kind of you,' Hattie replied in a voice dripping with sarcasm. 'I'll look forward to that.'

She heard Owen's exasperated sigh, and it did nothing to calm her temper. How dare he be exasperated with her! What sort of reaction had he been expecting when all this came out? Did he want her to be patient and understanding? Perhaps she would have been if he'd found the decency to be more honest with her in the first place. He might well have intended to finish things with this Neeve girl, but how could he expect Hattie to believe anything he said now?

'What do you want me to say?' he asked.

'How about sorry?'

'I'm sorry – you know I am.'

'And how about you follow that up with: I won't ever bother you again, Hattie?'

'That's it? You're dumping me?'

'I don't know what else you expected? Goodbye, Owen – have fun with whatever her name is.'

Hattie stabbed at the screen to end the call. First Jo and now this. Her day was getting better and better.

Hattie sat in her parents' garden listening to the birds going home to roost as the sun set over her dad's perfect rose bushes. Rhonda had been out with glasses of wine for them both and asked if Hattie was alright, and they'd talked for a while about this and that – about Melinda's pregnancy and Phyllis's latest disaster at the Willow Tree, about Rupert's leg and how long it was since his wife had died. Hattie didn't mention Owen to her mum. She didn't want to tell anyone about Owen because she felt too stupid, though she realised she'd have to tell people soon – especially Lance. She wondered whether Lance had known about this girlfriend tucked away in Dublin, but she'd known Lance a long time and was very fond of him, and she liked to think that he was very fond of her. She wanted to believe that he would never have tried to throw her and Owen together if he'd known. They were only second cousins anyway, and Lance had already said they rarely saw each other most years – perhaps they really weren't that close at all. One thing was for sure, it was going to make visiting the Willow Tree awkward for a while.

As the temperature dropped, Rhonda decided to go inside. She urged Hattie to do the same, but when Hattie told her that she'd rather stay out and make the most of the evening, Rhonda disappeared and returned a few moments later with a blanket, which she wrapped around Hattie's shoulders, along with the rest of the wine. Hattie gave her a grateful smile and watched as she went inside. She'd thought a lot about her parents lately and what they wanted from her, and about Charlotte. While she realised that they were never going to see eye to eye on her future, Hattie also realised that she was lucky to have them. It sounded, from what she'd said, as if Jo hadn't been so lucky. But then, if there had been any question of culpability in Charlotte's death, would her parents have done the same as Jo's? Hattie liked to think not, but she guessed she'd never know.

On reflection, it would have been healthier to talk to someone about Owen at least, because she was bottling up a lot of anger and hurt, and her mum really ought to have been that person. The worst of it was that she'd rejected Seth for someone who'd turned out to have less virtue in his whole body than Seth had in his little fingernail. Owen had said he'd been trying to break up with this girl – was that because he'd been caught or because he'd genuinely been trying to? Hattie recalled now the hurriedly rejected phone call in the Greek restaurant and guessed that might have been her. It didn't matter, because he shouldn't have been trying to break up with her while he was seeing Hattie; he should have done it before, and there was only his word that he'd ever intended to at all. Hattie didn't have much time for his word right now.

She gazed at the garden, bathed in golden light, and she hardly knew how she felt about anything right now; she only knew that she barely recognised her life at the moment. It was like leaving Paris all over again, only this time it felt far messier than a simple accident with some candles and dodgy curtain material.

But thinking of Paris made Hattie wonder whether perhaps Melinda had unwittingly hit on the solution after all. Maybe trying again in Paris wasn't such a bad idea. She still had connections there and it would be nice and distant – far away from Seth and Jo and Owen and the messes she'd made with all of them. Paris in the autumn… she'd always loved the riot of oranges and reds as the leaves fell and muffled the paving stones of the boulevards, and the sharp mornings that made her breath rise into the air like tiny clouds. She'd start the day with a strong coffee and a croissant from the patisserie just down the road from her flat, eating it on her balcony wrapped in a thick cardigan and listening to the sounds of the city. The thought of it sounded nice now, like a call to go home.

Hattie folded the blanket and took it inside with the empty wine glass and bottle. The sun was almost below the horizon now, mist settling on the fields beyond her parents' garden. It had brought her peace for a short while, but peace couldn't last forever. She needed to take action. Going to her bedroom, she picked up her phone from the bedside table and dialled.

'Alphonse…'

'Hattie? *Mon dieu!* It is Hattie!'

'Yes, it's me.' Hattie smiled. 'I just wondered… you remember you phoned me some weeks ago and asked if I would consider returning to Paris to work for you again?'

'Of course! But I have Colette.'

'I know and I wouldn't want to take Colette's job, but if you could perhaps see your way to… I don't know… finding another job that I could do…?'

'This surprises me!' Alphonse said.

'I suppose it would.'

'But why?'

'I'm ready to come back now, that's all.'

'You miss the little Paris sparkle, yes?'

'Yes,' Hattie said, laughing despite her misery. 'I miss the Paris sparkle. I could certainly do with some right now.'

'*Alors*... I will look at my books and I will let you know.'

'I'd love that,' Hattie said. 'Alphonse, if you don't have anything then I understand that. But maybe you might know somebody else who might want an assistant and you could put in a word for me?'

'Make you a gift for my rival?' Alphonse tutted loudly. 'Over my body!'

Hattie smiled. She could have corrected the phrase, but why would she want to ruin what was perfect despite its flaws?

'When will you come?' he asked.

Hattie sat on the bed and looked around at her room. She had brought few belongings back from Paris and had even fewer to transport back.

'As soon as I can,' she said. 'There's no point in hanging around here now.'

Chapter Twenty-Eight

'I didn't really want you to go,' Melinda said. 'I was only joking.'

'I know, but it actually makes a lot of sense,' Hattie said.

Stu was in the garden exerting a fair amount of crowd control on his family as they played on the swings, while Melinda entertained Hattie at their kitchen table.

'You look terrible, by the way,' Melinda added.

Hattie had slept fitfully, feeling impatient to move on now that she'd made up her mind, dreading breaking the news to her parents and having to tell them (some) of why she'd decided to leave Gillypuddle again.

'What an absolute bastard he turned out to be,' Melinda continued. Hattie had been there for fifteen minutes now and, since telling Melinda the whole story of everything that had happened and her recent decision to return to Paris, she had barely said two sentences – because Melinda was channelling her inner grump and using Hattie's misfortunes to complain about the world in general. Hattie guessed it was pregnancy hormones that had turned her friend from Mary Poppins to the Terminator, and she hoped it was only a temporary change, for poor Stu's sake.

'I don't know about that,' Hattie said. 'Maybe he *was* being genuine and just handled it badly. I must admit it's worn me out though.'

'You won't even be here to meet my new baby and it's all his fault!'

'Don't worry – I'll come home to visit when you've had your baby.'

'And you'll probably have to miss the christening. Does that man have any idea of the trouble he's caused? And what about Seth?' Melinda folded her arms. Beneath them the first tiny bump of her new pregnancy was just visible. Hattie couldn't deny that she was a little sad she wouldn't be around much for this new one again, or for any of Melinda's children for that matter – she'd become very fond of them over the summer months as she'd got to know them properly, as more than just a visitor who flew in and out for the odd day.

'What about Seth?' Hattie asked.

'Well, you're free now? Why on earth are you running off to Paris when he's right there?'

'I don't think that would work out,' Hattie said in a dull voice. 'I think maybe that ship has sailed, all things considered.'

'You told him the truth, which is more than Owen did for you,' Melinda insisted. 'I should think that puts you very firmly in the good books.'

'I told him the truth *after* I'd kissed him and let him think I was available,' Hattie reminded her.

'Technicalities,' Melinda said. 'You didn't go out with him and you didn't two-time him – that's what counts.'

'I'm not sure Seth would agree with you on that.' Hattie sighed. 'Look – it's just too messy. I'm ready for a clean break and I think it would be better all round.'

'Paris is hardly a clean break – you have history there, don't forget.'

'It's a different history; not nearly as complicated.'

Melinda huffed. Then her gaze went to the window and she leapt up from her chair and banged on the glass of the patio doors.

'Stu! Watch him!' she shouted. 'That swing is going way too high!'

Sitting down again, she fixed Hattie with a steely gaze.

'Remind me never to get on your wrong side while you're expecting,' Hattie said.

'Don't try to change the subject. I'm not happy about all this Paris business and I can't pretend I am.'

'I'm not sure I'm entirely happy if I'm honest about it,' Hattie said.

Melinda threw her hands into the air. 'Then why go?'

'I said – it's for the best.'

'For who?'

'For everyone.'

'For everyone or just for you? You want to know what I think?'

'I have a feeling you're going to tell me either way.'

'I think you're running scared because everything looks too big to sort out.'

'OK, yes, but I think everything *is* too big to sort out. What's more, it's mostly all my fault.'

'I hardly think so. You're not God, are you? Situations get spoiled just fine without your help. I mean, maybe you egg them on a bit but… you didn't make Owen a cheating pig, and you didn't make Jo's sister die in some horrible accident, and you didn't make her go mad with guilt, and you didn't make Seth all uptight just because you kissed him and then made yourself available in slightly the wrong order.' Melinda leapt up and rapped on the patio doors again. 'For God's sake, Stu! She's practically hanging off there!'

She sat down again and faced Hattie. But then the scowl lifted from her face and her lip began to tremble.

'Are you alright?' Hattie asked.

'Hormones,' Melinda said shortly. 'Oh, and you.'

'Me?'

'Yes – you're making me cry. There!'

'Why?'

'Because I don't want you to go to Paris, that's why. Paris can bloody well go swing for all I care!'

'I'm sorry,' Hattie said. 'But I've made up my mind and nothing is going to change it now.'

'Not even your best friend?'

Hattie gave her a sad smile. 'Sorry, Mel. Not even you.'

Her parents had taken the news that Hattie was headed back to Paris badly too – and they didn't have hormones to blame for their reaction. Rhonda had wept and asked when on earth her daughter was ever going to settle in one place, while her dad felt duty-bound to remind her that her last stay in Paris hadn't ended well and why did she think that this time would be any better? It was time to find a proper job, he said, rather than messing around with informal agreements with this or that person. The annoying thing was, Hattie could see his point, but her mind had been made up and there was little point in him trying to change it. Besides, Alphonse had been true to his word and had carved out a little job for her in his mini empire. It wasn't very glamorous – more or less a glorified clerk taking care of his admin, such as his admin ever was – and she suspected that the job had never really existed at all, but that Alphonse had created it out of the goodness of his heart to help her out. It wasn't as well paid as the one that Colette had inherited from her either, but it would be enough to begin with.

She'd booked her flights for the following weekend, which would give her time to wrap things up in Gillypuddle, including a goodbye for the people who meant the most to her. She'd been to see Rupert and had spent an evening with him and Armstrong, his ancient cat, which he seemed to enjoy very much, and she'd been to see other friends throughout the village, including Lance and Mark. Lance had heard from Owen that Hattie had dumped him, though Owen had pretended not to know why. Hattie thought that was silly because it should have been obvious to Owen that Hattie would tell Lance everything, so if it was an attempt to save face, it was a misguided one. Lance had apologised profusely when he'd heard the truth, sorry that he'd ever introduced them at all. Even though he'd heard Owen could be a ladies' man he'd never believed it to be true, and he was sorry for that too. Hattie told him not to feel bad and she kissed him on the cheek and told him that he and Mark were welcome to see her in Paris any time. He would, he said, if they could be certain Phyllis wouldn't try to man the café alone in their absence and accidentally burn it down.

She thought about going to see Seth, but in the end she didn't. By the end of the week the whole village knew that Hattie was leaving; Seth would have heard about it from someone and if he cared at all he'd have come to say goodbye. He didn't, and so Hattie took that as a fairly reliable sign of his feelings on the matter. There didn't seem any point in subjecting him to an awkward meeting that he probably didn't want. She couldn't deny that it stung, though. Maybe she'd never really meant as much to him as she'd imagined, and if he hated her for leading him on, maybe she deserved it.

It was Friday evening and she was packing the last of her clothes when the knock came at the door. Her parents had gone to play bridge with their friends in the neighbouring village, which they did on the last Friday of every month and nothing would ever change that, not even Hattie's imminent departure. But they'd promised to be home early so they could spend a few hours with her on her last evening in Gillypuddle. Hattie sensed some reluctance on her dad's part, but it was probably only frustration that he'd failed to make her see what he thought was folly in her decision to return to Paris.

As she placed the last shirt into her case, the sound of a fist on the front door echoed through the house. Hattie froze. It sounded aggressive, and she was in alone. She went to the window and looked out, her breath catching as she noticed Seth's car. Had he finally come to say something – anything – about her going? Would it be like one of those romantic movies where the hero rushes in at the last minute and begs the heroine not to leave because he loves her?

Hattie raced downstairs, her heart beating wildly, and flung open the door.

'I need your dad,' Seth said urgently.

Hattie's hope collapsed like a punctured airbed, but she had the presence of mind to maintain some semblance of calm in the face of her disappointment. She simultaneously longed for him and hated his guts right now, but she was in agreement with herself on one thing – it would have been better if he hadn't come if this was the best he could do.

'He's not here. I can give him a message when he gets back or you can try his mobile, the number's—'

'What do you make of this?' Seth shoved a sheet of paper at Hattie. On it was a letter, written by hand. She'd seen that writing before, and it didn't take her long to confirm her suspicions when she read the sign-off at the end.

'Rehome the donkeys?' Hattie stared at Seth, all thoughts of how much she loathed and detested him for not kissing her right there on the doorstep forgotten. 'Why?'

'Your guess is as good as mine.'

Hattie looked at the letter again and read it carefully, unable to believe the contents.

'I thought you might have more of an idea than me,' Seth added. 'After all, you know her better than anyone else in Gillypuddle.'

'Maybe, but don't forget that she threw me out,' Hattie said, choosing not to add *twice* to the end of her sentence. As far as she knew, Seth was unaware of Hattie's second attempt to make peace with Jo, when she'd tried to get her to open up about her sister.

'What about the bit at the end?' Seth asked. '*If you see Hattie, tell her I'm sorry for everything...*'

'I don't know. I guess she realises she gave me a hard time?'

'She wouldn't part with those donkeys for the world – you know that as well as I do.'

'Then why write you a letter to say that's what she wants you to do?'

'Because she knows I'll go up there... Listen, she posted it through the door after surgery hours. Any other Friday night I'd have been on my way home, but it just so happened I had accounts to do and I was still in the office tonight. I don't think she was expecting me to pick this up until tomorrow morning.'

'Your Saturday surgery?'

'Exactly. I'd get this and I'd open it up and after I'd seen my patients I'd phone the farm. I'd get no reply and then I'd drive up there just to see what the hell this is about and—'

'Why no reply?'

'What?'

'Why would you get no reply when you phoned?' Hattie frowned. 'Do you think she's leaving Gillypuddle?'

'Yes.'

'To live somewhere else? Without the donkeys? It makes no sense...'

'I agree – it's completely out of character. You know how she feels about those animals.'

Hattie's mind raced. Why would Jo do this? Seth was right – it was totally out of character and out of the blue. Was it a reaction to Hattie's last visit? Was she moving away because Hattie had discovered her secret?

No, she decided. Jo would never leave the donkeys like that. If she planned to move away she'd rehome them herself. She'd want to see that they went to a good place and she'd want to wrap everything up properly. Hattie cast her mind back to that last visit. Jo wasn't herself at all. Things were… not as they ought to be. Hadn't Jo been in bed at some strange hour? And a mess in the house unlike Hattie had ever known. Jo hadn't been coping at all.

'Unless…' she said slowly. 'She was struggling – last time I saw her. She didn't seem herself.'

'Down? Not coping so well?'

'Yes.'

Seth nodded. 'What do you think it means?'

'I don't know. I can't… Seth… you don't think things have got so bad that…?'

'I'm afraid I do. I didn't want to think so, but if you think so too…'

'I don't know what to think – it seems so unlikely.'

'It's the only explanation. This letter…' Seth snatched the piece of paper from Hattie's hand and waved it desperately in front of her face. 'It's a suicide note!'

Chapter Twenty-Nine

Seth muttered under his breath as he drove. Hattie couldn't make out much of it, but she was certain there was a fair amount of cursing and blaming, and questioning people's stupidity. He was scared, and Hattie was too. She held the letter in her hands and looked down again at it now as Seth took the road to Sweet Briar.

Dear Seth

I need your help. I need you to come to the farm. I need to find new homes for the donkeys and chickens right away. I have instructions for each one, because they need special care, and you can get them when you come.

If you see Hattie, tell her I'm sorry for everything.

Jo Flint

The last time she'd been up there Hattie had wondered whether Jo was managing as she ought to be, but she'd never imagined it was this bad. But now, the evidence had been there all along. Or had it? Was it a crazy overreaction to think that she might take her own life? After all, she'd been so dedicated to her animals that Hattie couldn't imagine a circumstance in which Jo would want to entrust them to anyone else. And although she lived a life of isolation, she seemed to like it that way.

Hattie had thought her the toughest, most stubborn, most determined woman she'd ever known. And Hattie had thought that Jo loved her life up at the farm. Had it all been a lie? If she'd really been happy, why would she have been asking for a live-in assistant when Hattie first got the job? Had it been because she really wasn't happy at all? Had it been a cry for help, for someone to understand her? If it had, then Hattie had stepped up to the plate but, ultimately, she'd been found lacking. If anything had happened to Jo, it would be Hattie's fault. Hattie didn't dare dwell on the possibility. She clung to the hope that if Jo were to do something awful, she'd want to see the animals safely in their shelters first, which meant that they had… minutes? Dusk was already covering the land, the skies shell pink and iced blue, and there was a good chance Jo had taken the donkeys down already.

She glanced across at Seth, his concentration steady and purposeful as he took the bumpy road to the farm at speed, his lips still moving sporadically as he cursed or prayed or maybe even encouraged himself to see this through.

'Do you think we might be wrong about this?' Hattie asked.

'I don't know.'

'Jo won't appreciate us barging in if we are.'

'Think about it for a minute,' Seth said, as if Hattie had just made the most stupid comment he'd ever heard. 'Think about what's in that letter.'

Hattie looked at it again. Jo was a woman who wasted no words when she spoke and it seemed she was the same when she wrote them down. There was really nothing in the words she'd written, but it was the words she hadn't written that were the worry. Despite what she'd just said to Seth, Hattie couldn't help but feel he might be right about this.

At the entrance to the farm, Hattie leapt out of the car and opened the gates to let Seth drive into the courtyard. As he parked up, she ran to the house. The door was open, as always, and she went into the kitchen and called out for Jo.

There was no answer. Hattie rushed upstairs and checked the rooms, her own now an empty, cold shell. Jo's bed was unmade and the sheets were grubby, and on it lay a photo album. Hattie's eyes filled with tears as she glanced at it to see pictures of a woman who was unmistakably related to Jo, smiling out at her, but there was no time to dwell on it.

As she got back to the kitchen, Seth was snatching up a sheet of paper from the table.

'Instructions,' he said tersely. 'For the animals, just like she said.'

'I can't see her upstairs,' Hattie replied. 'Maybe she's putting the animals to bed.'

'You check the orchard and I'll go to the stables.'

Hattie nodded and went outside.

The plum trees were heavy with fruit, though much of it still needed time to ripen, and she could hear the chickens fussing. She looked into their enclosure to see they'd been fastened in for the night.

'Jo!' she called. 'Jo... are you here?'

There was no reply and Hattie didn't waste any more time there. She raced to the stables and met Seth on the way out.

'Donkeys are all in,' he said. 'What now?'

'She's not there?'

Seth gave his head a grim shake and Hattie realised that it was probably a stupid question but she was stuck. If Jo wasn't in the house, the orchard, or the stables, then where? Had she guessed people would come looking? Had she hidden herself where nobody would find her? The idea appalled Hattie and yet, knowing Jo, she had to consider it.

'Maybe she's not on the farm at all,' Hattie said. 'Maybe she's packed up and left.'

'Did the house look packed up to you?'

'Well, no…' Hattie thought about her own suitcase, still open on her bed at home. 'But she might not have taken much.'

'She'd never leave without rehoming the animals first.'

'But she'd never do *anything* without making sure they were alright first in any event.'

'Unless she was very desperate,' Seth said.

'Unless she wasn't really in her right mind?'

'Exactly.'

Hattie wondered if Jo had been in her right mind at all in the time she'd known her. Was the woman Hattie had lived with the real Jo Flint? Or was she the post-traumatic Jo Flint, the woman who couldn't move past her sister's death and the idea that she'd caused it? What if the woman the whole of Gillypuddle knew wasn't her at all?

Hattie had no idea, but she knew one thing: they had a duty to find out, to save her if they could – whatever that meant. She didn't care how angry Jo might be this time, because things had gone too far to worry about that.

Seth was silent, staring across the courtyard. And then he turned to Hattie and they spoke as one.

'Cliffs.'

'We'll take the car,' he said.

Hattie ran, clambering into the passenger seat, barely in before he'd started the engine. The car threw them around as Seth took the narrow, winding path at speed. It wasn't really a road, and it had never been designed for cars, but to walk it would take precious minutes Hattie was scared they didn't have. They passed the top field, empty now as darkness crept over it, and Seth pulled up in a clearing at the cliff edge. Hattie tumbled out, looking frantically left and right. Seth appeared at her side. The light was fading, but following his outstretched arm she could see now what he had seen: a figure further along the line of the coast, looking out to sea.

Hattie opened her mouth to call out but Seth slapped a hand over it.

'If she knows we're here she'll jump.'

Hattie stared at him.

'It might not even be her,' he added.

'What do we do?'

'Get closer, check who it is, talk to her then if it's her. She won't have as much time to decide she doesn't want to talk to us.'

'She might jump right there and then if she really doesn't want to talk to us,' Hattie said, shivering at the words that had just come from her mouth. In her wildest nightmares she could never have imagined that one day she'd have to deal with a moment like this.

Hattie followed Seth as they circled back to approach the figure from behind. If they were quiet enough, Seth said, maybe they could get close without the person noticing; close enough to see if it was Jo or not. It all felt faintly ridiculous and yet utterly terrifying, and Hattie's heart was beating like the wings of a trapped bird as they negotiated the uneven ground as quickly as they could. It was hard going, and it took a couple of minutes, and every agonising second came with the fear that they might be too late.

As they drew closer there was no mistaking Jo's outline. A few feet away, Seth opened his mouth to speak, but Jo turned around. Her eyes were swollen and red, and her usually proud shoulders were slumped.

'Come away from the edge,' Seth said.

Jo shook her head.

'Please…' he added. 'Just for a minute so we can talk.'

'So you can talk me out of it?' Jo said.

'We don't know what *it* is,' Seth replied.

Jo looked at Hattie. Perhaps she was expecting her to add something, but Hattie didn't know what to say.

'Don't feel guilty,' Jo said to her finally. 'There's nothing anyone could have done, not even you.'

'I don't understand—' Hattie began, but Jo took another step closer to the cliff edge.

Hattie watched in horror as Jo took a breath and closed her eyes, and she began to tilt forwards, so slowly that it felt like time had gone wrong. In the next second, Seth lunged forward, grabbed Jo's arm and yanked her away. She fell to the ground with a howl and he went with her.

'No! Let me go!' she cried, desperately trying to pull away.

'If you go,' Seth said, steel in his voice as he continued to grip her arm, 'then I'll go with you. Do you really want that?'

Jo looked up at him. 'No,' she sobbed. 'But I don't want to be here either.'

'Why?' Seth panted. Hattie could see it was taking every ounce of self-control he possessed not to let the situation break him. 'Give me one good reason why I should let you do this and, if I'm convinced, I'll let go.'

'You won't let go,' Jo cried.

'No, I won't, because we could sit here for ten years and you'd still never be able to give me a convincing reason.'

Jo looked up at Hattie. 'Please...' she said. 'You know everything. You know why.'

Seth looked at Hattie now, his expression demanding an explanation. He looked angry and afraid and lost, and Hattie knew that it was going to look bad that she hadn't told him what she'd known about Jo, particularly now, when it might have helped.

'I do,' Hattie said. 'But I'm with Seth – it's still not a convincing reason to let you do this.'

'I have nothing,' Jo said. 'You saw it – you know.'

'I'm sure it felt like that,' Hattie said, 'but if you'll let us, we can show you that it's simply not true.'

Chapter Thirty

The bunting was wonky.

'If you want something doing, do it yourself,' Hattie sighed as she adjusted it.

'There was nothing wrong with that,' Jo said as she walked past with another armful. 'And it will still look ridiculous whatever you do with it. People are coming to see a farm, not a carnival.'

Hattie smiled as she watched her walk away. Some things would never change, no matter how much counselling, no matter how many nights you spent talking until your voice was hoarse.

The winter had been long and slow and sometimes very dark, and there were many days when Hattie wished she'd got on that plane and gone to Paris, as she'd planned. But she stuck it out because, finally, she had found the thing she'd been looking for her whole life, the thing that mattered. She had found Jo and Sweet Briar Farm and this time she was going to get it right.

She'd also found Seth.

His hands closed over her eyes now. His scent was unmistakable.

'Guess who.'

She peeled them away and turned to look up at him.

'Lance wants to know if there's enough canapés,' he said with a grin.

Hattie rolled her eyes. 'I told him there was enough before he went dashing off to get more.'

'You know Lance. There ain't no party like a Lance Holt party.'

Hattie giggled. 'You say you were cool in the nineties but I know you weren't.'

'No kids were cool in the nineties; that's why.'

'I wasn't even around in the nineties,' Hattie said. 'Well, maybe just.'

'Don't remind me of how much older I am,' Seth said. 'It's just not fair.'

'Go and tell Lance that the food he's brought up will be just fine. I'm not even sure we'll get the numbers the Facebook event has shown – people sign up to this stuff and they don't come. If they do…' She shrugged. 'It's free food anyway so they can hardly complain if we run out. It'll be first come first served and they'll have to lump it.'

'Ouch – you've got tough over the winter.'

'Somebody has to manage this place.'

He smiled. 'Jo's lucky to have you; making you site manager was the best thing she could have done.'

'I know,' Hattie said with a grin. 'Things are a lot calmer now she can finally accept help and she's not trying to control everything herself all the time.'

He left her with a kiss and a warm feeling in her chest and went to find Lance. Hattie took a moment to look around. Even though they'd had little money to do anything much to the exterior of Sweet Briar farmhouse, it somehow looked brighter and more welcoming in the spring sun than it ever had during all the months Hattie had lived here. Perhaps because today was a celebration of all that they'd overcome and all that they hoped to achieve. Perhaps the prospect of a brighter future lent today a brighter hue.

There were lines of candy-coloured bunting around the courtyard and Lance and Mark had set up a small refreshment tent stocked with homemade goodies from the Willow Tree. Seth and Hattie's dad had extended the courtyard between them to create a run from there to the stables, and the donkeys had been given outdoor stalls as well as indoor ones so that the visitors could come and meet them today more easily. When the visitor aspect of the farm was up and running properly, they could let people walk up to the top field where they could meet the residents of Sweet Briar Sanctuary and also enjoy the cliff-top views. Hattie planned to set up picnic tables there – Jo hadn't been overjoyed by the idea and she was still suspicious of visitors' intentions, but when Hattie had enlisted the help of her dad and promised that when the field was open to the public, he'd be stationed up there to keep an eye on things, she relented. It would only be a few days a week and Nigel seemed happy to oblige. Like Hattie's mum had said, he was bored and driving her mad at home anyway, so she'd be glad to see him keeping busy.

Next to the refreshment stall, Rupert was setting up a tombola to raise some funds for the sanctuary's upkeep. Hattie watched as Phyllis came out of the tent with a cup and a slice of cake on a plate and gave them to him. He looked up at her and winked, and she giggled like a dizzy girl.

Were they *flirting*?

Hattie grinned. Good for them if they were – the whole village had been trying to persuade them for years that they were made for each other.

'Boo!'

Hattie spun around to see Melinda, Stu and the kids behind her. 'Hello,' she said. 'How's it going?'

'Good,' Hattie said. 'No major disasters yet. I wasn't sure you'd make it.'

'Not witness my best friend's finest hour? Try and stop me.'

'I know, but I thought you might have your hands full.'

'Oh, this one…' Melinda smiled down at the tiny baby in her arms. 'Sleeps like a dream. You could have an orchestra doing the 1812 symphony, cannons and all, and he'd sleep through it like a… well, like a baby.'

'What's this one called again?'

They turned to see Jo looking at the baby, this time arms empty of bunting. If she'd finished putting it up she'd done it very quickly, and Hattie made a mental note to go round and check what it looked like.

'Dustbin or something, is it?' Jo continued.

Melinda scowled but Hattie laughed. 'She's winding you up.'

Jo went over to take a closer look at Melinda's newest arrival. 'You should have called him cute.'

'We haven't called him anything yet,' Stu said. 'We'd better do it soon, though because he has to be registered.'

'Why haven't you named him yet?' Jo asked. 'Can't be that hard to think of a name.'

'It's not hard to think of a name but hard to agree on one,' Melinda said.

'I wanted Nathan,' Stu said.

'But that doesn't go with the others at all,' Melinda scolded. 'It's far too normal.'

'That's because you got your way with all the others,' Stu pouted.

'But you get to a certain point where you have to stick with it because anything else will sound lame. You can't go and give one of them a normal name.'

'We should have given them all normal names.'

'Then you shouldn't have let me have Sunshine in the first place.'

'Yeah, well, I felt sorry for you after I'd watched you give birth.'

Hattie raised her eyebrows at Melinda. 'Any ideas at all on this one?'

'I was thinking Thor,' Melinda said. 'Like thunder but cooler.'

'Makes him sound like a Viking,' Jo said. 'I like it.'

Without waiting for anyone's verdict on her comment, Jo wandered off.

Ocean tugged on Hattie's hand. 'Can we see the donkeys?'

'Seth and Jo are supposed to be putting them in their enclosures any time now,' Hattie said. 'Maybe you and your dad and sisters want to go and help him?'

Ocean nodded eagerly and Melinda smiled her agreement. They watched as Stu led them away to follow where Jo had just gone. Just then, baby-possibly-called-Thor started to grizzle.

'I knew he'd do this,' Melinda said. 'I bet he wants a feed. I tried to get him to take extra this morning so he'd last but he didn't want to know.'

'You can use my bedroom if you need to – shouldn't be disturbed there. The house will be unlocked until the visitors start to arrive so come and go as you please until then.'

'Thanks,' Melinda said, kissing her on the cheek before she left, her baby now starting to sound quite cranky.

Hattie watched Melinda go into the house. But then she noticed Lance standing at the entrance to the tent. He beckoned her over.

'I'm sorry,' he said in a low voice. 'Owen called – he says to send his apologies that he couldn't come and cover your grand opening.'

'I didn't think he'd be able to anyway,' Hattie said. 'But thanks for trying.'

'If you ask me he's too chicken to face you.' Lance folded his arms tight across his chest. 'And I'd get him to come anyway because he owes you big time.'

'I wouldn't blame him for that but if he thinks I still have bad feelings about what's happened then you can tell him that I don't.'

'I should think not. I know he's family, but I have to say that I think the best man won in the end.'

Hattie grinned. 'I didn't realise there'd been a competition.'

'Oh, I think our sexy Seth has been pining after you for a lot longer than you might realise.'

'Really?'

'Trust me, I know these things.'

'I'll take your word for it,' Hattie said with a laugh.

'It's nice to see you happy. But I still think you're a little loco…' Lance twirled his finger at his temple. 'That woman… that Med—'

'No!' Hattie warned.

'*Jo* then,' Lance corrected, rolling his eyes. 'She's just been in here trying to tell me how to do my job! I mean, what does she know about catering? I told her straight – you stick with your donkeys and I'll take care of the cakes.'

'You didn't shout at her, did you?'

'Of course I bloody well did!'

'Oh God!' Hattie's face lost a shade. Of all the things she'd needed today, one of them was for Jo to stay focused. She was getting better, but she still went back into her dark place from time to time. Hattie just didn't need that time to be now. 'Where did she go?'

Lance shrugged. 'As long as it's out of my way I don't care.'

'I'd better find her.'

Hattie dashed from the tent.

'Did you see where Jo went?' she asked Phyllis and Rupert.

'Who?' Phyllis asked.

'The stiff woman,' Rupert reminded her. 'Didn't notice,' he said to Hattie.

'Did she look OK?' Hattie asked.

'How should I know?' Rupert shrugged. 'She looked like she always does.'

'Right… OK.'

Hattie scanned the courtyard. But then she saw Jo with Seth by the new enclosures. It looked as if Melinda's kids had found them, and if Jo had been upset by her run-in with Lance, she wasn't showing much sign of it now. She was telling a story about one of the donkeys, the kids listening, still and silent as they gazed up at her. Seth glanced across and caught Hattie's eye. He sauntered over.

'You need to have a word with Lance,' he said quietly.

'I already have,' Hattie said. She sighed. 'I suppose you can't expect miracles right away. They've got some very strong opinions of her and it's going to take some time for people to realise that she's got a lot to offer the community.'

'I don't think she always helps her cause,' Seth said.

'Again…' Hattie smiled. 'Maybe we can't expect miracles straight away.'

'But…' Seth grabbed her around the waist and planted a kiss on her lips, 'she is looking happier than I've ever seen her. As am I,' he added, 'and it's all because of a certain young woman.'

'Phyllis?' Hattie grinned. 'I'll be sure to tell her what you said.'

Just then, Hattie noticed her mum across the courtyard, looking as if she was trying to explain something very complicated to her dad. There was a sort of hand semaphore whenever she did this, a very deliberate set of gestures that got bigger and wider the more frustrated she got.

'I'd better go and see if my mum and dad are OK,' she said. 'I think something is kicking off.'

'Right; go and referee,' he said with a grin and another kiss.

Hattie went over to her parents, leaving Seth to go back to helping Jo entertain Melinda's kids.

'Today is not a day for arguments,' Hattie said sternly as Nigel and Rhonda turned as one, guilty looks on their faces. 'Today is about harmony, and I'll be throwing out anyone ruining the ambience of the grand opening party, family or not.'

'Your dad's just eaten the biggest cream cake,' Rhonda complained. Hattie looked at her dad with raised eyebrows.

'You know what the GP said about your cholesterol.'

'I *am* a GP!' he said. 'I know about cholesterol!'

'Then you should know that a big cream cake is not going to help it come down,' Rhonda fired back.

'It's too late now, Mum,' Hattie said wearily. It's gone and he looks like the cat that got the cream – literally. Looks like you'll have to get him back on the wagon tomorrow.'

Rhonda glared at her husband, but he only looked supremely pleased with himself.

'So, now that you two are sorted…' Hattie began to walk away, but Rhonda called her back.

'We did want to give you something,' she said. 'Before the festivities start.'

Hattie turned back with a vague frown. Her eyes widened as Rhonda pulled a faded jewellery box from her handbag and opened it to reveal a heart-shaped locket.

'But that's…' she said slowly, looking up at her mum and dad.

'Charlotte's – yes,' Nigel said. 'We thought you ought to have it.'

'But you've kept that ever since…' Hattie stared at the locket.

'Charlotte would want you to have it too,' Rhonda said.

'But I can't take this—'

'You can,' Rhonda cut in. 'And we want you to.'

'You always thought you were the disappointing child,' Nigel said, 'and perhaps the blame for that belief always lay with us. But the way you've grown up, the way you've handled yourself this past year, the things you've achieved and the people you've helped… well, we couldn't be prouder of you if we tried. You were never the disappointing child; you were just yourself. It was always us who needed to try harder.'

Hattie's eyes filled with tears as she took the box.

'Do you want to put it on?' Rhonda asked uncertainly.

Hattie gave a mute nod. She had no words; she could only hand the box back and watch as Rhonda took the necklace out and fastened it around her neck. Charlotte had never been gone from Hattie's life, but now it felt she had a real piece of her. But it also felt like a huge moment with her parents. This was the locket Charlotte had worn until she died, and Hattie knew that her mum looked at it every night before she went to sleep. If Rhonda had been willing to part with it finally, to give it to Hattie… well, it meant the world. It meant more than Hattie could ever express.

Rhonda handed her a tissue from her bag.

'Buck up,' Nigel said as Hattie took it and dried her eyes. 'You've got a job to do – can't take your eyes off the ball now.'

Hattie smiled through her tears. 'I love you both, so much.'

'And we love you too, though we're sorry we never said it as often as we ought to have done.'

Seth came bounding over. 'Have you seen the time—' He stopped and stared at the scene. 'What's wrong?'

'Nothing's wrong,' Hattie said, a heart already bursting with love swelling with a little more at the tender concern in his eyes. 'Everything's perfect.'

And it was.

A Letter from Tilly

I want to say a huge thank you for choosing to read *Hattie's Home for Broken Hearts*. If you did enjoy it, and want to keep up-to-date with all my latest releases, just sign up at the following link. Your email address will never be shared and you can unsubscribe at any time.

www.bookouture.com/tilly-tennant

I'm so excited to share *Hattie's Home for Broken Hearts* with you. It's my eleventh novel for Bookouture and I loved every minute of writing it, especially the bits where I got to research donkeys all day! I truly have the best job in the world and I've been so proud to share every new book with my lovely readers.

I hope you loved *Hattie's Home for Broken Hearts,* and if you did I would be very grateful if you could write a review. I'd love to hear what you think, and it makes such a difference helping new readers to discover one of my books for the first time.

I love hearing from my readers – you can get in touch on my Facebook page, through Twitter, Goodreads or my website.

Thanks,
Tilly

Acknowledgements

The list of people who have offered help and encouragement on my writing journey so far must be truly endless, and it would take a novel in itself to mention them all. However, my heartfelt gratitude goes out to each and every one of you, whose involvement, whether small or large, has been invaluable and appreciated more than I can say.

There are a few people that I must mention. Obviously, my family – the people who put up with my whining and self-doubt on a daily basis are top of the list. My mum and, posthumously, my dad, who brought me up to believe that anything is possible if you want it enough, no matter how crazy or unlikely it seems. My ex-colleagues at the Royal Stoke University Hospital, who let me lead a double life for far longer than is acceptable and have given me so many ideas for future books! The lecturers at Staffordshire University English and Creative Writing Department, who saw a talent worth nurturing in me and continue to support me still, long after they finished getting paid for it. They are not only tutors but friends as well.

I have to thank the team at Bookouture for their continued support, patience and amazing publishing flair, particularly Lydia Vassar-Smith – my incredible and patient editor – Kim Nash, Noelle Holten, Peta Nightingale, Leodora Darlington, Alexandra Holmes and Jessie Botterill – collectively known as Team Tilly! Their belief, able assistance and encouragement mean the world to me. I truly believe I have the best team an author could ask for and I could not continue to do the job I love without them.

My friend, Kath Hickton, always gets a shout-out for putting up with me since primary school. Louise Coquio also gets an honourable mention for getting me through university and suffering me ever since, likewise her lovely family. And thanks go to Storm Constantine for giving me my first break in publishing. I also have to thank Mel Sherratt and Holly Martin, fellow writers and amazing friends who have both been incredibly supportive over the years and have been my shoulders to cry on in the darker moments. Thanks to Tracy Bloom, Emma Davies, Jack Croxall, Clare Davidson, Angie Marsons, Christie Barlow and Jaimie Admans: not only brilliant authors in their own right but hugely supportive of others. My Bookouture colleagues are all incredible, of course, unfailing and generous in their support of fellow authors – life would be a lot duller without the gang! I have to thank all the brilliant and dedicated book bloggers (there are so many of you but you know who you are!) and readers, and anyone else who has championed my work, reviewed it, shared it, or simply told me that they liked it. Every one of those actions is priceless and you are all very special people. Some of you I am even proud to call friends now.

I'd also like to mention The Donkey Sanctuary at Sidmouth for being so generous with advice and information on caring for donkeys. If you loved the donkeys in *Hattie's Home for Broken Hearts*, please consider going to visit them or perhaps making a donation.

Last but not least, I'd like to give a special mention to my lovely agent, Madeleine Milburn, who always has time to listen to my gripes and does so with a smile on her face.

Made in the USA
Coppell, TX
01 January 2022